This book is pure fiction. It should not reflect on the excellent work the Los Angeles Police Department and its courts systems provides.

Dedicated

To my wife Sung Hui

Whom I love

And adore

Detective Harriet Brown

These are the other books in the series I think you will enjoy.

Detective Harriet Brown 2 The Cruise

The story introduces Harriet to her first real love. It throws her off balance because he is their mark. She must stop the man trying to blow up the cruise ship, and then she must drive for her life when she becomes the mark.

Excerpt:

Blinding headlights behind, now beside her. Curve ahead, she slams the brakes. It misses, smashes through the rail. She hears it strike the rocks below. Silence, only the darkness. Her arms shake. In the city, headlights again. The ship, the Marines will be there. She skids to a stop at the gangplank, no one. The black car pulls up behind her, doors open. She accelerates, as bullets take out the windows. She stops at the edge of the pier. It's quiet, she hears footsteps. Raul why, I love you.

Detective Harriet Brown 3 Kidnaped

Harriet's detective agency sets off to rescue a young lady kidnaped in Puerto Quetal, Guatemala. The rescue is successful, but Harriet is left stranded with no money, phone, or passport. She has a price on her head because she was responsible for the previous drug cartel demise. The police department is tainted, where can she go?

Excerpt:

She had 300 thousand in her briefcase, the compliments of Senor Gutierrez. He could be generous after completing a four million drug deal. She had a plane. She was flying home after she drop him off at the Rafael Nunez airport in Cartagena Columbia.

She brought the plane to a stop five-hundred-feet from his black limousine. Senor Gutierrez stepped out of the plane, walked towards the limo, stopped, turned, tip his hat, when four men stepped out of the limousine with automatic weapons. He took ten bullets before his replaced his hat.

Startled, Harriet could not move until they pointed their weapon towards her. Closing the door, she ran to the cockpit taking a bullet in the leg and arm as the windows shattered from the bullets. She pushed the left throttle turning the plane as one of the assassins ran towards the cockpit spraying it with bullets. She took one bullet across her forehead, rendering her slightly dizzy as the left propeller caught the assassin. She felt the thump as his body passed through the moving propeller leaving him scattered over the wing. Concentrating, blood flowing over her eye, she starts the remaining engine. The plane picks up speed towards the runway as the limousine continues to pepper the plane with bullets. The plane reaches the runway finally leaving the limousine behind.

Detective Harriet Brown 4 The Prince

Raul has married and has a child. She must move on. She finds herself protecting the Crown Prince of Saudi Arabian. The CIA wants him dead to accommodate the cousin of the King, Prince Fahd. He promises a decrease in oil prices along with an increase in the supply of oil when he becomes King, but first, he must have the current Crown Prince removed. Harriet's company is trying to prevent the assassination.

Excerpt:

Harriet was already out of the car when the black van bump the smaller car hard jarring the car and Raul forward. She ran back to the black van and hit the opening front passenger door with her shoulder.

A hand with a gun in it had been coming out when the door slammed into it. The gun fell into Harriet's hands as she moved past it. The man screamed in pain.

The back-passenger door was opening. It had a leg and an arm in it when Harriet slammed into it with her back. The man screamed in pain and dropped the gun in his hand. It fell back by the rear wheel.

Detective Harriet Brown 5 Marriage

Harriet marries Raul, the Crown Prince's bodyguard, only to have it end in tragedy. She is pregnant, but she must face her old nemeses, Prince Fahd who is out to kill her and her child

Excerpt:

Harriet lifts off from the King Abdulaziz Military Air Base in the Gulfstream 630. She heads north over the Red Sea. She had an uneasy feeling and noticed a blip some distance behind her. She opens the missile bank Raul had installed on the plane. She had three missiles on each side of the fuselage. The small blip suddenly became larger, and two smaller blips appeared. They were missiles coming her direction.

She pressed the red button twice releasing her two missiles when the blips were almost on her. The explosion rocked her plane as she dove for the sea floor below. The black Panther Jet flash by as she leveled out going south twelve feet from the water. She cut the throttle back to 70 miles an hour and flipped on the automatic pilot. The flat surface of the water kept her in the air.

The Panther coming back saw only a boat on the radar screen going south on the red sea. He was satisfied he had killed her and headed bhome.

Detective Harriet Brown One

A Mystery

By Christopher Charles

Contents

Prologue

A pampered, sensitive young lady learns her family
has been murdered. Suddenly she finds her world
upside down and must now struggle to survive.
Assassins are trying to kill her, but she does not know
why

1 Things Change

Matlin Mc Craw, a strong woman, five-foot-seven, early thirties, pulled into the South Coast Plaza Shopping Mall, the largest in Southern California. She parked her car in the upper level near Nordstrom's and walked towards the entrance. She saw the black limousine coming towards her and waited. It stopped beside her.

She opened the door, climbed inside, and took the seat across from Mr. George Brown, a tall strong willed cultured man. She could see the uneasiness in his face, "I'm expecting the money within the hour, sir. Have you heard anything on the product?"

"Not a word," George said. "We should have had something by now." The limousine moved on through the parking lot making a large circle.

"It's a large shipment to move, sir," Matlin said.

"I don't like holding 800 million dollars," George said. "It makes me a target."

"We will protect you sir," Matlin said. "Now, after I receive the location of the money, where do you want me to send it?"

"Send it to my E-mail address. It is secure." He immediately knew he would be wiring it to his personal secure account.

"Yes sir, this will shut down their drug operation for at least a year."

"They may not like us confiscating their product, especially one this large. We should expect some reprisals," Brown said.

"When the Cartel cannot pay their people, the people may take care of the problem for us."

The black limousine had completed the circle and stopped beside her car. "I think this is where I get out." She looked up at his chauffer, Stanley, a broad-shouldered man. She knew he was undercover DEA, "You will take care of him?"

"Yes madam, the whole staff is alerted," Stanley said. He quietly pressed the send button on his phone and slipped it into his pocket unnoticed.

She stepped out of the limousine and climbed into her car as she heard it drive off. She pulled out of the parking lot and headed for the freeway. She thought she saw a black sedan pull out behind her, but when she entered the freeway, she lost it.

She planned to leave the Drug Enforcement Agency when this was completed. She married Tim Mc Craw, a detective for the Los Angeles Police Department, a year ago promising him she would quit. He thought she did, but she did not want to leave Mr. Brown exposed. The case had been dragging on, but now she could see the end. We will have the money today. The drugs should be here after that, then it will be over.

She pushed the garage door opener as her phone dinged telling her she had a text message. That was probably it.

She drove into the garage, closed the door. She walked quickly into her suburban house and sat down in front of her laptop computer in the kitchen.

Opening her phone, she saw the message. "You have the money!"

Excited, she opened her computer, and went to her Email. There staring at her was the bank routing number, account number, username, and password to 800 million dollars. For a brief-second she looked at it before her shaky hand punched the forward button sending the message on to George Brown's computer. She immediately pressed the delete to remove it from her E-mail.

She heard a car come in the driveway. She was not expecting anyone. Her husband was not due home for another two hours.

She glanced out the window. It was a black sedan. The doorbell rang. She started to reach for the door, when someone tried to kick it in. Locked, it rattled from the force. She could not move for a few seconds staring at it. Finally realizing what was happening, she turned, and ran for the back door.

The assassin's second kick sent the door flying open. He saw her running down the hall towards the kitchen. He took a long shot nailing her in the back.

She fell to the floor wounded. She heard his footsteps until he stood over her. She felt the second bullet an instant as it pierced her heart. The other two bullets she did not feel.

The assassin went to the hall closet, removed the tape to the security cameras, and looked around. He found Mc Craw's second gun in an unlocked box. He removed the gun, placed it in Matlin's right hand, smiled, and thought, "A nice touch."

He picked up the laptop computer from the counter and left the way he came in leaving the front door slightly ajar with the lock hanging loose. Removing the silencer, he holstered his gun.

He looked back before he stepped into his black sedan. Smiling, he thought, "Perfect." He threw the laptop into the front seat, eased the car out of the driveway, and drove on down the street.

A few blocks from the University of Southern California campus

Matlin's husband, Timothy Mc Craw, a tall muscular black man began staking out an alley. His informant had told him a buy was going down. Fifteen minutes ahead of the three o'clock buy-time, he looked for a concealed spot in the alley.

He found some boxes beside a trash bin. He looked inside pulling out some more. Then he made a stack of the boxes, hid behind them, and waited. Twenty minutes earlier, he had beaten his informant severely to get this information. Then right on time, a male twenty plus years old walked into the alley. He stood within three feet of his boxes. A teenage girl entered from the other end of the alley. She looked around apprehensively. Slowly she walked towards the trash bin.

Still apprehensive, she held out two hundred dollars. Her hand shook as she asked, "You got it."

"Yeah, I got it," the young man said reaching into his pocket. He pulled out a small folded piece of paper and handed it to her.

"This stuff is clean?" She asked. "The last stuff you gave me almost killed me. I was in the hospital for three days."

"It's clean. I take the stuff myself," he said as he took her money handing her the folded piece of paper.

As she took the piece of paper, the boxes exploded. Mc Craw had the young man by the throat holding him up against the wall. The money floated to the ground.

The girl dropped the piece of paper. In shock, she peed her pants. Then realizing she was still free, she reached down, picked up the two hundred dollars, and ran up the alley.

Mc Craw held the young man against the wall of the building, "You gonna try and lie out of this one?"

The young man, shaking hard, managed to squeak out, "Look, I don't even have the money."

Mc Craw turned his head, looked at the ground, he noticed the money missing, and the teenage girl running out the end of the alley. He turned back to the man up against the wall, "I still got you." He punched the young man in the stomach a few times, then he asked, "Were you selling drugs to that girl?"

"You still got nothing!"

Mc Craw released him slightly. Then he nailed him hard in the face loosening some teeth and breaking his lip open. Shoving him against the wall, he asked, "Did you give that girl drugs?"

Breathing heavy with tears flowing, he said, "Yes sir, please don't hit me again."

Mc Craw pulled him from the wall and hauled him back to his car outside the alley. Thirty minutes later, the undercover patrol car pulled up to the police station. Mc Craw jerked the young man from the back seat taking him inside. He cropped him into the chair in front of his desk, pulled out the confession form, and began typing.

The young man with blood dripping from his lip and loose teeth looked at the floor until Mc Craw shoved the paper in front of him, "Sign it!" The young man looked up. He saw the temper in Mc Craw rising again.

"Do we have to go back to the alley?" Mc Craw asked.

The young man shook his head. He signed the paper.

Mc Craw came around his desk, took the young man by his jacket, and jerked him up from the chair. Two minutes later, he returned from the cellblock to finish his paperwork. Done, he took it to Chief Don Morales, a large man, thin hair with a bulging stomach hidden beneath his uniform. He handed him the signed confession, "Another one off the street for a while, sir."

"He didn't look all that good coming in here," Chief Morales said. "What happened to him?"

"He made a run for it. I had to tackle him. He hit the concrete a little hard."

"It seems most of your collars come in this way."

"They're off the street, sir. My arrest record is one of the best."

"That it is, but I wonder at what cost?"

"I can let the bastard go, sir," Mc Craw said. "He was giving contaminated drugs to a young teenage girl. She said the last batch put her in the hospital. He doesn't deserve any sympathy."

Chief Morales shook his head, "Let's not be abusing their civil rights. We want the cases to stick."

"Yes sir," Mc Craw said. He turned and walked out of the station. He smiled to himself. His cases always stuck. Feeling good, he took another scumbag off the streets. The Chief may not like his methods, but he liked the results.

Driving home, Mc Craw thought of his wife. He married her a year ago, but it seemed like it was yesterday. He thought about calling her but changed his mind. He decided to buy her flowers and surprise her. He saw a flower shop. Pulling in front of a 'No Parking Zone', he turned on his flashing lights and entered the shop.

The shop owner looked up to see the police car in front of his shop. He rushed out to see what happened.

Mc Craw coming in said, "Easy Pops, I'm only buying some flowers for the misses."

Relieved, the shop owner said, "We have roses this month."

"Give me a dozen," Mc Craw said, then thinking a second, "No, make it two dozen."

"Yes sir," the shop owner said. He quickly packaged up two dozen roses. He knew this police officer. The whole neighborhood was frightened of him. He had beaten on most of the teenagers over the years. They could never do anything back to him because of his police officer status.

Mc Craw reached into his pocket to pay, when the shop owner pushed the flowers into his hand, "They are on the house."

Mc Craw smiled taking the flowers. He could feel the uneasiness in the man. "Maybe the message was getting out in the neighborhood not to mess with Mc Craw," he thought.

He climbed in his car and headed home. Looking at the flowers, he thought about calling his wife. He flipped open his phone, pressed speed dial. The phone rang, but no one answered. It went to message. He punched the speed dial a second time. The phone rang, but no one answered. Maybe she was in the shower or she left her phone in her car.

The smile disappeared from his face. He picked up the speed. Ten minutes later pulling into the driveway, he looked at the partially opened front door. His apprehension continued to build. The door should be closed unless she walked to the neighbor's house and left it open.

Christopher Charles

Not convinced, he pulled his gun, pushed the door open wider, thinking he might be making a fool of himself, losing-out on a romantic evening. "One does not come busting into the house with his gun drawn and expect love and kisses."

He thought about going back for the flowers when he saw her on the kitchen floor with four bullet holes in her back. She had his second gun in her right hand. She was trying for the back door.

He stood over her. He could not move. He stared at the blood oozing from her back. Slowly he placed his gun in his left hand, lifted the phone from his pocket, and dialed 911.

Then he moved carefully through the rest of the house checking the closets and bedrooms, but the assailant had come through the front door, and left by the front door.

Moments later the police arrived. An ambulance came taking the body after the lab people gave their okay. He did not sleep the rest of the night. He laid on his bed with his gun next to him praying the killer would return to take him on.

The next day he returned to work. He remained at his desk. They had given him desk duty not wanting him out in the field trying to solve the murder in his style. They told him to stay off the case and allow the other detectives to handle it. He knew what that meant. They would shelve it and write it up as a random shooting from a burglary that had gone bad. She had a gun forcing the burglar to shoot her.

Mc Claw, not buying it, left the office his usual time, eight o'clock at night. He drove home. When he reached his neighborhood, he slowed, and began looking at the houses for any unusual activity. He saw a shadow move in front of a house a block from his working a screen loose from a front window.

He parked his car a half block from the house. Stepping out, he approached the house quietly. The man had the screen off, and the window half open. When the man started to climb inside, Mc Craw charged! He pulled the man from the window and flung him up against the house.

Holding the man by his shirt, he yelled, "You gonna kill someone else tonight?"

The man tried to talk, but Mc Craw's huge hand against his throat prevented him.

Mc Craw hit him in the stomach three times before he worked on his face yelling, "Why did you kill her?"

The noise brought the other neighbors lights on. Someone called the police. They had been staying close in the neighborhood arriving in minutes. Mc Claw had the man on the ground kicking him hard in the side and head, when they arrived.

The officers pulled him off as he screamed, "He killed my wife!"

An ambulance arrived. They picked up the badly injured man lifting him onto a stretcher. The man regained consciousness slightly, opened his eyes, "This is my house. I left my keys inside." With that, the man passed out.

Mc Craw, handcuffed, taken into custody, slowly diffused his anger.

A week later, he found himself before the Judge Lawyin, a slightly built blond woman, to review his case before it went to trial. Mc Craw sat in court looking up at the Judge. He knew his fate lay with her. If she sent him to jail, he would not last four months. There would be no police department protecting his behind in jail. It would be their chance to even the score.

The Judge looked up, called out his name.

Mc Craw stood, and slowly walked to the front of the court. He stood in front of the judge with his head down.

The Judge studied the compliant in front of her. After a few minutes, she dropped the papers, looked hard at Mc Craw, "The plaintive says you beat him unmercifully without allowing him to explain why he was crawling back into his own house." She paused a moment, looked at him, "Did he threaten you in any way?"

"No madam," Mc Craw replied.

"It appears that is your standard method of arresting people. I am told most of your arrests that come into the station show signs of being severely beaten. Is that true Mc Craw?"

"Most of them are drug dealers, and difficult to apprehend. This sometimes requires force."

"Many of them come before my court with complaints of being roughened up by you to make them confess. Some of them to the degree, I have had to let them go to avoid a lawsuit. Now this last beating was an innocent man who had locked himself out of his house. Was it necessary to beat him to a pulp when you apprehended him? Again, was he endangering you in any way?"

"Just doing my job, madam."

"Your emotions were out of control. I know you recently lost your wife, but that is no excuse to beat up a civilian trying to enter his own house."

"Sorry madam, I sort of lost it."

"It's that temper of yours that is out of control. They gave you a desk job to keep you out of the investigation for good reason. You just could not leave it alone."

"Yes madam," Mc Craw whispered.

"I would like to detain you for six months in prison to let you cool off, but I don't think you would last more than two weeks. You have created too many enemies.

Therefore, I am placing you on probation for two years. You will give up your badge and gun. You will-not-be allowed to purchase or handle a firearm. Your driver's license will be revoked for the same period. You will attend anger-management-control classes at the local university, and report to your parole officer every month for the duration of your probation. It is either this or take your chances in jail for six months. If you break probation, you will go there automatically."

Mc Craw looked up at the Judge Lawyin, "I will take the probation your honor."

"Then we do not have to go to court for the legal side of this case, but the plaintive still has the right to file civil charges for the beating." She banged her gavel and left the courtroom.

2 Status Quo

Harriet Brown, slim five-foot four, blond young woman with a very submissive nature grew up in a fifteen thousand square foot mansion in Brentwood, California. She never left the perimeter of the estate.

She had home schooling until she entered college, but this they regulated to classes only. A limousine and driver would take her to school and be there to take her home at the end of her class.

She did not like this regimentation, but she was not strong enough to object to her father. She never felt close to him. He was away most of the time. Her only close friend was Nadine Quiver, her tutor.

Nadine Quiver, late thirties, petit, five-foot three, dark hair, played the part of tutor very well. She hid her talents as a mystic, but her quick wit, and general knowledge impressed George Brown, Harriet's father.

He liked her, thinking he might pursue these feelings upon the completion of the drug deal. Right now, he needed to protect his only motherless child. He lost his wife shortly after the birth of Harriet. The doctors said it was internal bleeding.

George, home for his daughter's graduation from the University of Southern California, she was to receive her Bachelor of Arts degree in piano, learned he could not attend. He had business pressures.

Harriet in her room putting on her commencement robe felt excited, and slightly fearful. Her education completed, she would be free of the confinement she has had to endure. She has never told anyone, not even Nadine how she felt.

Then quietly screaming: "I'm leaving this house!" There, she said it! Where, she was not sure yet. Twenty-three years old, no longer a child, it was time for her to explore the world.

Suddenly these thoughts shattered when her father entered her bedroom. His voice came ringing through her thoughts.

"I will not be able to attend your commencement dear, business again. We can celebrate when you come home."

Like a knife ripping through her heart. He could have at least attended one thing important to her. She allowed a tear to drop, swallowed, then in a meek voice, "It is okay father. Nadine will go with me."

"I knew you would understand, dear," Mr. Brown said. "It is only a ceremony. We will have plenty more of those. I hear your piano is coming along famously. I expect we will be hearing you play in the symphony in a few years."

"I like music papa, but there are other things I would like to try, maybe..."

"Nonsense child," he said interrupting her, "You were born for music, and that's where you will go. Besides, I have connections there. It would be a shame to not use them."

"Yes sir," she said as she felt her heart crumble.

Nadine walked into the room, smiled at Mr. Brown, "We need to be going, dear. You know how the traffic can be."

"You take care of her, Nadine," Mr. Brown said stepping closer to Nadine hoping for a slight hug.

Nadine sidestepped him, "I will keep her from harm, sir."

Harriet quickly left the room before she broke into tears. Nothing was going to be different. She would still be in her prison shackled to her piano. She would be playing even if her fingers wore down to nothing leaving her stubs to play with. Finally leaving the house, she shouted, "Please God, let me be free!"

In the limousine, she tried to smile slightly. She was getting away from the house if only for a few hours. She should enjoy this time. She also knew school allowed her a little bit of freedom, but now this would be closed.

Nadine sat beside her in the back of the limousine. She took Harriet's hand rubbing it, "Let's enjoy the day."

Harriet sat there a few minutes, then she blurted out, "Are you and my father going to get married?"

Stunned, Nadine could not say anything for a few seconds. Finally, she said, "Where did that come from?"

"I've seen how my father has looked at you."

"It doesn't mean I look at him the same way."

"It would be so neat if you were my mother."

"Really, you wouldn't mind."

"Of course not. You're the only mother I have ever known."

"You really don't know anything about me," Nadine said.

"I know I love you, and I think you love me."

"That may be so, but marrying your father is something else. He is a very busy man. I don't think he has time for marriage, and now you are all grown."

"I still need you."

"I will always be here for you, dear," Nadine said. She gave Harriet a hug.

The driver, Stanley, pulled up outside of Alumni Park. He came around to Nadine's side of the limousine, opened the door, "Miss Quiver, use your cell phone to call me when you are leaving, and want to be picked up. I must find another place to park."

"Thank you, Stanley," Nadine said stepping out of the limousine.

Harriet nodded, and followed Nadine. She took a deep breath, allowed the air to slowly release, "It feels so good to be free!"

"Let's enjoy ourselves," Nadine said placing Harriet's hat on.

Stanley watched them walk off. Then reentering the limousine, he pressed the speed button on his cell phone, "I have dropped them off, sir. Do you want me to remain here?"

"Give me until four," Mr. Brown said.

"Yes sir, but what do you suggest I delay them with?"

"She likes ice cream, give her a little bit of freedom."

"Yes sir, four o'clock."

3 Brown Detective Agency

Harriet received her diploma in the Bachelor of Arts. Hats were thrown, and Nadine called Stanley. Ten minutes later, they were in the limousine.

Stanley leaned back, "Who is up for ice cream?"

"We're going to celebrate with father," Harriet said.

"Yes, later this evening, but he asked if I could take you for ice cream. He was not quite finished with his business."

"Ice cream will be fine," Nadine said. "But find something closer to home."

"Yes madam, ice cream it is."

Stanley drove around for thirty minutes before he found an ice cream specialty store in the older section of Los Angeles. He pulled up in front of the store and opened the door for the two of them.

Harriet looked around at the other rundown stores. Men stood leaning against the building across the street. They made her nervous. When Stanley opened the door, she quickly walked inside. The people behind the counter seemed pleasant inviting them to sit at a table.

Stanley's phone rang. He said a few words and closed his phone. Turning to the girls, "I'll find a parking place, call me when you are ready." Not waiting for a reply, he returned to the limousine, and drove off.

Harriet immediately felt deserted, "Stanley's left!"

"He's just parking the limo dear," Nadine said. She felt the desertion too, but she did not want to add to Harriet's fears.

Trying to shake off the desertion feeling, Harriet turned, and ordered a banana split. Nadine followed suit ordering one.

Brentwood Mansion

George sat at his computer. Two weeks earlier, he had received the money, 800 million dollars to complete the biggest drug deal of the century with a large cartel in Columbia, but things had gone wrong since. Someone killed his handler after the money arrived. They gave him another handler, but this one seemed inexperienced to be handling a deal of this magnitude. Then suddenly the man he had been dealing with in the drug cartel also disappeared. The plan: bankrupt the Columbian Cartel and put them out of business as soon as he located their product.

He had been working up to this position for the last five years. The DEA gave him his mansion in Brentwood and paid for his staff. They all worked for the DEA except Nadine. He kept her separate along with his daughter, Harriet. Neither of them was aware of his business activities for their own safety.

All his hard work was about to pay off when suddenly new players became involved. They did not have the location of the drugs. He did not even know if the drugs had arrived in the United States.

Yesterday the DEA wanted the location of the money. This would take him out of the deal. Somebody had changed things. He was not even sure the E-mail came from the DEA.

He decided to give them the location. He punched it in, but not before he had wired the money to his new accounts, he had set up after his handler was murdered. The money would appear to be in the bank for a couple of more days, but he had it safely tucked away.

After Harriet had left for her graduation, he received an unlisted call on his home phone. When he lifted it to his ear, he could hear heavy breathing until it went to dial tone.

He debated what to do. It could be a scare tactic by someone in the cartel, or it could be someone checking to see if he was home.

Panicking, he dialed his handler, Detective Ramos on his phone, but he did not answer. Next, he dialed the Los Angeles Police department. The operator directed him around the department until Chief Morales picked up the phone.

Phone:

"Chief Morales here!"

"This is George Brown. I need to speak to Detective Ramos."

"He's not here at the moment, may I be of help."

"No, I need to speak to him. Could you tell him to call me immediately? It is an emergency."

"Yes, of course, as soon as he comes in."

"Thank you," George closed his phone. He needed help. He knew Harriet was through with her graduation. He had told Stanley to take her for ice cream. He needed to keep her away from the house. He opened his phone again, and punched speed dial.

Phone:

"Stanley here sir."

"Right after I transferred the money to the DEA, I was threatened by someone over the phone. I need you here immediately. I cannot find Detective Ramos."

"What about the young ladies? I have just dropped them off at the ice cream establishment."

"It is best they remain there. I need you here now."

"Yes sir, I am on my way." Stanley punched, "Message," on his phone, and pushed, "Send."

Twenty minutes later, someone pushed the gate button. George looked at his watch, smiled, and thought Stanley had made good time. He pressed the delete button erasing the location of the money from his laptop computer.

He started down the stairs when the doorbell rang. The housekeeper opened the door. He saw the gun pointing at him from the doorway. He tried to turn, but the bullets were faster, striking him in the chest. Everything went blank as he fell head first down the stairs.

The housekeeper screamed, turned, and tried to run, but she took a bullet in the back of the head.

The assassin quickly walked to the kitchen. He sent two more bullets into the back of another woman, running for the back door. He heard the limousine drive up and walked back to the front door. He noticed the shocked look on Stanley's face coming up the steps as he sent two bullets into his chest.

The assassin found the recording machine to the cameras and removed the tape. He climbed the stairs, bypassed George on the steps, and removed his laptop computer from his study. He already had the bank account number. He had to make sure no one else would have access to it. He left the house with the laptop, walked to his b ack sedan, removed his silencer, smiled, and thought. "That cleans up loose ends. Thank you, Stanley."

Ice Cream Parlor

Harriet and Nadine had finished with their ice cream, but Stanley had not come back.

"I thought he was only parking the car," Harriet said, "Maybe you better call him. We should be getting home."

Nadine nodded. Her apprehension increasing, she pressed her speed button. The phone rang, but no one picked up. She pressed it again, still no answer. The desertion vibes became stronger. She turned to Harriet, "Maybe we had better be going."

She dialed for a yellow cab and paid for the ice cream. They waited another fifteen minutes before the yellow cab pulled up in front of the ice cream store. Both quickly climbed in.

Riding back towards Brentwood, Nadine punched Mr. Brown's speed dial, but no one answer. She punched in Stanley's number again, but the same.

Harriet tried her speed dial, no one answered. She turned to Nadine, "Should we call the police?"

"Let's just wait until we get there," Nadine said. "We will know soon enough."

"But where is Stanley?"

"Maybe his phone is out of range."

Harriet allowed this to settle a moment, then she began to worry again, "Something has happened."

Nadine pattered her leg, "We'll see."

Ten minutes later, they were approaching the estate.

The police had the driveway taped off. The cab pulled over to the side of the road in front of the barricade. Nadine paid the driver, the two of them stepped out of the cab.

A police officer by the barrier came over, "You might as well go back with the cab, you cannot enter the property."

"I live here," Harriet said.

"This is a crime scene. You will not be allowed to enter no matter who you are."

"What happened?" Nadine asked.

"I can't tell you. This is an ongoing investigation."

Another police officer in plain clothes, Chief of Detectives Paul Ramos, late twenties, dark hair, and brown eyes, came out from behind the barrier, "I'll take care of this officer. These are important witnesses I need to question before they leave."

The police officer looked at him, shrugged his shoulders, "They are your responsibility."

The cab driver leaned out the window, "Do I wait or go?"

"Wait!" Nadine said. She turned back to the detective, "What's going on?"

"Who are you?" The detective asked.

"I am Nadine Quiver, Harriet Brown's tutor; I am employed by Mr. Brown. We have just returned from her graduation. Now who are you?"

The police officer raised his finger for her to wait, turned to Harriet, "And you?"

"Harriet Brown, Mr. Brown is my father. What is going on?"

"I am Chief of Detectives Ramos. I am sorry to inform you your father has been killed along with his driver, and two of his staff."

Harriet heard the words, but she was having a hard time believing them, "He can't be dead! You say everyone is dead?"

"Yes madam, it appears someone came through the front door, and started shooting. When his driver showed up, he met the same fate. He was killed at the front door."

Harriet could not say anything more. Her whole world had just collapsed. Too stunned to cry, she moved into Nadine's waiting arms. She began to feel guilty from her earlier rebellious thoughts. "He didn't have to die."

Nadine, holding Harriet asked, "Do you know who did it, and why?"

"We just started the investigation," Detective Ramos said. "Give me a call tomorrow, I will update you then." He handed her his card and backed away.

Nadine took the card. She moved Harriet towards the cab, "Come on dear, you can stay at my place. There is nothing we can do here tonight."

Chief of Detectives Ramos watched them enter the cab before he returned to the crime scene.

Chief Morales inside the house watched his men work. Mr. Brown laid on the staircase face down with two bullets in his chest. One woman laid on the floor in the kitchen with two bullets in her back. The other one laid face down in the living room with a bullet hole in the back of her head.

Chief Morales looked up when Detective Ramos entered. He did not like the college graduate. He had no experience. They gave him the Chief of Detective position because he had a master's degree in law bypassing more field-tested men in his department. He knew he would weed him out later. For now, he tolerated him, "Did you check out the driver?"

"Yes sir, he took two bullets in the chest as he came up the steps. It seems all the bullets came from the same gun, but we will know for sure when the forensic team is done."

"I want you to head up this investigation since you were his handler. Let's make the drug cartel pay."

"Yes sir. It looks like it was just one assassin, probably a hired gun."

"Probably right! Anything on the cameras?"

"No sir, someone removed the tapes."

"I should let you know he called the station earlier looking for you." Chief Morales said.

"Do you know why he called, sir?"

"He seemed quite upset he could not reach you. I'm sure he tried your cell phone."

"I dropped it yesterday. He didn't have my new cell number."

"That's too bad."

"Do you know what time that was, sir?"

"Four o'clock, they probably bought it right after that. I heard he had a daughter, but she wasn't here."

"She was at a graduation ceremony. I just met her a few minutes ago."

"She could be in danger. Do you have the address?"

"No sir, but she was not aware of Mr. Brown's activity with the drug cartel. He kept all of this from her."

"You are quite sure of this?"

"Yes sir, I am quite sure. It was part of the DEA's arrangement."

"She's in for a surprise."

"Yes sir, but there is time enough for that later, I thought it best for her to adjust to the death of her father first."

"Yes, you are quite right. This is your case. I want to be up-dated."

"Yes sir, I will keep you in the loop."

"Good!" Chief Morales said, tipped his hat, and left the house.

Detective Ramos turned, and went back to his investigation team analyzing the bodies.

Pasadena

The yellow cab pulled up to a house in the older section of northern Pasadena. These used to be homes of wealthy people, but now the age and the area caused them to drop in value allowing Nadine to buy one. It had a garage separate from the house located in the back of the property.

She had left her car at the estate. She did not want to push for it when she knew Harriet was suffering. She would pick it up tomorrow.

Harriet held her emotions in. She had not cried. She stepped from the cab with Nadine helping her. Nadine paid the cab driver and sent him on his way.

Nadine opened the door to her house, flipped the lights on, and allowed Harriet to enter first, "Don't be shocked by what you see!"

The living room had silk fabric hanging from the ceiling, a very large oak table in the middle with six high back chairs, and a fireplace with old décor.

Harriet had just walked into something very ancient. The old paintings on the walls showed people dressed in the fourteenth century style clothes. "Are you a witch?" Harriet mumbled out.

"I don't think of myself as a witch, just a person who enjoys ancient things and has some abilities. I don't go into making brews or spells to do people harm. Come on now; let me show you our bedroom."

She led Harriet up the old winding staircase to the second level. They entered Nadine's bedroom. The bed was large with old furnishings around the room. "You can stay with me tonight. Later, you can use the other bedroom down the hall."

Harriet went over, sat on the bed, "It is my fault my father is dead. I wanted to be free this morning. I prayed to God to be free. Look what I did! My father is dead." The tears began to flow slowly at first, then they took hold. She could not stop them.

Nadine sat down beside her, placed her arm around Harriet's shoulders, pulled her close.

Harriet fell on Nadine's lap. She continued to cry.

"You did not kill your father," Nadine said quietly. "Someone else did that. He had been in danger for some time. He protected you by getting you out of the house today. I think he called Stanley when we were at the ice cream pallor. He went back to help him, but they shot him too."

"Why?"

"Your father confided in me a few days ago. His business dealing had gone bad. He expected trouble. He has been keeping you protected for your own safety for some time. He thought they might try and kidnap you to put pressure on him."

Through her tears, "Who are they?"

"I don't know. I don't think your father wanted to get me involved. He told me to take care of you if something should happen to him. We are to see the Chief Detective Ramos tomorrow. Maybe he will know more. It's best we try and get some sleep tonight."

Los Angeles Police Department

The next morning Nadine made an appointment with Detective Ramos at the police station. They arrived close to noon.

The receptionist led them into Chief of Detective Ramos' office.

Ramos sat behind the desk after he had seated the two women in front of him. He looked at them a second, then said, "I knew your father. He was working for us. I was his handler. We had been working with this drug cartel group shipping drugs into the United States. Your father was their point man here in the states.

The house you grew up in, and all the furnishing inside belong to the Drug Enforcement Agency. These now will become state's evidence. You can no longer live there. Your personal belongings are yours but everything else is evidence.

That also includes all the bank accounts here and overseas. The only thing he bought on his own is the limousine. You may have that, and the office building in Pasadena where he had a private detective office at one time. It's run down, but you might be able to sell it for some money."

Harriet could not say anything. She had suddenly lost everything she knew.

Nadine taking charge, asked, "Is that all? The man gave his life, and all his country can give him in return is a rundown building with a detective sign over it."

"He knew the risks. It was voluntary. We tried to protect him. No one knew of his connection to us except me. I don't know how the leak got out. No one in the department knew. I intend to find out what happened."

"How is Harriet supposed to survive?" Nadine asked.

"I am sorry, but there is nothing left for her. The cartel did not know he had a daughter. That was to protect her. He could not set up an account for her without blowing her cover. Sell the building and the limousine. It will give her a few dollars to start-over. That's all I can do for you. I'm sorry."

"Do you have the address of the building?"

Detective Ramos wrote it on a card, handed it to her with two sets of keys, "This is the key to the building, and this is the key to the limousine. It's in the police parking lot. You will have to remove it today or it will be towed."

"Maybe we should be talking to lawyer," Nadine said. She took Harriet's hand leading her out of the office. Harriet was in shock. She had nothing. How was she going to survive? They went outside to the limousine.

Harriet looked at it, "I don't drive. I don't have a license."

"Then it is time you were getting one. You cannot survive in Southern California unless you can drive. Come on, let's go look at your building. I'll drive the limousine."

Thirty minutes later, they pulled up in front of a small rundown one-story building with boards on the windows and door.

Harriet stepped out of the car. She walked slowly around the building as Nadine began tearing the boards off the door.

Boards off, Nadine tried the key, the door opened, she walked inside. Harriet finished her walk around the building. She entered behind Nadine. Inside was small. It had a bathroom in the back beside the large private office. The reception area had a desk and six chairs against the walls with a large window next to the door facing out.

The large private office with a door extended to the right from there. The office had a desk facing the door with two chairs in front of it. It had a boarded-up window behind the desk. It smelled of old dust. The furnishings were old. Nadine looked around, "I like it."

Harriet had not said a word. She was still taking it all in. She walked behind the large oak desk in the office covered with dust, wiped the chair off, and sat down. There was nothing on the desk except a picture of her father, and another man dressed in a suit holding a baby. She looked at it a moment. She recognized her father on the left, but the one holding the baby she did not.

Behind them stood the building with the name, 'Brown's Detective Agency'. Finally, she reached for the picture, and brought it towards her.

The picture was slightly ajar in the frame. She opened the back of the picture to adjust it, a letter fell out. Slowly she opened the letter. Inside was a bank deposit key.

The Letter Read

I love you very much. I am your grandfather. If you are reading this letter, your father has passed away. Your father was very upset when your Mother died giving birth. He left the detective agency to work for the U. S. government. I could not talk him out of it. I told him he was going to get himself killed. I have tried to keep the company going, but my heart is about to give out any day. Without your father, I will be closing the agency. I am leaving the office for you. Maybe one day when you are old enough, you will take up the company's business.

The key opens a Crocker National Bank deposit box in Diamond Bar located on Diamond Bar Blvd. In it, you will find some seed money I was able to put away for you. It might help to get you started in the Detective Business. Hire good people. That is what makes it work. Your father has not allowed me to see you thinking it might put you in danger. I didn't understand his reasoning, but he is dealing with some very dangerous people.

Always love you,

Your papa

Harriet picked up the key, stared at it a moment, looked at Nadine, "We're going to Diamond Bar."

"What's in Diamond Bar?"

"A deposit box with money in it, I hope."

In minutes, they were on the freeway heading for Diamond Bar.

"What bank are we looking for?" Nadine asked.

"Crocker National Bank!"

"Wells Fargo Bank bought out Crocker Bank. The deposit box may be gone."

"We'll see."

Thirty minutes later, they pulled into the shopping center on Diamond Bar Blvd. The old Crocker Bank was gone, but the Wells Fargo bank was still there.

Harriet showed the key to the bank manager. She took her to the vault as Nadine waited outside. The key fitted the correct box.

Harriet opened it in the private room. Her heart began to beat fast as she slowly removed the lid revealing bundles of hundred dollar and twenty-dollar bills. She slowly lifted the bills out of the box and began counting until she reached fifty thousand dollars.

She placed the lid back on the box slipping the money into her purse. Now what to do with it? She gave the box back to the bank manager, walked quickly out to Nadine. She took her by the arm leading her out of the bank. She did not breathe normally until they were back on the freeway heading for Pasadena.

Finally, Nadine asked, "Okay, was the money there?"

Harriet nodded

"How much?"

"Fifty thousand!"

"I would say your grandfather liked you."

"Where can I hide it?"

"You should have put it in the bank while you were there," Nadine said. "They know where the money came from. Otherwise another bank is going to ask you questions where you got it."

"You really think I should put it back in the bank?"

"Yes, the sooner the better."

"Then let's go back."

Nadine turned the limousine around. They headed back to the bank. The bank manager smiled and took the money. She set up an account for Harriet and gave her temporary checks to work with. She had two accounts. One personal and the other one for the Brown Detective Agency.

Back in the limousine going towards Pasadena, Nadina asked, "Why did you set up an account in the detective agency's name?"

"I'm going to become a detective like my father and papa."

"Whoa there, do you know what you are getting into?"

"Papa left me the business, and the money to start up the business again."

"You know nothing about the business," Nadine said. "You are only trained in the piano, unless you are holding something out on me. That does not qualify you for detective work."

"I can learn," Harriet said. "It's in my blood. I only have to learn the mechanics. How hard can that be?"

"Your personality lends more to be a wife in the upper social circle. You want to be dealing with criminals that like to eat children for breakfast."

"That's a little severe."

"You know what I mean. You are not a strong person. Not that it's bad, but why don't you pick something more suitable to your personality."

"I can do this. Papa left the money for that purpose."

"He didn't say for you to start the business up with it. You can do anything you want with it."

"When I run out of the money, then what? I am still only a piano player. I might be able to get a job at the local pub and try for tips to live on. Starting the detective business will give me an income where I will control my destiny."

"If the detective business fails, which I am sure it will, then what? You will have spent the money."

"If I put the money in the stock market, I could lose it all too. If I place the money in a savings account, and get two per cent a year, it will not be enough to live on. I would-be forced to take out the principle depleting the cash until none is left. The business may succeed and give me a good living."

"There are other businesses to get into that are less dangerous."

"Probably, but I already have the office, and car for this one. Besides, papa would want me to take up the family business."

"You did not even know your grandfather," Nadine said.

"He loved me. You saw his letter; besides it is really his money. It should be spent for what he wished for."

"He wished for your father to come back to the business, not you."

"My father didn't. Now, I'll take his place."

"You're set on this, aren't you?"

"Yes!"

"Then we better be getting you a driver's license." She pulled off the freeway and located a DMV. Harriet read the booklet quickly. Her mind, used to memorizing book material, digested the information. She stepped out of the car an hour later and took the test. They gave her a learner's permit to start driving.

Nadine spent the next week in the limousine teaching her how to drive. Finally, Harriet drove it into the driving lane at the local DMV. She waited for the examiner. He came out and stepped back.

He looked at her, "You sure you want to take your test in this?"

"This is the only car I have."

Stepping into the Limo, he said, "Okay, let's go."

She started the limousine and drove it out of the DMV. She had them moving down the street when the light in front of her turned red. Hitting the brake, she started to come to a slow stop, when she saw this huge truck coming up behind her.

She heard his brakes squealing. Panicking, she took her foot off the brake, allowing the limousine to drift out into the cross street as the truck finally stopped a foot behind her.

The examiner looked back at the truck, wrote a note in his chart, "Let's go on the freeway."

Taking a deep breath, she had the limousine moving when the light turned. Entering the freeway ramp, she knew she needed some speed to be with the expected traffic. She put her foot to the accelerator. The limousine moved up the ramp. It entered the freeway at sixty miles an hour. She flipped on her turning light to make a lane change, when suddenly the traffic stopped in front of her.

There was no warning. It just stopped. She immediately took the limousine to the shoulder moving up beside the stopped car in front of her. The car behind her with no place to go rammed into the back of the stalled car.

The examiner began writing in his chart, "Let's get off the freeway, seems there has been an accident."

When the traffic picked up, a hole developed in front of the damaged car beside her. She moved into the lane taking the next ramp off the freeway. The light was green for her to move off the ramp, and cross the street, but a car had run the light forcing her to stop, but her rear-view mirror revealed another car coming off the freeway very fast. He also saw the green light. He was not stopping.

Harriet turned the limousine hard to the right to avoid the car going through the red light, but the car behind her did not. He barely missed the limousine, striking the car going through the light. Harriet continued with her right turn taking the limousine up the street.

The examiner was beginning to sweat profusely, "Let's try parking. Pull into the shopping center."

Harriet pulled the limousine into a crowded section. She looked for a place to park. Finding one between two cars, she pulled in, and stopped.

"Okay, take us back out of here."

She placed the limousine in reverse, and started to back out, when she saw the car behind her also backing out. She immediately pushed her horn and moved forward into her space.

"I said take us out."

Suddenly the woman's car backing out smashed into the car next to them. She left a big ding in the parked car and left.

"I think it is okay now, sir," Harriet said continuing to back the limousine out. She turned the wheel, and left the parking area, 'Where to now?"

"Take us back to the DMV please, and use the local streets," the examiner said in a shaky voice.

"Yes sir," Harriet said taking the limousine out of the parking lot. Approaching the DMV, she heard a siren in the distance, and took the limousine to the far side of the road to wait for the oncoming ambulance coming towards them to pass.

Another car coming out of the DMV parking lot did not hear the siren. Seeing the Limousine waiting on the road, the car assumed the limousine was waiting for them to come out. It kept coming. The ambulance squealed its brakes hitting the right fender of the car coming out. Harriet, seeing the other driveway open, drove the limousine into the parking lot. She pulled to a stop in the drive next to the building. She looked at the examiner, "Did I pass my driving test?"

The examiner did not say word. He stepped out of the limousine, walked into the building, dropped his chart on the desk, "I quit!" He left the building still shaking and headed for the nearest bar.

Harriet stepped out of the limousine, walked into the building to the front desk, "Did I pass my test?"

The woman picked up the chart, looked at it a moment, "He wrote 'Pass' on it with the suggestion you never take another test." Handing Harriet a card, she said, "Here's your temporary license. Your license will be mailed to you."

Harriet smiled taking the card, "Thank you."

Excited, she left the DMV, and headed home. She was a legal driver now. She avoided the freeway knowing there was an accident on it. She could not wait to tell Nadine. She parked the limousine in front of Nadine's house, ran inside. Seeing Nadine, she yelled, "I passed! I passed!"

"Congratulations, now you may join the rest of the insane people on the freeway."

"Now all I have to do is get my private investigator's license."

"That may not be as easy," Nadine said. "I've been checking, seems you need a bachelor's degree in police science, and 4000 hours in the field working for the police department, or another private investigator's office."

"That will take two years!"

"There's nothing you can do about it. You need the experience, and I don't see how you are going to get that."

"I'll have to sell the building and limousine," Harriet said depressed.

"Maybe, come on, let's go check the office again."

"What for?"

"I don't know yet, I'll tell you when we get there. You can drive now that you have your license."

Harriet drove them to the detective office. Nadine did not say a word all the way there. She opened the door and entered with Harriet behind her.

Nadine walked to the large desk in the office. She placed her hand on the wood. She moved slowly around it. Keeping her hand on it, she sat in the chair. Then leaning back, she closed her eyes. Her body seemed to crumble as she fell into a deep trance.

Harriet stared at her, but she did not say a word.

Slowly Nadine came out of her trance. She looked up at Harriet, "Your grandfather is alive. He has something in his chest that regulates his heart. He has been feeling depressed."

"Where is he?"

"I don't know for sure," Nadine said. "It looked small, maybe senior housing."

"We have to find him," Harriet said. She went to the desk and pulled out the phone book. She looked up senior housing and came up with three. She began calling. She found one with a Henry Brown, and another one with a Timothy Brown living there. She did not know her grandfather's first name. She looked up at Nadine.

Nadine looked at the two names, pointed to Henry Brown, "That's him."

Harriet quickly wrote down the address, "Let's go!"

"You sure you want me coming along?"

"I don't know which apartment he's in."

Nadine nodded following her out the door. She was still a little woozy from being in a trance. She allowed Harriet to drive.

After going the wrong direction a few times, Harriet pulled up outside the senior housing in South Pasadena not far from the office. They both stepped from the limousine and walked slowly into the complex. It had a locked gate protecting the entrance. She looked at the call list, sent the pointer down to the name of Brown, pushed the button, and waited. No one answered.

She waited five minutes and tried again. No one answered. Enough was enough, she jumped up on the gate, and worked herself half way over the gate when it opened.

Nadine walked inside. She watched the gate close again with Harriet still on top of it.

Slowly Harriet worked herself free of the gate and stood inside. She looked at Nadine, "I guess it worked."

Then becoming excited again, she moved off looking for her grandfather's apartment. She found it on the second floor and raced up the stairs.

Nadine remained below. She saw an older man walking slowly towards her. She knew instantly who it was. She smiled, "Are you Henry Brown?"

The old man stopped, looked at her hard, "Who wants to know?"

"Your granddaughter at the top of the stairs for one."

He looked up at Harriet a moment, turned back to Nadine, "I don't have a granddaughter. You must be mistaken."

"There is no mistake Henry Brown," Nadine said, "She is your granddaughter whether you accept her or not."

Harriet, coming down the steps, stopped halfway, "You're Henry Brown, right?" She could feel her heart racing.

"Could be, come here, and let me look at you."

Harriet slowly walked down the steps until she was face to face with Henry Brown.

He looked her over closely, "Come here child, and give your grandfather a hug."

Harriet ran, threw her arms around him. She buried her head into his shoulder.

Henry pushed her back after a few minutes, "Come on, let's go to my apartment. We have a lot of catching up to do." Leading the way, he took them up the stairs, and into his apartment. It looked well lived in showing an organized mess. He shoved some pillows off the couch allowing them to sit.

He went to the kitchen, "Would you like some tea? I also have some coffee left over from this morning."

They both said tea. A few minutes later Henry produced two cups of tea. Once they settled, he asked, "I guess this means my son is dead?"

"Yes sir," Nadine said. "Murdered along with his staff and driver. Harriet escaped the massacre because we were trapped in an ice cream parlor across town."

Harriet's tears began to flow.

Nadine continued; "The government confiscated all of the assets including the house, money, and artifacts. The only thing they left Harriet was the limousine, and the private investigator office building."

"I am very sorry to hear about my son. I knew this day would come. The office building and limousine belonged to me. When I closed the office, I had no need for the limousine, and gave it to him."

Harriet dried her tears, looked at him with her innocent blue eyes, "I want to reopen the office. I found the picture and the money."

Henry smiled, "The money is yours. You do not need to open the office."

"I want to open it," Harriet said. "I have no other prospects. I can go to school, but I have to acquire 4000 hours of experience before I can get my private investigators license. That means I have to work for someone. Realistically no one is going to hire me, so I need your license to open the business. Then in two years I can apply for my own license."

"I'm supposed to be retired. My doctor said no stress if I want to live longer. I simply cannot handle the office. That was why I wanted your dad to take it over."

"I can take it over if you help me."

"Have you had any training?"

"No, but I am fast learner."

"This is no easy job. It requires long hours, and training in self-defense, fire arms, and how to handle prisoners."

"I can get all of the training, but I will need your license to operate."

Henry looked at Nadine closely, "Are you planning on being part of this?"

"No sir, I am not cut out for it. I will stay in the tutoring business, but I will help from time to time if she needs me. I told her father I would look after her."

Henry could see more between the two of them, but he did not push it, "Okay, I will allow you to use my license on the condition you find the proper help to run it.

You can start by hiring my old girlfriend, Rose Blanchard. She needs the money since the government took her social security away. She's a professional hacker and got caught reading the President's E-mail. She told them she was only testing their security system.

They placed her on probation since she told them how she did it. To punish her, they took her social security. Don't mess with the government was the message."

"That's agreeable," Harriet said, "Anything else?"

"Keep me in the loop before you make a major decision, in other words, take advantage of my experience. I will check with Rose occasionally, but I do not want to be bothered with the day-to-day stuff. I am supposed to be retired."

"Done!"

"Then you may open the business after you have assembled your team. That means you will need to find someone with experience in handling the rough element in making an arrest. I don't want you taking on that element by yourself. You will use your brains, and not your muscle.

You will need a gun, but first you will need training. The law requires fourteen hours including six hours on the line. Get a gun you will feel comfortable with, and practice using it. The gun is your last resort. Use every other means before resorting to it. It's only meant to save your life. Your father might have survived if he had a gun."

"Yes sir," Harriet said. "I have a lot to do."

"You need it all in place before you open. Now when is your father's funeral?"

"This Sunday at three o'clock at the Presbyterian church."

"Then I will meet you there. I will bring Rose with me if that is okay."

"Yes, that will be fine," Harriet said standing. She gave her grandfather a hug, "Thank you for believing in me."

"I just hope I made the right decision," Henry said taking the hug. He gave Nadine a light hug, "Take care of her."

"Yes sir, but you have just made it more difficult."

"She has to grow."

"Yes sir, but why so fast?"

"We don't always choose our path," Henry said as he pushed Nadine away.

Nadine drove the limousine home.

Harriet was too excited. She was going to have her own private investigator business. She began thinking what she had to do next. She would fix the office up. It could use a good paint job inside and out. She had to conserve her money. It had to last until the business could start contributing. She needed to get into school, and work on her degree in police science. She would have to start that immediately.

Sunday, she meant Rose Blanchard at the funeral. She was definitely in her late sixties, but she had a youthful feel about her that made her younger. She did not wear makeup and wore an expensive suit to the funeral indicating she had money at one time. She still had her figure, her black hair had streaks of gray that fell to her shoulders. Her mother was Spanish, and her father was Arabic. She could speak both languages.

Rose shook her hand, "I am sorry for your loss."

"Thank you," Harriet said, and sat down beside Nadine. Rose and Henry sat down on the other side of her. Harriet noticed a tear developing in Henry's eyes. He blew his nose and tried to smile.

The minister came by, introduced himself, shook Henry's hand. Then he began the service.

While the service was in progress, Nadine closed her eyes. She could feel George's presence beside her. She cut it off when she saw Harriet crying. Trying to comfort her, he was making her more upset. Finally, he left, and Nadine could no longer feel him.

Chief Detective Ramos was the only other person to come to the funeral. Henry did not have friends, and his associates were in the drug cartel. They would not be showing. Harriet had to pay for the funeral. She kept the cost to a minimum.

After the funeral, Harriet cornered Detective Ramos, "Did you find out who killed my father?"

"It's going to take a while," Detective Ramos said, "We believe a professional did the actual shooting because he took out all the witnesses. We also believe the Columbia Drug Cartel hired the professional. So, you see none of this is going to be easy."

"Who is working on the case?" Harriet asked.

"Just me at the moment," Ramos said. "We have other murders with more evidence taking a priority. Even I am limited to how much time I can spend on it."

"You have done nothing, then?"

"We are hurting for any hard evidence to link it to anyone."

"Then I am going to hire a private investigator to give you a hand," Harriet said, "If that is all right with you." She was thinking her company.

"I'll take any help I can get," Ramos said backing his way out of the church thinking: "After you do the pathology, where do you take it if you have no suspects?" When he made it to the door, he quick-stepped outside.

Harriet felt depressed. She turned to her grandfather, "They probably shelved the case."

"They probably have. Their desks are full of cases, and all of them probably have more to go on than this case. If it gets solved, you will have to do it."

"I'll come over tomorrow to straighten up the office for you," Rose said.

"I really cannot pay you yet, maybe…"

"Don't worry about it," Rose said. "At least I won't be sitting home getting in trouble with my computer."

"Do you have a key?"

Rose took a hairpin out of her hair, "I always carry one."

Harriet smiled, the first time in a few days. "Then I am going to check into school tomorrow".

"Good, there is also a friend of mine I would recommend driving the limousine," Henry said.

"I don't think I should be hiring a driver," Harriet said. "I can drive."

"I heard about your driving test. I think everyone there would appreciate you finding yourself a driver."

Harriet smiled slightly remembering the accidents when she took her driving test.

Police Shooting Range

Chief of Detectives Ramos walked into the shooting range building. He met Mark Mathews, the thin, middle age shooting instructor, "Do I get the range all to myself today."

"Seems you're the only one qualifying today, sir."

"Any particular booth?"

"Take this one," Mathews said. "It's clean."

Ramos stepped into the second booth. He moved up to the range. He placed his gun on the shelf in front of him, "I'm ready."

"Go ahead, and good luck. Get them all in the bullseye."

Ramos took a deep breath. Allowing the air to escape slowly, he picked up his issued Police 38 Special, sighted down range at the bullseye, and fired six rapid shots. Replacing his pistol, he turned back to Mathew, "I think I qualified again."

Mathew pulled the target up, glanced at it, "You make it look easy, three in the bullseye, two near the bullseye, and one on the edge. That qualifies you."

"Thanks," Ramos said handing him a sheet of paper, "If you will sign it, I'll be on my way."

Mathew signed the paper, placed it in his folder, "I will have it mailed to you. Come back anytime, it gets lonely here."

Ramos nodded, "Fun time is over," He walked out of the gun range.

Christopher Charles

Mathew watched him leave. When the door closed, he took out his knife, and removed the six bullets in the target. He placed them in a bag and made a phone call.

Phone:

"Mathew here, yes sir, I have the bullets."

Pause:

"I'll bring them over," Mathew said. He closed his phone, left the gun range, and walked fast to the Police Station.

Cal State College

Monday, Harriet drove the Limousine to Cal State College. She remained on surface streets. She almost took out two cars when she made a wide left-hand turn. She managed the parking lot and found a space. It took her three tries before she had the limousine lined up right.

After asking four people, she found the administration building, and the Guidance Counselor. She found her Bachelor of Arts degree fulfilled the majority of the required courses. She just needed to take specialty courses related to police work. She had it set up where she could complete the program in one year taking three courses twice a week in the morning. She had missed a week of school, but her councilor did not see a problem.

She purchased her books, and paid the tuition costing her just under 2,400 dollars. She was rapidly using up her money. She finished her admission in time to make her forth class at eleven in the morning. It had already started. She did not have time to take her books back to the limousine. She could barely carry them.

Her first class was on the 'Rights of the Individual When Making an Arrest'. She tried to work the door open with her back, but it was not working. Suddenly she felt the door moving. Looking up, she saw a large muscular black man holding the door for her.

"Thank you," she said as she slipped into the room. She found a chair in back, plopped her stack of books on the desk, making a loud sound. The class in progress stopped, everyone in the class looked back at her trying to organize herself into her chair.

The large black man sat down beside her, "Do you need any help? The name's Mc Craw. Tim Mc Craw."

"My name is Harriet. Thank you, but I am fine," She said quickly.

The instructor cleared his throat, the class turned his direction. Then looking at Mc Craw, he said, "We are lucky to have former Detective Mc Craw of the Los Angeles Police Department with us. Would you come up to the front of the class and demonstrate the correct method of making an arrest."

Mc Craw, a little irritated worked himself to his feet, and started forward.

"You, young lady beside him, please come up here too."

Harriet looked up, pointed to herself.

"Yes, you, young lady, please come up here, and be our felon."

Harriet stood, balanced her shaking books on the desk, and followed Mc Craw to the front of the room. She was more than a little apprehensive.

While they approached the front of the classroom, the instructor said, "To arrest a felon trying to escape sometimes requires a little roughing up, but how do you arrest a young female without violating her rights?"

He handed Mc Craw a pair of handcuffs, "Arrest her for selling a package of spice on the street."

He gave Harriet a package of white powder, "What is your name?"

"Harriet... Harriet Brown, sir."

"Okay Harriet, you are our felon." He stepped away from her, "Mr. Mc Craw, make the arrest."

Mc Craw grasped the hand holding the spice, retrieved the sack of spice, "You are under arrest for selling drugs on the street." He began giving Harriet her rights as he turned her around. He took the wrist of her other arm closing the cuffs. He did a quick pat down causing Harriet to blush. He completed the reading of her rights, turned her around to face the class, and said, "She is ready for transport."

"Very good," the instructor said, "He did not use undo force. There was no need to slap her up against the wall to cuff her. This was a judgment call. She was not resisting, but you need to be ready if she does resist. You only use the force necessary to arrest the felon. Undo force will weaken your case in court and may even allow the felon to go free. You also noticed he protected the evidence."

Then turning to Harriet and Tim, "You may return to your seats."

Harriet tried to walk back with her arms pinned to her back.

"Wait a minute, we need the cuffs back," the instructor said.

The class laughed.

Harriet, embarrassed, looked back at the instructor for help.

"Come here Harriet, I think I have the keys to those somewhere here," the instructor said searching his pockets. Then he smiled, waved his hand, "They're kids play handcuffs. They will open without a key. Mr. Mc Craw please help her."

Mc Craw smiled and turned Harriet around. He tried to pull the cuffs apart, but they were stuck tight. The instructor came up handed Mc Craw the key as the class laughed.

Mc Craw, irritated, unlocked the cuffs, and handed them to the instructor. He suddenly realized the instructor knew why he was taking his class. He followed Harriet back to her seat.

"Thank you for releasing me," Harriet said. "Those cuffs pinch."

Mc Craw frowned and took his seat.

After the class was over, Harriet made a try for her books again. Picking them up, she headed for the door.

Mc Craw opened the door a second time, "Would you like some help?"

"No, I'll be okay," Harriet said, "I think I can manage." She headed for the parking lot and her limousine. She did not see Mc Craw following her. When she approached her car, she saw two men in dark suits standing next to it.

She walked by them to open the door. Suddenly she found her books on the ground, and her back up against the car. She looked up to see the larger of the two men staring her in the face.

"Where is it?" The large man demanded.

She could feel herself trembling. In a weak voice she asked, "Where is what?"

"The money your old man took!"

"I don't know what you are talking about."

The big man was about to slug her, when he found himself flying through the air. He landed on the pavement.

Christopher Charles

Mc Craw turned to the other man who immediately backed off running after the big man coming to his feet. They both ran across the parking lot.

Mc Craw turned to Harriet, "Friends of yours?"

Harriet, still shaking, "I have never met either of them before."

"They know who you are well enough."

"They seemed to think I had their money."

"Why would they think that?"

"My father died recently," Harriet said. "I think it has something to do with that."

"How did he die?"

"Someone shot him two times in the chest," Harriet said dropping a few tears. "The police are not investigating it, because they have nothing to go on."

"You are not talking about Henry Brown, are you?"

"Yes, he was my father. They said the drug cartel had him killed."

"Did they know why?"

"According to those men, he took their money. Now they think I know where he put it. I don't have anything except the limo, and a detective agency."

"A detective agency?"

"That's why I am taking these classes. I am going to operate it."

"You need a license to operate a detective agency."

"I know, I have one, or I should say my grandfather has one. I am using his."

"I think you are out of your league here. You should be attending tea parties."

"I can run a detective agency."

"You were not doing that well a moment ago."

"I just need to hire the right people to help me is all."

Mc Craw looked at her a second, "You plan on hiring help?"

"Yes, I need someone with experience immediately."

"Maybe I could be of some help. I am presently unemployed and could use the money."

"I thought you worked for the police department."

"That is not my present position," Mc Craw said. "I am willing to hear any offers."

"It will have to be on a commission bases, say fifteen percent of revenue you bring in."

"Mc Craw smiled, "That will be thirty-five percent of what I bring in."

"I have an overhead to pay for, it will have to be twenty percent, or I cannot hire you."

"Make it twenty-five percent, and I will help you find out who killed your old man for free."

"Deal!" Harriet said holding out her limp hand.

Mc Craw shook it closing the deal.

She handed him a card, "This is the office address, but it needs some paint and fixing up. Let's meet there tomorrow at nine to go over the details."

He nodded, "I'll follow you home to be sure those thugs are not following you."

"Thank you, but I will be okay now."

Mc Claw helped her pick up her books, "I cannot carry a gun. I just wanted you to know that."

"Then I should have said twenty percent," Harriet said, and smiled. "I need your phone number in case those men come around again."

"Let me have your phone." She handed it to him, he placed his number on her speed dial. "There, just press two, and you'll reach me."

"Thank you," Harriet said placing her books into the limousine. She walked around to the driver seat, and climbed in.

"You need a driver for that thing," Mc Craw yell.

"I know, I am getting one," Harriet said as she started the limousine. It jerked back, almost hitting the car behind her. Somehow, she barely managed to miss another parked car when she made the turn with her long vehicle.

Mc Craw shook his head and headed for his truck. He had heavy shocks installed, that lifted it a foot and a half higher. It also had a large grill bumper protecting the front end. He climbed up into the truck and followed the limousine out of the parking lot keeping some distance behind it. Easy to follow, she was not driving fast.

He held back, and noticed another car following it. He watched the man in the passenger seat with his window down talking on his phone.

The limousine pulled up to stoplight. The black car pulled up behind it. Mc Craw stopped behind the black car. Irritated the two men continued to follow his new boss; he jumped out and ran to the passenger side of the black car. He ripped the phone from the man's hand and leaped back into his truck.

The light changed. The limousine and cars started forward. The lane freed up on the driver's side of the black car.

Mc Claw pulled his truck up beside the black car as it pulled away from the light. Holding the phone up, he waved it in the air.

The driver in the black car rolled his window down and pointed his gun out the window. He was no longer watching where he was going. Mc Claw swung his truck hard into the black car.

The huge grill struck the black car on the driver's side door. The force loosened the wheel from the man's hand shoving him forward against the dash. The black car out of control swerved hard to the right. It smashed into a light pole as his gun went off.

The bullet struck the driver in the chest rendering him unconscious. The other man, shaken, staggered out of the car. He did not see what was in Mc Craw's hand. He only saw it pointing at them. Believing Mc Craw had shot his partner, he ran off down the alley. The horn in the car continued to blare until the police arrived a few minutes later to turn it off.

Mc Craw placed the stolen phone to his ear. He heard the voice on the other end. It sounded familiar, but he could not place it. The man on the other end realizing no one was talking hung up. Mc Claw placed the phone number into his phone. He would call it later.

Mc Craw continued to follow the limousine until he felt she would be safe, then he turned around, and headed back towards the wreck. The police had the area secured. The ambulance was pulling up.

He recognized Chief Detective Ramos coming away from the wreck, and yelled out the window, "What happened?"

"Some guy took a bullet hole in the chest," Ramos said, "Looks like he was trying to commit suicide. Witness said he was driving when he shot himself, but I hear there was someone else in the car. It could be a murder attempt, and the gun planted in his hand."

"Interesting, let me know how it turns out," Mc Craw said. The traffic began to build up behind him. He nodded and moved on down the street with a slight smile on his face.

He had a phone to decode. He would find out who they were working for. First, he had to get rid of his grill with the black car's paint on it. It took him an hour, but he had it off. He threw the grill into a dumpster after his had wiped it clean. He knew some kid would be picking it up.

Later that night the man from the black car finally stopped running. He had made a call on a pay phone. Now he waited in a dark alley downtown, their usual meeting place. The man said he would be there in twenty minutes.

Finally, a car entered the alley. "About time," he thought. He flicked his cigarette and started walking towards it. Suddenly the car picked up speed coming straight towards him. He turned and began running up the alley. He saw the end of the alley. Kicking in harder, he could feel the lights behind him. Suddenly he felt himself in the air before the left fender and door struck him in the legs and back sending him against the wall of the building. His lifeless crumpled body slipped to the ground.

The car screeched its brakes, stopped, reversed, and came back to the crumpled body. A man jumped from the car, ran to the body, and went through his pockets. Taking a handful of items, he climbed back in the car. It sped out of the alley onto the main street.

"Did you get his phone?"

"He didn't have it on him."

"That's too bad, he was talking to me." The car continued to move into the night.

4 The Team

At nine sharp the next day, Harriet arrived at her office. She saw three cars parked next to the building. She pulled the limousine in front of the office and went inside. Rose sat at the reception desk working on her laptop computer. Mc Craw stood beside the desk holding his phone to his ear. A medium built middle aged Korean man dressed in a brown uniform sat in a chair in front of the desk waiting for her.

Harriet smiled as the Korean man stood, "You're the chauffeur my grandfather sent over?"

"Name Youngsu, Mr. Brown say you need driver." He extended his hand.

Harriet extended her limp hand, "Welcome aboard. Have you met Mr. Mc Craw and Rose?"

"I worked with Rose before."

Mc Craw nodded, "We've met!" Then turning to Harriet, he said, "I have the phone of the man who tried to slug you yesterday. He has some interesting phone numbers here."

Harriet smiled, released Youngsu hand, turned to Mr. Mc Craw, "How did you get his phone?"

"He had an accident, seems his partner shot himself, and sent his car into a light pole. The police said it may have been a murder. They believe the guy shot the driver, put his gun in his hand, and left the scene."

"I have it on the police report," Rose said. "They're looking for him."

"Wait! Wait!" Harriet shouted. "You are all going too fast for me." She looked back at Mc Craw, "That still does not explain how you possess the man's phone."

"I took it from him while they were parked waiting for the light behind you." Pausing, he continued in a low voice. "I saw them following you. I noticed him on his phone, his window was down. I jumped out of my truck, reached in, and took his phone."

"He just let you take it?"

"When the light changed, I pulled up beside him, and showed him the phone. The driver pulled a gun. I rammed his car to avoid taking a bullet and sent them into a light pole. The man, intent on killing me, didn't see the pole, and shot himself when the car impacted the pole. The guy with the missing phone took off down the alley."

"Okay, Rose, your turn?"

"I hacked into the police computer and found the incident report."

"Is that against the law?"

"It is if you get caught."

"I don't think we can afford to hire a lawyer if you get caught," Harriet said. "Now, what did you find?"

"The man who shot himself died on the way to the hospital. This morning they found a homeless man dead in an alley ten blocks from the scene. They are calling it a hit and run."

"Did they find out who they were?" Harriet asked.

"They had no identification on them, or if they did it is not in the police records."

"How about the gun or a phone on the one who shot himself?" Mc Craw asked.

"A throw away gun, and no phone. He's a John Doe."

"The man on the other end of the phone number," Harriet said, "He's still alive." She allowed that to settle.

Continuing, she said, "Okay, first we need to get this office organized. We need the boards off the windows, paint, and a general clean up. You two," pointing to Mc Craw and Youngsu, "Work on that. I'll get the phones working, and the electricity turned on." She pulled out five hundred dollars, "Here, this will get you started." She turned and left the office.

It took her most of the day, but she managed to get everything working. She had to leave deposits to speed things. When she came back to the office, the sun was setting.

Exhausted, she noticed everyone had left, but the office looked clean. She unlocked the door, went inside. Closing the door, it locked automatically. She slipped her keys in her pocket and turned the lights on. They worked. She went to her office. She saw the John Doe's phone on her desk.

She dropped her purse on the desk, flopped into her chair, and looked at the phone a moment. Suddenly car lights pulled into the parking lot piercing the slightly opened window behind her drying the paint.

The car turned its lights off but kept the motor running. She heard two men walking around the building to the front door.

She dropped the phone in her pocket, quickly locked the office door, and ran to the window. A nail held it open. She waited a moment. She had to time this. She had trouble breathing.

When she heard the front door being smashed, she raised the window. The pounding on the door covered the sound of the window opening. She climbed outside. She could feel her heart pounding harder. Her dress caught on the nail holding the window up. Ripping her dress, she pulled herself free as the front door gave way.

She noticed the license plate of black car and memorized it. She felt her car keys in her pocket, started for the limousine, when she stopped.

Her mind working again, she had to keep them from coming after her. She ran back to the black car, reached in, turned the motor off, and removed the keys. She pressed the remote. The car door locked.

She ran for her limousine parked in front of the office. She noticed the kicked in front door. She opened the limousine door on the driver's side and slipped behind the wheel. She could not find the keyhole with her hand shaking.

Inside the two men had kicked the office door in. They saw her purse on the desk. One of the men lifted the purse high, the contents fell on the desk. Harriet's phone fell out. He quickly placed it in his pocket.

The other man looked out the window, "She went out here." Then looking out the window, he asked, "Did you leave the car running?"

"Yeah, why?"

"Damn, it's not running now!" He turned and ran out of the office with the other man following him. They made it to the front door when the limousine pulled out from the curb.

Inside the limousine, Harriet dialed 911 on the John Doe's phone as her hands continued to shake.

A woman came on the phone:

"Two men have broken into my office," Harriet said.

"Address and any other information, please."

Harriet gave her the license number of the car, and her address.

"Where are you now?"

"I am driving away from the office."

"Good, do not go back, I will send a patrol car over."

"Yes madam, thank you," she closed her phone. She wanted to call Mc Craw, but she did not have his number. It was on her phone. She drove straight to Nadine's house.

The two men walked up the street away from the office.

The younger man said, "We can't go leaving the car?"

"What would you suggest? Sit there and wait for the police to arrive."

"But they will trace the car."

"Yeah, we'll have to fix that," the older man said.

They turned the corner as the patrol car pulled up in front of the detective agency. The two police officers stepped out of the patrol car with their guns drawn. They saw the bashed in door.

They checked the office, saw the open window, and the desk spewed with the contents of Harriet's purse.

One of the police officers pulled his phone to talk with the dispatch office.

"There was a break in, but no one's here now." He looked out the window and shined his flashlight outside. He immediately saw the black car, "The black car with the license number you gave is still here. We're checking it out."

Christopher Charles

"Stay where you are," the dispatcher said. "I am sending a tow truck to pick it up."

"Yes madam, standing by."

Nadine's House

Harriet pulled up in front. She saw Nadine waiting for her at the door. She ran into her arms, closed her eyes, and continued to shake.

Calming her some, Nadine took her inside, sat her at the table, and made her a cup of tea. Finally, she asked, "What happened?"

"Two men broke into the office while I was there. I went out the back window. I saw their car running, removed the keys, and came here."

"Did you call the police?"

"Yes, they said they would send a patrol car."

"Then we had better call Mr. Mc Craw. I don't want you going back there until he's checked it out."

"I don't have my phone. I left it in the office."

"I have his number," Nadine said. She found her phone, dialed him, handing the phone to Harriet.

Phone Conversation:

"Mc Craw here."

"This is Harriet Brown. Someone broke into the office. I escaped out the back window and took the keys to their car. The license number is PDJ820. The police should be there, but Nadine thought you should go back and check it out before I did."

"She thought right," Mc Craw said. "You stay put."

Twenty minutes later Mc Craw pulled up in front of the detective office behind the police car, but the black car was gone. He recognized one of the police officers, Jed Black, waiting in the office.

"Mc Craw, what are you doing here?"

"This is where I work, Jed. What happened here?"

"Seems two men broke in, the lady called 911, and escaped out the back window."

"I know, she also said there was a black car in the parking lot. Where is that?"

"They just towed it away."

"Who towed it?"

Jed looked at him a second, "It didn't have a name on the door. You'll have to ask the dispatcher."

"Didn't he give you a receipt?"

"I called the dispatcher," Jed said. "She said to give the car to them. It seemed a little irregular, but that was my orders. I didn't get a receipt."

"I don't suppose you searched the car?"

"It was locked," Jed said. "I was told they would check the car out in the yard."

Mc Craw walked into the office. He saw Harriet's purse, and the contents spread out on the desk. He swept everything back into the purse and closed the window.

Jed looked in, "We'll be leaving. I would recommend placing an alarm system in here, something with a loud siren."

"Yeah, thanks," Mc Craw said. He found the hammer and nails as they were leaving. He placed the boards back up on the door, and nailed it closed. He drove to the Pasadena police yard to check on the car. He did not expect to find it.

He stood outside the locked gate, flashed his flashlight around. He only saw a few cars with dented fenders.

He drove to the Los Angeles police department's parking lot on a hunch. He saw a tow truck leaving. He spotted a black car sitting at the end of the parking lot. He flashed his light on the license plate. It checked.

He dialed Nadine, "Call Rose, and tell her to bring her computer. Then have that Youngsu guy meet us at your place. I am coming there. What's your address?"

Nadine gave him her address. Thirty minutes later, all of them were arriving at Nadine's house.

Mc Craw walked in, looked around, "Are we having a séance?"

Nadine ignored the comment and led him to the kitchen.

Rose, already there, continued to work her computer.

Mc Craw handed Harriet her purse, "Check what might be missing."

Harriet took her purse and began checking. She looked up, "Only my phone."

"You still have that guy's phone?"

Harriet held it up, "Yes."

"They found you a little too easy. Let me see it." Taking the phone, he tried taking it apart.

Rose watched him a minute, "Hand it here." Taking it, she asked, "What are you looking for?"

"The chip!"

She stuck her fingernail into the side of it. It popped open. She looked it over, found the chip, flipped it out, and handed it to Mc Craw.

He started to smash it against the table.

Harriet stopped him, yelling, "Wait, that's the tracking chip, right?"

Mc Craw nodded.

"Then let's use it to our advantage," Harriet said. "Let's place it on something that moves around the city. Let them follow that and leave us alone."

"What would you suggest?"

"Maybe a police car."

Mc Craw smiled, "I'll be back in a few minutes." He left the house, drove into downtown Pasadena. He spotted a patrol car and pulled up a half block away. The police officer was in the process of making an arrest. The passenger's side window was down. He threw the chip through the window. It landed on the floor in the back seat. He turned and walked back to his truck. A half hour later, he pulled into Nadine's driveway. Youngsu had arrived.

Nadine let him in and led him to the kitchen where everyone was.

Rose looked up, "I traced the license plate of the black car before they erased it. It belongs to the Los Angeles Police Department."

"Figured," Mc Craw said.

"Why would the Los Angeles Police Department want to kick in my office door?"

"That's a good question," Mc Craw said.

"And more importantly we will all have to remove the chips in our phones," Rose said.

They all looked at her.

She continued, "They have Miss Brown's phone. That means they have all of our phone numbers. The police have access to files in the phone company. It is no problem for them to access the chips in our phones."

"Do you really think the Los Angeles Police Department is out to get us," Harriet asked.

"They broke your office door down," Rose said.

"What about the Pasadena Police Department?" Mc Craw asked.

"You tell me."

"Here's my phone," Mc Craw said.

Rose began taking the chips out of the phones. She handed them to Mc Craw, "That's the last of them."

"Where do you want me to place these?"

"On anything that moves," Harriet said. "Let's give them something to keep them busy."

Mc Craw took them and left. He taped his chip up under the back end of a large trash truck. He found two police cars for Rose and Youngsu. He threw Nadine's into a delivery truck. Feeling better, he headed back to Nadine's house.

Rose began working her computer. She wanted to find out whom the police department had issued the black car too. She had the Los Angeles Police computers on line when Mc Craw arrived. When he entered the kitchen, she had the name of the police officer. Looking up, she said, "The police car was issued to Detective Ramos."

"He's Chief of detectives for the Los Angeles Police Department." Mc Craw said.

"He's supposed be handling the murder of my father."

"And the murder of my wife," Mc Craw added.

"Why would he be breaking into my office?" Harriet asked.

"We only know the car was assigned to him," Rose said. "We don't know it was him driving it."

"I'll find that out tomorrow," Mc Craw said.

"We also have the car key here," Rose said. "There's a smudge of a fingerprint I was able to pick off with scotch tape. I need to ink it when I go back to the office."

"That will need a new door, and an alarm system." Mc Craw said.

"That's a good idea," Harriet said, "I'll look into one. Mc Craw will check out Detective Ramos. Try not to show our hand. Especially how we came about acquiring the knowledge it was his car. Rose, continue with the computer. See who was working that night and had cars. The ones that didn't may be our police officers if it wasn't Ramos."

"What makes you think it wasn't Ramos?"

"It didn't feel like him," Harriet said. "These were mean men intent on doing me harm. Ramos would not have needed to break into the office to reach me. I would have allowed him to enter, and he knows this."

"I'll see what I can find out," Mc Craw said leaving.

They all began filing out behind him leaving Harriet in Nadine's hands.

Harriet took a deep breath, relaxed as the door closed. She needed a gun. She needed one immediately.

The next day Mc Craw called Detective Ramos and made a lunch appointment with him at a little outdoor restaurant on Colorado Boulevard in Pasadena. They were both detectives before Ramos received his promotion to Chief of Detectives two weeks before he became Mr. Brown's Handler.

Mc Craw took a table facing the street. He stood when Ramos arrived. They shook hands as they both took their seat. They gave their orders, and talked a few minutes about old times on the force, when Mc Craw asked, "Where was your car last night?"

"Why at my house. I drive it home every night. You know that."

"Then why is it in the police parking lot?"

"Are you checking up on my driving habits?"

"There was a break-in, and the ones doing the breaking in drove your car."

"That's impossible. My car remained in my driveway all night. I drove to work this morning."

Mc Craw pulled out the slip of paper with the license plate number on it, "Is this yours?"

"That was the car I turned in two weeks ago. I drive a SLK 230. It's twenty years old, but it drives nice."

"Then who's driving your other car?"

"I don't know, but I could check it out for you."

"Thanks, the guys driving it, smashed into a detective agency in Pasadena last night."

"Maybe they were trying to make an arrest."

"You don't go smashing doors down in another city without notifying the locals. This was no arrest attempt. They wanted to do harm to the young lady inside."

"Did she get hurt?"

"She escaped out the back window, turned their car off, took the key, and left in her car. The tow company took the car back to the Los Angeles Police parking lot like nothing happened. We ran the plates. They came up yours."

"Do you have some connection with this lady?"

"Yeah, I work for her."

"You got a job then?"

"Yes, thanks to her, but this is the second attempt to do her harm."

"You going to tell me?"

"This has to stay between you and me."

"It stays!"

Mc Craw nodded, "That guy who shot himself, and his buddy, the one you found in the alley tried to beat her up earlier. The bigger guy, the one who shot himself, was about to smash her in the face when I stopped him."

"Is there more?"

"Yeah, they drove off in the same car that was in the accident. I assume the one in the alley was his partner. Can you give me any information on them?"

"No, they both are dead. We have no leads. I have other cases I need to look into."

"Don't you think it's weird no one has identified them. They have finger prints and wallets with ID's in them."

"You know we are overloaded. We have to be selective in what we investigate."

"I think you ought to be checking them, since there seems to be a connection between the two. I like to keep my boss alive."

"Sorry Mc Craw, I closed the case," Ramos said.

"You don't mind if I protect her?"

"Go ahead! If you find anything, give me call, and I will look into it."

"I'm going to hold you to that."

The food arrived, the conversation turned to lighter subjects.

Finally, Ramos asked, "You're not driving, are you?"

"Well some. I need to get around to work and take the damn classes."

"The judge took your license away. You're driving without one. You get caught, you go to prison."

"I know, I'll be careful."

Ramos shook his head, "You have to stop now! It only takes one little thing. The boys are wagering how long it's going to take."

"Okay, okay, I'll stop."

5 The Gun

Harriet finally fell asleep. The next morning, she woke up, and made her way to the kitchen. She had the coffee going and headed for the shower. She slipped on a pair of pants, worked her hair, and placed some makeup, but she would not be ready until she had her coffee. Today was gun day. She could not depend on Mc Craw coming to her rescue every time she found herself in trouble.

Nadine came into the kitchen, took advantage of Harriet's coffee, "Where are you headed today?"

"I'm going to see about an alarm system and get some protection. Last night showed how vulnerable I am. I'm going to change that today."

"You're going to wait for your chauffeur?"

"I really don't need a chauffeur."

"You would not have been alone last night if he was with you."

"I don't know what he could have done last night."

Christopher Charles

"Don't underestimate him," Nadine said. "Your grandfather would not have sent him otherwise."

"Okay, you can call him. I don't mind being pampered."

Nadine picked up her phone, called Youngsu. Ten minutes later, he pulled into the drive. Harriet just had time to write down some gun shops she found on the internet. She also needed another phone.

Rose arrived at the office as Mc Craw finished replacing the door. She had been in her computer trying to trace the whereabouts of Harriet's phone. She worked her way through the phone company's security system, but it took time.

Harriet had her chauffeur stop at her second gun shop. The first one only sold rifles. He suggested he had some pistols in the back, but something did not feel right. He made a phone call when she left.

She walked up a half block to her waiting limousine, "I think we had better be moving."

"Yes madam, where to now?"

"The next address on the list."

"Yes madam."

Harriet liked having the limousine and driver. It made things much more efficient. She no longer had to find a place to park the long Limousine.

They arrived at the second gun shop. This one looked cleaner and newer. She felt better and went inside.

The man behind the counter polishing his rifles looked up, "How can I help you Miss…a"

"Harriet Brown, I want to purchase a pistol for protection."

"Do you have any experience using a pistol?"

"No, but I plan on taking the required fourteen hours to learn how."

"You do not need the fourteen hours unless you plan on concealing it."

"I am a private detective. I need it for protection, and I plan on concealing it."

He pointed to the bulletproof case in front of him, "These are all good weapons for young ladies."

Harriet looked them over, "Will these stop a large man?"

"It would if you were very accurate, and shot him in the head," the man said.

"If I am not very accurate?"

"He would still be able to do you harm."

"What do you have that would stop him no matter where I shot him?"

He turned pulling out a drawer revealing a large military Colt-Forty-five. He took it from the drawer, placed in on the counter, "This was made to stop anything it hits."

Harriet looked it over closely, then she looked up at the man, "Can I touch it?"

"It's not loaded," the man said. "Go ahead, lift it, get the feel for it. This is a relic now. The army has not used these since World War II, but there are a few of them left around."

Harriet picked the gun up. It felt heavy, but she could hold it with two hands. She moved it around aiming at things. She could not keep pointing the gun for long, because the weight caused her arms to tire.

Turning back to the man behind the counter, she asked, "It will stop anything it hits?"

"That it will. They don't make guns like this anymore. This is no pansy gun. This will stop anything."

"Show me how you load it?"

The man took the clip out of the box and loaded it with bullets. He slipped the clip into the gun, released the safety, "It is ready for use, madam."

"Let me try it,' Harriet said.

The man removed the clip and handed her the gun.

She practiced loading the clip and removing it until she had it down. She loaded the chamber. It was ready for use.

"Do you want more ammunition for it?"

"That I do."

"How many boxes do you want?"

"I need some for practicing, maybe four boxes."

"That will be six hundred dollars."

"Harriet wrote him a check and placed the gun in her purse."

The man started to tell her she could not conceal it yet, but then she did say she was going to take the fourteen hours. He took the money, smiled as she left. He had been trying to unload that relic for years.

"I need a telephone next Youngsu, take me to this address." She handed him the address of a Verizon store. Thirty minutes later, with fifteen hundred dollars missing from her checking account, she emerged with her new satellite phone. She called the office and Rose answered.

"I have my new phone," Harriet said, and gave her the number.

Rose wrote it down, "I already have the alarm people here. It's an old company your grandfather used to use. Thought it best to get someone we could trust."

"Yes, thank you."

"The door is fixed. I also have a lead on that fingerprint I found on the remote. His name is Jose Morales. I gave Mc Craw a picture and an address. He's checking it out."

"He can't be running off on his own. We need to plan these things."

"He's just following a lead, dear."

"Has he called in?"

"No," Rose said.

"What is the address?"

Rose gave her the address, "It's in the warehouse district in south LA. I don't know why he would be living there."

"We're heading there." She nodded to Youngsu, "You heard."

"Be careful, dear, there could be more there."

"We're only checking on Mc Craw."

South Los Angeles

Mc Craw drove through the industrial complex. He spotted the address parking his truck two buildings over. He walked by the large tilt up buildings meaning they pour the concrete on the ground, and then lift them to place.

They had a large garage door, and a smaller side door opening. They also had a few windows at ground level, and a couple up near the roof. They usually had a small office up the side of one wall that stood ten feet from the floor.

Mc Craw walked up to the small door and pounded with his fist. The door opened, a man in his thirties looked up at Mc Craw.

"I'm looking for Jose Morales." Mc Craw said.

The man turned, and yelled, "Hey Morales, there's someone here looking for you!"

"Send him up here!"

The man opened the door. He pointed to the office to his right. Mc Craw entered looking around slowly as he walked towards the steps. He had an uneasy feeling that he had just walked into something. He spotted two trucks, and some boxes in the dim light, the only light source coming from the overhead office.

He started up the stairs, and noticed another man coming out from behind a truck. He had his hand in his coat pocket. The man who opened the door followed him up the stairs. The door to the office hung open. He walked in to see a big man with black hair, and a mustache sitting behind a desk with his right hand below the desk.

The man looked at him hard, "Who sent you?"

Mc Craw glanced around, looked at the man behind the desk, "You Morales?"

"Could be, again, who sent you?"

Mc Craw could see the right arm move slightly. He knew there was a gun in it. "The guys' downtown wanted to see how you're doing?"

"We're ready, if that's what you want to know."

"Yeah, I think that was it," Mc Craw said, and started to leave the office.

The man following him up the stairs blocked the door, "You didn't answer the man's question."

"I told you the guys uptown, now get out of my way," Mc Craw started to grab the man when a bullet grazed his ear.

He froze waiting for another bullet.

"Back in here, and take a seat," Morales said, "Search him!"

When the man at the door started to search him, Mc Craw grabbed the man, swung him around, and threw him at the desk. All in one motion, he jumped out the door, and started down the steps when he ran into the gun muzzle of the third man at the bottom. He stopped placing his hands in the air.

"Bring his ass back up here," Morales yelled from inside the office.

Mc Craw turned slowly, walked back up the stairs, and entered the office with his hands in the air.

"Search him and see if he's carrying." Morales said.

The two men with guns drawn began searching Mc Craw. They came up with a wallet, some loose change, and a comb. They threw the contents to Morales.

"Sit down!" Morales commanded as he picked up the wallet.

The two men shoved Mc Craw into the chair in front of Morales and began tying him up with a rope.

Morales went through the wallet. He pulled out Mc Craw's license that had "Expired" across it. Looking up, Morales said, "So you're Detective Timothy Mc Craw LA Police."

"Was', is the operative word!" shouted Mc Craw. "They kicked me out two months ago. Now I'm looking for work. You have any suggestions?"

"Depends, what did they kick you out for?"

"For being a little rough on my arrest, somebody complained." Mc Craw said. He was thinking fast.

"That's easy enough to check out," Morales said. He pulled out his phone and made a call. No one answered. He left a message, put his phone away, looked at Mc Craw, "You have a few more minutes of living. You have anything else to say?"

"I'll wait for your confirmation."

Christopher Charles

Morales nodded to the two men, "Soften him up a bit. Maybe he will feel more like talking."

The two men began beating on Mc Craw.

Limousine

Harriet's limousine was speeding down the Harbor Freeway south as she loaded the 45 clip. Twenty minutes later, they arrived in the warehouse district. Her clip loaded, she pushed it in place as they passed the large warehouses. They made a turn and saw Mc Craw's truck parked outside a warehouse.

Youngsu pulled the limousine in beside it. He checked the building, no security cameras. After he helped Harriet from the car, he went to the trunk, taking out a small bag and a stepladder. He pulled out two pairs of gloves, gave one pair to Harriet, "Put them on, don't want fingerprints, Miss Brown."

Harriet felt the heavy gun in her purse. Youngsu carried the stepladder and his small bag. They moved quickly between the buildings staying away from the security cameras.

When they reached the address, Youngsu stopped, pointed to the security cameras on the buildings nearby. He reached into his bag and took out a set of rods that locked into place giving a forty-foot extension. He attached a black spray can to the end of this.

Then he lifted the spray can, and the forty-foot extension up to the security camera. Pulling a trigger at the bottom, the black paint came out of the can, covering the camera lens.

Approaching the target building, Youngsu pointed to the window on the side of the building. He held her back, pointed to the two security cameras on the side of the building pointing toward the window. He went to one, sprayed it, and then the other one. Finished, he quickly folded the rods, placing them along with the black spray can into his bag.

He pulled out a glasscutter and went to the window. He saw the sensor fixed to it. His mind registered old alarm system. Using the glasscutter, he cut a circle around the sensor. Then tapping it with his knuckle, he knocked it loose from the window.

Next, he pulled out a large suction cup. He placed the cup against the window, and pumped the air out freezing the cup to the glass. Putting the glasscutter to the edge of the window, he cut the window out while holding the cup. A slight jerk, and the window came loose. Easing the sensor through it, he took the window out, placing it alongside the building.

Releasing the suction cup, he placed it in his bag, and took out a piece of tape. Moving the piece of window with the senor on it to the side, he taped it against the wall. They could now enter.

He placed the step stool beside the window and leaped inside with his bag. He turned and helped Harriet through the window. When she was inside, he reached over, and picked up the stool. He motioned for her to follow him.

Harriet took out her pistol, released the safety. They moved deeper into the warehouse. The only light came from the office on the far wall. It gave them enough light to move below. They worked their way toward the office. They had to move between two trucks, and hundreds of four by four boxes stacked three deep. One open box revealed two-pound bags of a white substance.

Youngsu slipped a knife from beneath his uniform, stuck it into one of the bags. Retrieving it, he put the blade to his tongue, tasted it. He looked back at Harriet, "Cocaine."

Youngsu moved on until they could see the office clearly. They stopped and watched two men beating on one man tied to a chair.

Harriet instantly knew it was Mc Craw in the chair.

Youngsu leaned closer, whispered, "Count ten then shoot Miss Brown. Shoot at window, ceiling, use all bullets up."

Harriet nodded. Her heart beating fast, she watched Youngsu disappear into the darkness. She looked up at the lit office. She could see Mc Craw take another punch to the jaw.

Counting, she pointed her gun at the lit office. Finally, she reached ten. She aimed her gun with two hands at the office glass and fired. The recoil from the pistol sent her arms straight up and back. The barrel of the gun struck her up beside her head knocking her to the floor. Recovering, she remembered Youngsu saying she had to keep shooting.

Pointing the gun towards the ceiling, holding her arms straight up, she fired again. The recoil sent the gun, and her arms flying up over her head. Hanging onto the gun tight, she kept firing into the ceiling or anywhere her arms went.

The bullets ricocheting off the steel beams in the ceiling began striking the small office.

The first bullet pierced the glass window shattering it. Continuing, it took off the corner of the Morales' desk, and embedded itself into the wall across from him.

The sound from the small cannon vibrated through the building becoming louder with each blast. More shells ricocheted into the small office.

Morales, with fear in his eyes, headed for the stairs, yelling, "I'm getting the hell out of here!" He pushed the other two aside and blasted through the door. Going down the steps into the darkness and safety, he did not see Youngsu waiting for him.

Youngsu came out from between the trucks, hit the big man in the legs. He did a twist with his body sending the man to the concrete face first. The blow rendered him unconscious with a broken nasal, and zygomatic bones (facial bones).

The other two men recovering followed Morales out the door as two more bullets whizzed through the glass. The first one coming down had his gun pointing out into the darkness. When he reached the large truck, he found himself flying. His gun flew to the ground as his chest smashed into the door. Unconscious, he slipped to the concrete.

The third man felt a bullet coming off the ceiling whizz past his ear and strike the concrete. He did not see the leg coming up out of the darkness striking him in the chest. The blow stopped his heart a few seconds rendering him unconscious. He fell to the concrete on the spot.

The bullets stopped. Harriet slowly raised herself from the cement floor and walked into the light. Her head was bleeding from where the barrel had struck her, and her dress was dirty from being on the floor.

Youngsu turned to her, "Miss Brown all right."

"Yes Youngsu. The gun hit my head. Did we get everyone?"

"Think so," Youngsu said. "Rescue Mc Craw now." He turned and ran up the stairs. He found Mc Craw on the floor looking up at him.

"What did you bring with you, the cavalry?"

Youngsu smiled as he cut him loose, "Miss Brown, she cavalry." Then taking the rope, he turned, and disappeared.

He passed Harriet going up and began gathering up the men on the floor. He took their shirts off and blindfolded them.

Next, he took off their belts, lowering their pants to their ankles. He used the belts to tie their hands behind their backs. Making a loop, he placed both hands in the belt loop, tightened it, placed a hole with his knife, and dropped the buckle lever into the hole. Then he went between the wrists with the belt placing half hitches.

He took all three to the steps and wrapped them tight to the metal upright with the rope.

When Harriet entered the office, Mc Craw was coming to his feet. His face, bruised, and bleeding in spots.

He looked at her, "I see one of them got you too."

"No, I did this to myself." Then turning to him, "What are you doing coming here on your own with no plan. You could have been killed."

"They weren't going to kill me," Mc Craw said, "Maybe beat me up a bit."

"Do you know what is down there?"

"A couple of trucks and some boxes."

She went to the light switch, flipped it on, "Look! All those boxes contain cocaine! Youngsu tested one of them."

Mc Craw looked out over the floor. It was full of four by four boxes stacked three deep. He allowed a whistle.

"There's got to be over half billion-dollars-worth of cocaine. You were not going to walk out of here, and we may not either unless we can think of something."

Youngsu came up the stairs with the phones, and wallets of the men below. He deposited them on the desk, walked to the computer, "Better get what Miss Brown want, and leave quickly." He placed his thumb drive in the computer and began downloading it.

"What do we want," Harriet asked. "What are we going to do with all of this cocaine?"

"We can't keep it, or even make anyone aware we had anything to do with it." Mc Craw said.

Harriet thought a moment. Then she said, "Give the glory to the police. Call Detective Ramos and give him the credit for finding the cocaine."

"That would only make him the target."

"We'll call the news people too. Give the tip to them and Detective Ramos."

"Yeah, that would take the heat off him. He just got a tip like the press did."

"That puts us still in a bad position if anyone finds out we gave the tip."

"No one find out," Youngsu said pulling the completed thumb drive out.

"Those guys down there are going to say we knew," Mc Craw said.

"How much did you tell them?"

"They got my wallet. They know who I am."

"Okay, you call Detective Ramos," Harriet said, "Give him the location, and of what's here. If he asks how you knew about it, tell him to look up Morales' ID. It's his address."

"That might work."

"Then let's use their phones to make the calls," Harriet said. "Detective Ramos will cooperate" She flipped one of the phones to Mc Craw, "Call Detective Ramos."

Then turning to Youngsu, "Make it look like we were never here."

"Yes, Miss Brown," he said, and began removing all the security tapes from the cameras. Done, he went below, and collected all the empty shell casings from Harriet's gun.

Using one of the other phones, Harriet called information. They gave her the number of the Channel Seven News station. She called and left the tip.

Mc Craw had Detective Ramos on the line:

"That's right, a half a billion at least, but you got to keep me out of it. I am just someone giving you a tip from the inside."

Pause:

"Source? Look up Jose Morales' ID. It's his address."

Pause:

"Channel Seven News team has been tipped."

Pause:

"Yeah, a circus you could use. I'd recommend getting down here. Three of their men are tied to the step rail."

Pause:

"Yeah, anytime." he looked at Harriet, "Done!"

"Then let's get out of here," Harriet said, "Take their wallets and phones. Let's meet back at the office."

"Leave way we come avoid cameras," Youngsu said.

"Then we follow you," Harriet said.

They descended the stairs following Youngsu. Easier now with the lights on. When they reached the window, Youngsu placed the footstool on the floor in front of it and jumped through. Harriet used the stool and climbed out the window with Youngsu's help on the other side. Mc Craw handed out the stool and climbed out.

Following the route coming in, they made it back to their vehicles. Taking the lead, the limousine left the complex, entered the freeway with Mc Craw following.

Harriet called Rose's, "We have Mc Craw."

"Anybody hurt?"

"A few bruises, but otherwise okay."

"Good, are you all coming back here?"

"Yes, but you might want to take a look at channel seven. It should be interesting. Tell my grandfather to watch it too. We should be there in twenty minutes."

"Okay, will do."

A few minutes later they heard a line of police cars moving south on the freeway. Twenty minutes later Harriet and company were driving into the parking lot beside the detective agency.

Rose had the Channel Seven News on her computer when they walked in, "Were you guys involved in this?"

"What are they saying," Harriet asked.

"It's real live drama," Rose said. "The news people were there ahead of the police. They filmed them charging the building and breaking the door down. Guys with guns were all over the place. They took three men away in a police van. The news people are not going to be allowed inside I don't think. No. I am wrong. They're letting them. Hurry, you guys have got to see this!"

The news people had their cameras rolling as they entered the building. The cameras showed the broken glass, and bullet holes.

The news commentator said, "There appears to have been a gun battle in here, there's bullet holes everywhere."

The camera switched to the four by four boxes and showed the open one. Chief of Detectives Ramos standing next to it looked up when the news camera came towards him.

"What's in the boxes, Detective?"

"It looks to be cocaine," Ramos said as he picked up a sac from the open box and showed the camera.

"How much is in here," the commentator asked.

"Hard to say, maybe half a billion dollars, but you will have to wait until the investigation is over for an accurate account. Now you people will have to move back outside. You have had your peek, now we must preserve the evidence."

The camera slowly backed out the door while it focused on the four by four boxes three deep going to the back of the building. The camera resumed its position beyond the roped off area.

Rose turned to the others watching the news, "You people were there, right?"

"Don't answer that!" a voice said coming through the door. It was Henry Brown. He entered his office, "You three in here!"

Henry took the chair behind the desk, and shouted, "Close the door!"

Mc Craw closed the door and turned back to the man in the chair.

Henry looked at Mc Craw turning around from the door, "You're the only one I don't know."

"Name's Timothy Mc Craw. I've had twenty years with Los Angeles Police Department."

"And," Henry asked.

"I was fired for roughing up a felon that was feeding bad spice to a teenager, and a man entering his house."

"And," Henry asked.

"I'm on probation, I cannot carry a gun, and I lost my driver's license."

"Is that all?"

"That about does it."

"I bet my granddaughter didn't know all of this when she hired you."

"She didn't ask, and I didn't say."

"You have twenty years on the force, and you pull a stunt like this today. Man, what were you thinking? You had no back up! What were you going to do when you found Morales, beat him up to get some information, information that could not be used in court. Worse, did you know that Morales is Chief Morales' brother?"

"No sir, there's a lot of Morales around."

"Now you've got the drug cartel looking our direction to get even."

"I think your granddaughter fixed it, sir"

He turned to her next, "Calling in the news media was your idea?"

Harriet could feel a tear developing, and said in a soft voice, "The police department is dirty. They have already killed two possible witnesses and lost all of their paperwork. I thought by keeping everything out in the open, it would be harder for whoever is controlling things to cover it up."

"It's out in the open," Henry said. "And that brainless Ramos already said it was cocaine. Gees, it wasn't tested, and whose to know what was in the other boxes. He better hope they were all filled with cocaine. Then he allows the media to mess up his crime scene."

"Again, my fault," Harriet said, "We were there rescuing Mc Craw. I shot the place up with my gun. I put a hole through most everything there."

"I tell Miss Brown shoot until no more bullets, sir," Youngsu said. "They scare plenty. We rescue Mr. Mc Craw."

"Now we come back to Mr. Mc Craw, the one who put you all in danger by going head long into something without thinking it through. This office is teamwork. We do things by the book. No individual initiative required. We do not place our members in danger because we do not think things through."

Christopher Charles

"I thought I was working for Miss Brown?" Mc Craw asked.

"She is using my license, and I would like to keep my granddaughter around a little longer if that is okay with you."

"If you don't want me working for you, say the word, and I am out of here?"

"Can you control you temper, and work as a team?"

"I am working on the temper management. I can handle the team thing."

"Then you may continue working for my granddaughter." He turned to the other two, "You all did well in getting out of a sticky situation. I don't mean to demean that, but it should not have happened to start with. Bringing the press in was a good idea. There is a problem in the police department. You should continue to use Ramos. After tonight, you may be his only ally. I am sure Chief Morales is not going to like what he sees tonight."

"We did stop a whole bunch of cocaine from reaching the streets," Harriet said.

"That you did. It was accidental, but you were able to function under the pressure. I am very proud of you Harriet, but you will be spending time at the shooting range for a while. We can't have you shooting up the ceilings."

He looked at Youngsu, "Thank you for pulling everyone out of this."

Then leaning back in his chair, he said, "This is a good team, but you need to work together." Then coming forward, he said, "Now, where are we? How much will the police department find out?"

"They will know I was there if they question Morales," Mc Craw said. "He looked at my wallet and got my name."

"Then they will be calling you in for questioning?" Henry said. "What are you going to say?"

"What they already know, I went there looking for Morales. I had no idea it was a cocaine dump."

"How did you know he was there?"

"His address was on his ID. The guy was dumb enough to put that address on it."

"Good, that shifts the fault to them for losing the cocaine." Now looking harder at Mc Craw, he asked, "How did you get there?"

"A... A I took a taxi."

"Which taxi company?"

"Okay, I took the bus?"

"No bus stops there."

"Okay what would you suggest?"

"So far you are breaking your probation. Maybe you should say you were taken there in the limousine. The rest of your team was there."

"They would back me up?"

"We are a team, though I do not like letting them know all of you were there."

"They will be probing until they find out, sir," Mc Craw said. "It might be better to come right out with it."

"If you can make them believe it was only a rescue, and not a raid," Henry said. "You should consider placing your truck in storage until you are allowed to drive again. It will delay future temptations."

"Yes sir," Mc Craw said.

"Now I am going home and let you people figure out your next move."

6 Repercussions

With the cocaine building locked down and under tight security, Chief Don Morales' called Chief of Detectives Ramos into his office.

Ramos took the chair across from the Chief and waited. He knew the questions would be tough.

Chief Morales cleared his throat, looked at Ramos after he adjusted his chair, "Did you know you ruined five years of work trying to catch the people operating drug trafficking in the United States."

"No sir. I had no idea."

"Exactly, that's why we have the Drug Enforcement Agency and the Southern California Drug Task Force. We can't have people doing things on their own. You should have coordinated the bust with them. The bait was huge by any standards. It drew people to it, some of them coming out in the open to get their share. Then your bust ruins the whole thing. Now it's all hot. You only managed to capture three men low on the ladder, and one was our own agent, my brother, Jose Morales."

"The news people already had the leak," Ramos said. "They were there waiting for us. We had no choice but to proceed."

"Where did this leak come from?"

"An accident, sir," Ramos said. "It seems someone traced your brother. The address was the warehouse. He had no idea it was loaded with cocaine."

"My brother? How?"

"Check his ID, it has the warehouse address on it."

"You're saying this was a by chance thing. No one was aware of the cocaine?"

"The man only did his job tracking your brother and found the warehouse. Your brother evidently out of control threatened the man and ended tied to the steps beside the office. Probably seeing all that cocaine spooked him. He called the press and me."

"And who's the guy doing the tracking of my brother?"

"Why it's one of our own, Timothy Mc Craw, sir, doing his job. Seems your brother became careless breaking into a detective agency the best I can figure it."

Chief Morales looked up at the ceiling, and said in a low voice, "You may go Ramos, have them pick up Mc Craw."

"Yes sir," Ramos said standing.

Thirty minutes later Mc Craw walked into Chief Morales' Office. Morales nodded for him to sit. Mc Craw took the chair opposite him.

Morales looked at him a moment, then said, "I hear you have a job, Mc Craw."

"Yes sir, and they know about my probation."

"Have you been driving that truck of yours?"

"No sir! That was part of my probation."

"Then how did you follow up on your lead to the warehouse?"

"The company I work for has a chauffeur, sir. I ride in the limousine."

Morales allows this to settle a moment, then he asked, "Do you know what you stumbled into?"

"I was not the one who got rough this time, sir. I was only following the lead of the man who smashed the door down at the Brown's Detective Agency to do harm to one Harriet Brown who is an innocent child of circumstances. He also bashed my face in."

"I hear he is the one complaining of being attacked."

"I didn't tie him to a chair, and pound on him, sir."

"Why did you call the press?"

"With that much cocaine, someone's gonna to be angry, sir. I thought it best everyone knew I had nothing to do with it."

"I think you accomplished that. Did you know the cocaine was a plant to attract buyers? That you stumbled into a sting operation, Jose Morales, my brother was running. He thought you were a spy for a drug cartel."

"Yeah, well he didn't start slugging me until he found out I was a former cop."

"I think he paid for that," Captain Morales said. "Your crew was very efficient."

"He didn't pay for the damages to the detective agency. He smashed two doors costing over two thousand to fix. Does the detective agency send the bill here?"

"He'll pay for the doors," Captain Morales said. "Is there anything else?"

"No sir."

"You know, Mc Craw, I've always liked you. You're a little heavy handed at times like my brother, but you get the job done. Maybe when your probation period is completed in two years, we can reinstate you back into the department."

"That would be appreciated, sir."

"Good, you may go, Mc Craw. I am presently surprised you have found a job."

"Thank you, sir." Mc Craw said as he stood and left the office. His mind kept trying to get around the idea Jose Morales was the Captain's brother. He still did not say why his brother was breaking down doors, and threatening Miss Brown.

Coming out of the Police Department, his phone rang. It was Detective Ramos. Answering, he asked, "What is it?"

"I'll pick you up."

"Okay, where?"

"Stay where you are."

A Sport Mercedes drove up. Mc Craw stepped into the car. Small for his big body, his kneecaps pushed into the dashboard.

Mc Craw ducked his head as he closed the door. He tried to ignore the closeness of the car. Looking over at Ramos, the car seemed to fit him.

"Where to?"

"Brown Detective Agency in Pasadena."

The small Mercedes sped off towards the freeway. After a few minutes, Ramos asked, "How much cocaine do you really think was in that warehouse?"

"We only saw the one box open. One of my team tested it, and said it was cocaine. That's all I know."

"They didn't give me a chance to check it out," Ramos said. "The DEA had me out of there in ten minutes after we broke in. What can you tell me?"

"The room was full of boxes. I don't know if they had coke in them. The alarm system was old. My team disabled it fairly easily."

"That's the problem, if you had a billion dollars-worth of cocaine wouldn't you protect it better?"

"I see your point, so you're thinking that wasn't the case."

"All we know for sure was the one box that was opened."

"The DEA guys know what they have in there."

"Maybe," Ramos said. "I would bet you'll find only the one open box with any cocaine, and that will be only a few bags."

"If that's not so, then what? Did the DEA guys steal it?"

Thinking, Ramos said, "It's hard to come up with that much cocaine without being noticed. I would say only the one box had any cocaine."

"Why did Jose Morales attack Miss Brown?"

"I thought you knew. There's eight hundred million dollars of drug money missing. Someone killed George Brown because of it. His overseas accounts are empty. His house appears to be empty. No one knows where he put it. Everyone figures he left some clues for his daughter."

"Why did they kill him before they recovered the money?"

"It could be the killer thought he had the location of the money, but it hasn't turned up anywhere so that may not be the case, or they could have been a dispute in the ranks. I'm still checking."

"What about my wife's murder?" Mc Craw asked.

"She was Brown's handler before me. They were both killed by the same gun."

"She wasn't working for the DEA. I would know."

"What did you really know about her, and why do you think she married a policeman?"

"She loved me?"

"Maybe she wanted protection, and she wanted to remain close to the police department in case things went bad, but the missing money bought them both dead."

"I'm not buying this. If she was Brown's handler, I would have known."

"Suit yourself, you can check it out."

"Yeah, maybe I will."

"By the way thanks for giving me the tip."

"The Captain didn't seem all that thrilled about it."

"That's because he's thinking I might be after his job. I did get good press for making the largest drug bust of all time," Ramos said.

"Yeah, now they have the problem of how to get rid of it."

The Mercedes pulled up in front of the Detective Agency as Ramos said, "I think this is where you wanted to go."

"Yeah, thanks."

"If you find out anything on the murders, you're going to let me know?"

"If you can keep your source quiet. You didn't this time."

"Sorry, the Captain wanted to know my source. To avoid him looking for it, I told him to direct the fault to his brother."

"Yeah, that's why he had me brought in for questioning."

Christopher Charles

"I gave you a ride home."

"Thanks," Mc Craw said stepping out of the car."

Police Station

Jose Morales walked into Captain Morales' office. His nose had a splint, and a bandage covering most of his face. His mustache was gone. The tissue around his left eye revealed a large bruise. He took the chair in front of his brother, "You wanted to see me?"

"What's this I hear of you taking a police car from the lot, and using it to smash in a detective office without a warrant or identifying yourself?"

"I was looking for the money," Jose said. "I know she has it. She's the only person he would give it to."

"That may be so, but you got caught. Now you will pay the damages of two thousand dollars."

"I haven't got two thousand dollars."

"Then I will pay it and take it out of your salary."

"I didn't do that much damage."

"What were you planning on doing when you got her?"

"Make her tell me where her old man hid it."

"If she didn't know?"

"She knows. It takes money to open a Detective Agency. I know she didn't have any money before, I checked."

"We don't operate like that in this department."

"The DEA's looking for it, and I'm working for them."

"She cannot hide that kind of money. Check her bank accounts, and such, but you go manhandling her, you're going jail. Being my kid brother, they will throw away the key. Do we understand one another?"

"Yes, I get the picture, but what about the guy who gave me this?"

Captain Morales looked at his face, "What were you doing prior to this?"

"Just trying to get some answers out of a guy who likes to rough people up."

"Yeah and look what happened to you. I don't think you have a case."

"I know Mc Craw is connected."

"Let's see, you break into a detective office threatening to do harm to an innocent young lady who barely manages to escape. Then you pound on one of her detectives who only wanted to ask you a few questions. Does this sound like you have a case? Before you are done, you will find yourself in jail; or at the very least kicked out of the force like Mc Craw. Am I making any sense?"

"Alright, I get the picture."

"Do you really get this picture? Then why in hell did you give the warehouse address as your place of residence for your ID?"

"I was living there at the time," Jose said. "I didn't have another address."

"Gees! Why didn't you tell the DEA boys about it? We could have gotten another warehouse?"

"I didn't think anyone would be checking."

"Now we have a useless pile of hot cocaine to get rid of. Do you know how much money is being lost here? Someone is going to pay. Right now, that someone is you."

"Me, I didn't go busting in there, and calling the press."

"They will be looking for someone to blame. You're a loose-cannon, Jose."

Christopher Charles

"Am I being kicked out of the DEA?"

"What do you think?"

"I'll go talk to them. This was all an accident."

"Good luck!" Captain Morales said as he waved him away from his desk.

Slowly Jose stood as he felt the rejection from his brother and walked out of the office.

Captain Morales watched him leave, smiled to himself. "Yes, the DEA boys knew of your warehouse address. Now their boxes will be worth the advertised eight hundred million, and maybe draw out the money old man Brown hid."

Detective Agency

Mc Craw walked into the detective agency. He noticed the Limousine was missing, "Where is our leader off too?"

"She's at the firing range trying to shoot that cannon of hers, but Mr. Brown is in the office."

"Thanks," Mc Craw said, and walked that direction.

Inside the office, Henry Brown stared at his lap top computer as Mc Craw walked in. He motioned for him to sit down with his right hand but continued to look at the screen. "Glad you're here, Mc Craw. We've been looking at those phones you brought in from the raid. Some of these numbers keep coming up."

"Any names to the numbers?"

Looking up, "Rose put together a list. We have an address on some of them. You'll be looking into them when Youngsu gets back from the range."

"I rode back with Detective Ramos," Mc Craw said. "Seems everyone is looking for eight hundred million dollars your son stashed somewhere including the DEA."

"I knew he was working for the DEA, but I never knew they gave him eight hundred million dollars."

"We don't know if it is in dollars," Mc Craw said. "It could be in those boxes of cocaine we found at the warehouse."

"Then the DEA already has the money," Henry said.

"I don't think so, or they would not have sent Jose Morales to find Miss Brown. Ramos thinks there was only one box of cocaine, and that box only partially filled. He also thinks the killing of my wife, and your son were connected. Do you know anything about that?"

"He didn't confide in me, but if Ramos was his handler. He would know," Henry said.

7 Firing Range

Harriet entered the firing range. She had taken the eight hours of hands on and classroom study. Now she would actually shoot her cannon. She knew the others in the class had placed bets she would not pass this phase of the class.

Each of the six students at the range had a booth. The one instructor, Mark Mathew, walked behind them giving instructions.

She had her gun on the board in front of her pointed down range at the target. She had the clip in, and one bullet locked in the chamber.

The instructor, Mathew, walked up to each student. He showed them how to hold their gun, and fire at the target. He fired the first bullet with them. Then he allowed them to fire two more rounds on their own correcting their stance and positioning their feet.

He finally reached Harriet's booth on the end, "Pick up your gun, Harriet, and point it down range."

Nervous, she did what the instructor said. She had not shot the gun since the warehouse. She knew it had a kick. Holding the gun with two hands, she pointed it downrange.

The instructor adjusted her arms making them straighter. Stepping back, he said, "Fire!"

The target seemed to be moving all over the place. The heavy gun would not stay still. She squeezed the trigger the gun flew backward taking her arms with it. The barrel of the gun struck the instructor up beside his head. He fell backwards struggling to keep his balance.

Recovering, he shouted, "Keep your gun pointed downrange!"

"Yes sir, sorry sir," Harriet said bringing her gun up in front of her with her arms shaking.

"Now take two more shots, but keep the gun pointed downrange!" He shouted again wiping the blood from his forehead.

Controlling her shaking arms, concentrating, Harriet brought the gun back into her sights, but she found she could not hold it steady on the target. She had to allow it to move through the target and fired the gun when it passed over the target.

Her arm flew up over her head, but she held onto the gun. The first bullet missed the target because she waited too long to fire. She had to be pulling the trigger before she reached the target. Bringing her arms back down, she fired her second shot. She missed the target again. That was too soon. She had it now, but he said only two shots.

She laid her pistol on the board, "I would like to try again, sir."

"That will be all the practice I will give you," Mathew said, "This time it is for real. If you miss the target entirely as our

Miss Brown has done, you will not pass this course. If you get all of your shots in the bullseye, you will have the opportunity to be one of our 'Marksman'.

Okay, everyone on the line. You will take six shots. If you need to reload, do it now. It will be one shooter at a time, and keep your gun pointed downrange at all times. Do not turn around unless the gun is on the board, and pointing downrange, any questions?"

No one asked a question.

"Okay, shooter number one, line up on the target, and began shooting."

The students began shooting one after the other. A couple of them managed to hit the bullseye with one or two bullets, but most of the bullets struck the target wide of the bullseye.

Finally, Harriet's turn. She had her gun moving over the target. It passed the bullseye twice before she fired. She nailed it. Her arms flew up, but she managed to keep from striking her head. Her pistol coming down, passed over the target once, coming back she fired, and nailed another one.

She did this six times striking herself up beside the head twice with her arm, and once with the barrel of the gun. By the sixth shot, she learned how to control the recoil taking her arms only a foot and half off the target. She felt battered, but she smiled. All six shots were in the bullseye.

Mathew pulled the target up and removed it from the rack. Shaking his head, he handed her the target, "I don't how you did it, but you may be our only 'Marksman'."

Then turning to the class, he said, "Unload your weapons, and keep them unloaded. We will be going through the simulations next. Remember what you have learned in class. This is recognizing who you should shoot, and who you should not shoot. You are allowed only one mistake. More than that, and you will not be allowed to carry a concealed weapon, any questions?"

No one said anything.

"Okay, let's line up. Load your gun at the beginning of the course, and unload your gun at the end of the course, everyone understand that?"

Everyone yelled out.

"Okay, the first one in line, load, and move out!"

They began moving through the complex structure. Harriet could hear gunshots inside. Finally, her turn, she slipped the clip in, and loaded the chamber. She removed the safety and entered the building. The lights immediately dimmed making it difficult to see.

Suddenly a child jumped out from a corner wall partition and crossed in front of her. Next would be a bad-guy. Sure enough, a bad-guy with a mask and a revolver jumped out at her. She fired sending the bullet into the mask figure ripping it apart. It sent her arms flying backward. She heard another gun being fired and felt a sting on her right arm.

"It fires back," she thought. She did not know they made it this realistic. She would have to be more careful. Instead of just walking though, she began to look for places to take cover.

She ran to one wall as a silhouette popped up of two women, and a bad-guy behind them. A bullet grazed the edge of the wall as she dropped behind it. Coming back around the bad-guy was gone, but the silhouette of the two women remained.

She moved on to the stairs. Shaking, she began talking to herself, "They're only trying to make it seem real. They wouldn't actually shoot me." She looked at her right arm. It was bleeding. A piece of flesh was missing.

Mathew, watching her on the monitor, did not see the shooter, but he could see Harriet jumping back behind the partitions. "She's really taking this serious," he said to the young man on the monitors.

"Yeah, some people like to think this is real. It takes all kinds."

Below Harriet checked the stairs keeping her eyes focused for anyone looking around the corner. Keeping her gun pointed upward, she started up. Reaching the landing, she found herself in a long hallway with doors on each side leading into rooms.

Keeping her left arm against the wall, she pointed her gun down the hall. A silhouette of a bad-guy dressed in tee-shirt, pointing a gun jumped out of the room across from her. She turned slightly and fired.

The bullet destroyed the silhouette and went into the room. She ran quickly for the room. Stepping in front of the silhouette, she leaped inside, moving her 45 revolver around the empty room.

Nobody, she felt safe for the moment. Taking a deep breath, she turned quickly back to the door. She could feel her heart pumping fast. Glancing out, she saw a man entering the end room on the left. Now, she had him located. Impressed, he seemed so real.

Stepping out of the room, she moved quickly to the far wall, lined her gun up against it. She pointed it towards the door where the man had disappeared. Her arm continued to shake. She did not know if the heavy gun caused it, or the pounding of her heart.

Suddenly another bad-guy silhouette jumped from the room across from her. She did not move from the wall, and kept her gun pointing towards the door.

The man in the room knew she was in the hallway. He waited just inside the door. He had his gun in his left hand. He did not want to expose himself by using his right hand. He knew the next silhouette would be popping out from the room across from him. It would direct her attention enough for him to get off his shot.

He heard the silhouette man popping out. He leaned into the hallway exposing his left shoulder. "She was not across the hall, but on his side pointing her cannon right at him." He fired, but it was hurried. The woman's cannon exploded. It felt like someone had hit him with a steel pipe in the left shoulder. The force sent him flying backwards into the room.

Harriet had seen the man's gun pointing at her and fired. She heard his gun go off as her arm flung upward across the wall. She felt a sharp pain in her right side. His bullet had struck her beneath her arm putting a crease on her rib cage leaving a gaping hole.

She pushed herself away from the wall and drifted to the opposite wall of the hallway facing the door where the gunman had fallen back inside. Frightened, she became emotional. She began firing into the room starting at three feet.

The man on his back took the gun from his helpless left hand, crawled up closer to the wall facing the hallway, and pointed it towards the door. He would nail her when she came through the door. Suddenly a portion of the wall blew out and sent the debris on his face. Another bullet whizzed past his stomach.

Panicking, he yelled, "Stop! Stop! I give up! I give up!"

Harriet stopped firing, and yelled, "I'm not coming in there! Ten seconds, and I'm firing again."

"I'm coming out. I'm hurt!"

"The gun?"

"Coming out now," the man said.

She saw the gun slide out of the room. She did not pick it up, "The other one!"

"That's only one I have."

She fired two more bullets into the room. One just missed the front part of the man's head taking out a square foot of plaster filling his face and hair. The second one passed over his chest.

"Okay, Okay!"

She saw another gun come sliding out into the hall.

"Now it is your turn," She whispered. She could feel the blood flowing from her side.

She heard the man crawling. She aimed her gun at the door. Her arms shaking hard, she kept them moving across the target coming towards the door.

Mathew heard the excessive gunshots. He could see her shooting into the wall. Thinking he had to calm her down, he turned the lights up, then over the speaker, "That is all Miss Brown. You can put your gun down and remove the clip."

The man had reached the door. He began pulling himself through. He saw his guns on the floor, and thought about reaching for them, but she still had her gun on him.

Mathew seeing only her said, "Miss Brown, place your gun on the floor, and walk away from it. Do it now!"

Harriet slowly lowered her gun to the floor.

The man seeing his opportunity started to reach for his guns.

Harriet ran across the hall and kicked them away from him.

Seeing he was about to be discovered, he worked himself to his feet, and staggered down the hall. Holding his useless arm, he disappeared behind a false partition.

Harriet heard people coming up the stairs behind her. Her side bleeding profusely, emotionally exhausted, she staggered back across the hall, and collapsed to the floor in a sitting position with her back against the wall.

Reaching her, Mark Mathew, and the monitor man stood over her. Looking around, they saw the big holes in the wall across from her, and two revolvers lying on the floor. Mathew looked in the room and saw blood on the floor.

He came out of the room, "What were you doing? Whose blood is in here? Did you shoot someone?"

She looked up at them holding her side, and whispered, "Why did you let him shoot me?" At that, she passed out. The loss of blood, and all the emotion had taken its toll.

Downstairs Youngsu watched a man work his way out of a partition and go out the back door. Holding his shoulder, the man could barely walk. He heard the shooting upstairs, and the instructor demanding she put her gun down.

Now when he saw someone injured, he knew something was wrong. He jumped to his feet, ran into the building, and up the stairs.

He saw Harriet on the floor with the two men standing over her. Pushing them aside, he checked her bleeding side. She had a bad flesh wound. The bullet had passed through.

He placed his phone to his ear called 911 as he eased Harriet to the floor. "Police gun range, woman shot, need ambulance, and police." He placed his hand on her side and pushed in to stop the bleeding.

Then looking up at the men, "Why did man shoot her?"

"Who, we didn't see anyone on the monitor," Mathew said.

"Maybe she shot herself," the monitor man said.

Pointing to the guns on the floor, Youngsu asked, "Who those?"

They heard the siren in the background. Both men shook their heads.

The police arrived and took charge. They placed Harriet in the ambulance as Detective Ramos arrived.

Youngsu approached him, "Two guns upstairs belong to man who shoot Miss Brown, blood of man in room, Miss Brown blood in hallway. Man escape out hidden partition with bleeding shoulder."

Detective Ramos nodded, "Anything else?"

"No, take Miss Brown to hospital now."

"Okay, I'll be by to get her statement later." He watched the ambulance close up after Youngsu climbed in back. He would protect her, he thought.

He headed for the building. They directed him upstairs. He checked the room and hallway. He saw the blood and made sure the lab people had a sample. He took the two guns and picked up Harriet's cannon. He would have the two guns checked for fingerprints.

He pulled Mathew and the monitor man aside, "You were observing her the whole time, and you did not see the other man shoot her."

"We only saw her," Mathew said. "We only became aware something was wrong when she began shooting into the wall. That cannon of hers was tearing the place up. When we got here, she was sitting up against the wall barely conscious."

"I am sure you have footage of what happened."

"I'll make you a copy," Mathew said." He nodded to the monitor man.

The monitor man started to leave when Ramos clasped his arm, "I will know if any of it is erased. We don't want to make you an accomplice. I want it to go back an hour before she started through, and up until now. I want to see everything in-and-outside the building, all your cameras!" The monitor man nodded and took off running.

Looking back to Mathew, he asked, "Is it possible for him to wear something that would make him impossible to see."

"It's possible."

"I was told the man came out of the partition. Do you have hidden staircases and hallways?"

"Of course, we are always changing the structure inside depending on who is going through ranging from an easy course to a hard one. This one was an easy one."

"Yeah, that's why we are sending her to the hospital." Ramos said. He had the monitor man make up two thumb drives with the camera footage. He remained another hour looking at the footage on the screen. He could see a silhouette moving at times, but you had to know where to look to see it. He did not pick up anyone entering or leaving the building.

After Ramos left, Mark Mathew reached behind the computer, pulled out the thumb drive, and placed it in his pocket. Relieved, he left the building quickly. He touched his speed dial, a man answered.

Phone:

"Mathew here, he only wounded her."

Pause:

"I don't know where he is, but I think he's wounded. She nailed him in the shoulder with her Colt 45."

Pause:

"Yes sir, I have the thumb drive in my pocket."

Pause:

"Yes sir, I know the location. I will be there in ten minutes." He closed his phone.

Thirty minutes later Mathew was still waiting on the corner of a dark alley. Nervous, they said to meet them here. Then he saw the black undercover police car come around the corner. Relieved, he stepped to the curb as the black car's side front window partially opened. He could not see inside. The dark glass prevented it.

Mathew handed the man inside the thumb drive, "It's the only one." The window immediately went up as the black car moved on down the street. He felt relieved. He pushed the walk button and waited for the light to turn green. "Walk!" The street recorder said.

It had been a long day. Thankful to be heading home. He thought of the forty thousand going into his Bahamas' account tomorrow. Halfway across the intersection he heard a large truck. It seemed to come out of nowhere. He managed to turn in time to see the huge headlights and register his last thoughts as the huge bummer sent his body fifty feet across the street, and headfirst into the curb.

Hospital

Ramos headed for the hospital. Maybe the victim could talk now. He wanted to get her statement while it remained fresh in her mind. He saw her people in the waiting room and moved quickly to the receptionist. He flashed his badge, "I have to see Miss Harriet Brown."

"She's in the prep room waiting to be seen by the doctor."

"Is she conscious?"

"She is at the moment."

"Then I need to talk with her."

"It's very irregular."

"A gunman shot her an hour ago, and he is still loose. I want a policeman by her side at all times, and I want to talk to her before you put her out."

She motioned to one of the guards by the door, "You're to go with this man to the prep room. You are to stay with Miss Brown until you are relieved."

The guard nodded, "This way!"

Detective Ramos followed the man down a hallway, and into a room with patients on carts waiting to be seen by the doctor. He saw Harriet on a cart against the wall waiting her turn. They had her wearing a hospital gown. A large blood-soaked bandage covered her right side, and another one covered her right arm. She was awake.

The big guard took his position at the foot of the bed.

Ramos walked up beside her, "You remember me, Detective Ramos, I am investigating your shooting."

Harriet's eyes began to swell, "I didn't kill him, did I?"

"No, no, nothing like that. We haven't found him yet. Do you think you would recognize him again if you saw him?"

"I shot him in the left arm. He's bleeding badly." Letting some tears go, she continued, "He tried to kill me."

"They did not see him on the monitors," Ramos said, "They only saw you shooting."

"He shot me," Harriet said raising her right arm.

"It's obvious something shot you, I'm not doubting that. I want to hear your side of it now, from the beginning."

"Yes sir, from the beginning." Then looking at him, she asked, "Starting from the gun range?"

"Is that important?"

Christopher Charles

"I got 'Marksman'."

Ramos smiled, "Start when you entered the building."

"I was fired upon when I first entered. It grazed my right arm. It didn't go deep, but I became more cautious thinking that's what the shot was for. I began hiding behind the partitions. I heard another shot, and part of the wall splintered in front of me. At that point, I took everything very seriously. I was not sure if the monitor was doing this, or someone else was in the building.

I went upstairs, and saw a criminal silhouette jump out of the room on my right. I took a shot, blasted it to bits. Taking advantage of the blast, I ran into the room with my gun in front of me, but I didn't see anyone. Then going back to the door, I looked out carefully, and saw a man running across into the room on the left at the end of the hall.

Now I knew where he was. I ran across the hall, moved towards the room. I kept my gun against the wall on the left side when suddenly another criminal silhouette jumped out from the door across from me. I ignored it keeping my eyes on the door at the end of the hall. It happened so fast.

When the criminal silhouette jumped out the man came out of the room, and fired his gun at me, but I had already pulled my trigger. His bullet got me here in my right side. My bullet got him in the left shoulder flinging him back inside the room. You know I was aiming down the wall.

Anyway, he was inside the room. I was not about to walk in there. I moved to the other side of the hall and began firing into the wall going progressively lower until the man yelled out. He threw his gun out, but I felt he had another one. I fired two more times before he produced the second gun. He finally crawled out of the room after I threatened to shoot again.

I had him in my sights when my instructor told me to put my gun on the floor. He yelled at me to put my gun down twice. Now confused, I thought maybe this was all part of the training. I had just shot a man.

Anyway, I put my gun on the floor. The man started to crawl towards his guns. I ran over and kicked them away. Maybe it was over, but he shot at me, and I wasn't going to give him another chance to do it again. I watched him crawl away into the partition. He disappeared, my instructor, Mr. Mathew, came up the stairs all excited."

She looked up at the detective, "Am I in trouble?"

"You are here with two wounds, and he is gone," Detective Ramos said, "I think he is the one in trouble."

The nurse came up beside them, "It's time. We have a room for her now, if you will excuse me." She started to move Harriet, when she said, "If you are a relative, you may come with her."

"They are outside. I'll send one of them in here," Detective Ramos said. "I want someone with her at all the times. Someone just tried to kill her."

"I'll stay with her until they come," the nurse said moving Harriet inside the operatory.

Walking out into the waiting room, he saw Nadine. He waved to her, "You are to go in and stay with her. Be careful who you let near her, I would not trust anyone at this point."

"Yes sir," Nadine said walking quickly past the nurse's station.

The rest of them stood. Seeing Mr. Henry Brown, Ramos walked over, handed him a thumb drive, "See what you can make of this. Her assailant appears to be invisible. Maybe you can bring him to light."

Taking the thumb drive, Mr. Brown asked, "How is she?"

"She has some nasty wounds, but she will be all right. I am more concerned for her safety. This is a second attempt on her life."

Christopher Charles

"Her instructor is saying she shot herself."

"A real person shot her. I have his guns, and we have his blood. By tomorrow, we will have his fingerprints and DNA. She also shot him. Therefore, he needs medical attention. He'll have to come out of the shadows soon to survive."

Night, Downtown Los Angeles

A man limped along a dark street near an alley holding his shattered left arm. The pain had left leaving a numbed feeling. Losing blood, he needed help. He had called the emergency number they had given him. Now he waited beside the alley. He knew better than to go into it. He heard about the other man's alley accident.

He finally saw the black car approaching slowly. It came up to him and stopped. The left window rolled down, a gun with a silencer on it appeared, a bullet pierced his head. He fell to the street dead. The black car's window closed, and the car moved on down the street.

They sent fingerprints through all the agencies and came up with a possible match. Detective Ramos picked up the match after they notified him of the street homicide. The man had a blown-out shoulder. The prints matched, but he was a little late.

He made a trip to Pasadena to check on Harriet. He heard they released her from the hospital after they sutured her wounds. Nothing critical, the hospital did not want the responsibility of protecting her. He heard she was at her office.

He pulled into the parking lot beside the Brown Detective Agency. He saw the black limousine parked beside the curb. He entered the office to see Rose working on her computer, with Youngsu standing by. Mc Craw stood behind Rose.

Harriet with Mr. Henry Brown following came out of her office to see Detective Ramos. She smiled slightly.

"I brought your cannon back," Ramos said reaching into his pocket. He handed her the heavy gun, "I see you are up and around already."

"Yes, thank you for returning my gun."

He reached into his coat inside pocket, took out an envelope, handed it to her, "I think you earned this."

She took the envelope and removed the paper inside. Looking at it, she realized it was her gun permit, "They let me have my permit?"

"I don't think they wanted you going through their course again. That gun of yours torn things up a bit, and of course it helped when you came out a 'Marksman'." He smiled.

"Thank you," Harriet said. She started to hug him when she changed her mind, embarrassed.

To relieve the awkward moment, Ramos turned to Rose, "What did you find on the thumb drive?"

"I found your invisible man," Rose said. "He was wearing a device that made the camera unable to see him. If you go looking inside their computer, you will probably find a thumb drive that doesn't belong there."

Ramos immediately thought he should have taken the computers from the gun range. Probably too late, he placed his phone to his ear, "Go over to the gun range, pick up their computers, and dust everything inside and out for fingerprints."

Pause:

"Yes, do it now!"

Pause:

"Yes, especially inside, also see if there is a thumb drive or a small box that should not be there, but dust for prints first."

Finished, he put his phone away, looked at them, "You cannot leave her alone. Someone is trying to kill her. It's probably connected to her father's murder."

"I don't know anything," Harriet said.

"It has to be the missing money."

"If I don't know where it is, then what does killing me accomplish?"

"That's the point, someone knows where it is, but if he reveals it, you may be able to take possession of it."

"Maybe we should fake my death, and see what happens," Harriet said.

"A good idea, but not just yet," Ramos said, "We don't know where the money is, or who might have knowledge of where it is. He does not have to have you dead for long to change overseas bank accounts. Then he is gone, and out of our reach. All I know is your father, working for the DEA, was supposed to make a buy from the drug cartel. It never took place, and now he's dead, and the money is missing."

"Maybe somebody in the drug cartel has the money, but never delivered the drugs." Henry Brown said.

"That's possible. I know the money was real for a short time. I know your son had it in his possession just before someone shot him. Then he was dead, and the money gone."

"Then whoever shot him has the money," Mr. Brown said.

"Maybe, but that would not explain why they are trying to kill Harriet."

"Could the drugs at the warehouse be part of the buy?" Harriet asked.

Ramos turned to her, "That was a set up, but the cartel is not in the habit of delivering before they are paid. It is more the DEA trying to draw the money out."

He looked at his watch, "I need to get going." Turning back to Harriet, "I'll work with you on this if you keep me in the loop. I can also send you a bodyguard or place you in protective custody."

"I think I rather be here doing something. Protective custody sounds too much like prison."

"Very well," Ramos said, looked at the others, and continued, "You will need to keep her safe. Someone thinks she is very important."

"We can take care of her," Mr. Brown said.

Ramos nodded, and walked towards the door. He liked Harriet. He felt the urge to protect her. Maybe it was her innocent nature and fragility.

When he reached the door, he turned, "One of the accomplices of Jose Morales, Raymond Hernandez is being set free this afternoon at five. Their attorney made the case, if they allow Morales to be free, then he should be. I think he made a mistake. He was safer in jail." He turned and walked out the door.

Henry Brown turned to Mc Craw, "How reliable is our Detective Ramos?"

"He's one of those college grads that's still wet behind the ears. I think they gave him your son's case to keep him out of their hair, but the DEA has taken that over. I think he's just scratching to see what he can find. We use him right, he could be useful like today. He seems to like you, Miss Brown."

Harriet blushed slightly.

"Let's get down to business," Henry Brown said. He looked at Youngsu, "Do you think they would recognize you again from the warehouse?"

"No sir, I blindfold them good."

"Okay, we need to plant a bug on our Raymond Hernandez. We do it when he leaves the police station. Set up a receiver in the limousine."

"How far can the audio reach," Mc Craw asked.

"About a hundred yards for voice, but two miles for location."

"You want us to follow him?"

"That's the idea and plant a bug on anyone he meets if you can, but don't overdo it," Henry said. "We need information here." He looked at his watch, you have an hour before five, and you have traffic."

Mc Craw started for the door with Youngsu carrying the receiver behind him. Harriet stated to follow them, when Mr. Brown pulled her back, "You stay in the limousine."

"Yes sir," she said, and followed them.

8 Moves and Counter Moves

Forty-five minutes later the limousine pulled into a parking space a block from the police station. Youngsu jumped out of the car and made his way towards it. Then right on time, the big man, Raymond Hernandez, left the building. Coming down the steps, he bumped into Youngsu who slipped a bug into his coat pocket.

Youngsu walked on up the steps, and into the police station. Once inside, he turned around, and walked quickly back to the limousine. He turned the receiver on and waited. They could see Raymond moving down the street. He stopped at the local pub on the corner, took a seat at the bar.

They could hear his voice coming in very clear. Then they heard another voice. It was Jose Morales sitting down next to him in the bar.

"I see they let you out," Jose said.

"I'm not doing this anymore Morales. I've had enough!"

"No one walks away. You know that."

"I can walk away. I am not going to tell anyone what I know. I am just going to leave."

"You have too much information."

"You know what I know, just tell them to change things, and leave me alone." Suddenly feeling a little uneasy, he looked around, "You come in here alone?"

"Now, I wouldn't do anything to a buddy," Jose said.

Raymond dropped a bill on the bar and began moving towards the door.

Jose watched him leave and picked up his new phone. He hit speed button, and a man on the other end answered

Phone:

"He's panicking and wants to quit."

Pause:

"That's not my area. I don't do that!"

Pause:

"Yes sir, I'll get it done."

Jose left the bar as another black car pulled in front. He climbed in, "His car is in the police yard, he'll be coming out any second. We'll do this at his house in Chino. I was told to keep it clean, and neat, and out of the city."

The man nodded as Raymond pulled out of the police parking lot. They followed him to the Pomona Freeway going east.

Youngsu had the receiver hooked into his GPS system. He followed the beep unaware that another car was following Raymond.

Thirty minutes later, dark, the three cars pulled off the Pomona Freeway. Youngsu remained a hundred yards behind Raymond's car. Since he had the bug working, he did not need to be right on him.

The limousine drove down a neighborhood street. Small houses occupied each side of the street. Youngsu pulled the car into parking space a block from where Raymond's car stopped.

Coming out of the limousine, Mc Craw and Youngsu ran down the block stopping next to Raymond's house. They saw his car parked in the driveway, and another black car parked across the street watching the house.

Youngsu pointed to the car and motioned for Mc Craw to remain there. He worked his way back up the street and crossed to the other side.

Working his way towards the car, he watched a man take something out of the trunk and run across the street carrying it.

Jose Morales on the passenger side, his attention on the man, did not see Youngsu plant a bug under the back bumper.

Youngsu wanted to get something inside the car, but all the windows were up except for the front wing window. It remained slightly open.

Keeping low, Youngsu worked his way up the passenger side. Using his fingertips, he eased a bug through the window while Jose watched the man placing something beneath Raymond's car. The bug fell into Jose's coat pocket.

Moving fast, Youngsu worked his way up the street. He crossed back over in the dark as the man left Raymond's car, and ran to the waiting black car.

Quietly the black car moved down the road, and around the corner.

Youngsu leading, Mc Craw followed him back to the limousine. Inside, Youngsu began working his receiver. He

Christopher Charles

picked up the frequency to his second bug and turned the recorder on.

The Two Men Were Talking

"It's going to blow when he starts the car."

"How can we be sure it is him who starts the car?"

"You can't be sure," the man said. "I'm not God."

"Maybe we should stick around to be sure it blows," Jose said.

"This is Chino," the man said. "I'm not sticking around. As soon as this blows, the place will be full of cops asking questions. The police station's just down the street. They don't know us. Besides, he may not start the car until morning."

Limousine

After hearing the man, Harriet said, "We have to warn him."

"That's not going to be easy without getting involved," Mc Craw said.

"You and I will go," Harriet said to Mc Craw. "He will know you. Youngsu, you remain here as our back up, and in case our bombers come back."

Climbing out of the car, Harriet walked fast down the block. She passed the car in the driveway and rang the doorbell.

A young woman of Mexican decent opened the door.

"We need to see your husband immediately," Harriet said.

"No husband here," the woman said.

Harriet looked at her, "Two men have just wired your car to explode. Please tell him immediately."

Raymond opened the door wider, and looked at Harriet, then he recognized Mc Craw, "You here to take revenge on my family?" He moved the shotgun in his right hand forward.

"Only to save your life," Harriet said. "There's a bomb planted beneath your car."

"Seems your buddies don't like you anymore," Mc Craw said.

Raymond pushed Mc Craw and Harriet from the door. He walked to his car, looked under it, he saw a blinking blue light. "Damn, I didn't think they would go this far?" Working himself back to his feet, "Did you see who did this?"

"You know who did this?" Mc Craw said. "You have two choices, one, go to the police, or two get the hell out of here."

"How can I get that bomb off my car?" Raymond asked.

"You willing to give us some information?" Harriet asked.

"You can get it off?"

Harriet lifted her phone to her ear, "Bring the limo up, Youngsu."

The limousine pulled up in front of the house.

"Follow me," Harriet said, "I want you to know we had nothing to do with this."

Raymond looked around cautiously following Harriet to the Limousine, "You sure they have left?"

Harriet looked at Youngsu. He nodded. She turned back to Raymond, "We're sure. Play the recording Youngsu."

Youngsu reached back inside and turned the recorder on.

Raymond immediately recognized Jose's voice, "Okay, what do you want to know?"

"What do you know about the murder of Mr. Brown?"

"That wasn't my area," Raymond said, "In fact no one knows much about that. He was to make a buy, but something went wrong. He ended up dead."

"How about my wife?" Mc Craw asked. "Who killed her?"

"She was the inside contact with the cartels. I don't know more than that."

"How involved is Jose Morales?" Harriet asked.

"They think the cartels own him."

"His brother, Chief Morales?"

"I don't know. He seems clean. He had been pulling his brother out of one jam then another."

"Were all the boxes in the warehouse full of cocaine?"

"I was told they were, but that don't mean nothing. I only checked the one."

"Was the DEA using the drugs to draw out the cartel?"

"Hell, the DEA is the cartel. At least most of them are."

"Then who is trying to kill you," Mc Craw asked.

"The cartel, who else. We're talking eight hundred million dollars here. The DEA doesn't have that kind of money."

"We'll need your computer." Harriet said.

"Okay!" He said and glanced back at his wife.

Harriet turned to Youngsu, "Disarm it!"

Youngsu nodded and headed for the car. He slipped under, turned the switch off, the blue light went out. The car did not blow up. He disconnected the wiring and retrieved the bomb. He came back smiling.

"Okay, you are free to go," Harriet said, "But I would be leaving the state as soon as possible. When they find out the bomb didn't work, they will be coming back."

"Thank you," Raymond Hernandez said. "I plan on leaving tonight."

Hernandez's wife was at the door. She handed Harriet the laptop computer, "I am glad to be rid of it."

Chino Hills

A small lake occupied a clearing between Chino Hills and Diamond Bar. A motorcycle drove down the dirt road and stopped beside a small garage. A man stepped from the motorcycle, opened the garage door. He pulled out a small aircraft with a twelve-foot wingspan, attached a missile in the nose. He turned the plane down the small dirt road, flipped a switch, and turned the propeller a few times. He was ready.

Los Angeles

In the penthouse at the top of the Biltmore Hotel, a man in a black suit looked out at the city lights below. Tonight, he would be cleaning up some loose ends. Hernandez was in the process of being taken-care-of. He smiled as he thought of Jose Morales getting his hands dirty. He needed more loyalty from the man.

He picked up his phone, dialed a number.

A voice came on, "Yes sir."

"Get rid of those interfering pests!"

"Yes sir, consider it done." The man said and hung up the phone. He had been expecting the call. He brought up his computer. He already had his access to the phone company's tracking satellites.

He punched in Mc Craw's phone number and sent the information to the computer in Chino Hills. He placed his cell phone connector into a small box that disguised his voice and punched in his speed dial.

He heard a man answered, "Ready here, sir."

"Let's get her into the air and find them. I sent you the locator's information. It's in your computer."

"Yes sir," the voice said. He placed his phone in his pocket, and adjusted his computer placing the information into the drone guidance system. He pressed the start button. The propellers came alive taking the drone down the dirt road.

In the garage behind the drone, he directed it up into the sky. The camera in the nose of the drone allowed him to see the terrain. He turned it towards Los Angeles. Fifteen minutes later the drone picked up Mc Craw's sensor. The man followed the sensor as the target moved slowly around the city.

He pulled out his phone, dialed the number, "It's in the air, sir, and I have spotted the target. It is moving slowly around the Biltmore hotel. It stops like it is investigating something."

"Don't hit it until it leaves the city," The man said. "Let's cut down the collateral damage."

"Yes sir, it seems to be moving up on the freeway now. I will stay with it."

"You sure Mc Craw is in the limousine?"

"Yes sir, I checked his house, his truck is there with a for sale sign on it."

"Good, maybe we can remove our whole problem."

"It's going off the freeway now, sir. It looks like Puente Hills. I think there is a dump out there somewhere."

"Good, send it when he is off the freeway."

"Yes sir."

Detective Harriet Brown One The Mystery

Puente Hills Dump

A trash truck brought its load up the dirt road towards the city dump. It pulled up behind another truck awaiting its turn. The driver jumped down from his truck and walked to the truck in front of him.

He knew the man, "It's going to be awhile again.'

"Yeah, looks that way," the other man said, "Want a cigarette?"

"Sure," the man from the back truck said.

The man handed him a cigarette from the package, but his eyes were on something coming out of the setting sun. A small plane seemed to be coming straight for them. "What the hell?"

The other driver looked up. He saw the plane coming in, yelling, "Hit the dirt!"

They both dove for the ditch beside the road as the missile slammed into the back truck blowing the metal and trash out over the landscape. They felt the debris fly over their heads as the second explosion took out the rest of the truck. The second truck took damage, but it could still be moved.

A half hour later Ramos arrived. He saw debris spewed over two thousand square feet. He looked the truck over, then he went over to the two men by the fire engine, "Whose truck is it?"

"Mine sir," One of the men said.

"Did you pick up a bomb?"

"No sir, we both saw this little plane come out of nowhere and fly right into my truck. We hit the ditch. Metal and debris flew everywhere."

"You sure it was a small plane?"

"Yeah, one of them drone things," the man said.

Ramos took their phone numbers, and addresses, "If I have any more questions, I will give you a call."

"Yes sir, are we free to go home?"

Ramos nodded, handed them his card, "If you think of anything else give me a call." He watched them leave, checked the damage once more, and left, asking himself, "Why would anyone destroy a dump truck unless they made a mistake. He would have to get the man's route tomorrow."

He received a call from the Detective Agency saying it was urgent. He took the 605 freeway north and headed for Pasadena.

Coming up to the Detective Agency, he noticed the limousine parked in front. He pulled into the parking lot. Coming inside, the whole gang was there.

He smiled, "What's so urgent?"

"They tried to blow up Raymond Hernandez car at his home," Harriet said. "It was Jose Morales."

"Do you have proof?"

"We have a recording, but he had another man place the bomb."

"Seems to be a lot of bombs today, a city dump truck was attacked by a drone. It blew it to bits, but no one was killed."

"Why would anyone bomb a city dump truck?" Harriet asked.

"Maybe to get to us," Mc Craw said. "I placed my phone chip on a city dump truck, a few days ago."

"That might explain it." Ramos said. "Okay, where is our Mr. Hernandez?"

"I suspect he is halfway to Arizona by now."

"I would have liked to question him," Ramos said.

"We did," Harriet said, "And we have a nice set of fingerprints of the man who placed the bomb under his car. We have Jose Morales on tape discussing the placement of the bomb admitting his involvement."

"I think we had better sit on it," Ramos said. "There's more involved here, and his brother is the Chief. We need a solid case against him, but more importantly we need him to lead us up the ladder."

"Bug still working," Youngsu said.

"Then we're back in the limousine," Harriet said.

"Wait a minute," Rose said. "I posted an Email from Hernandez's computer to Jose's computer saying he wanted to talk. He took the bait and opened the E-mail. Now I am in his computer. What would you like to see first?"

"Who's he been E-mailing to?" Ramos asked. "Maybe we'll get a break."

"He's been looking at a lot of porn, but let's see… Here's his most recent E-mails." She sent it to the printer and made a copy of the list. Next, she began going down the list opening the mail.

She found an interesting one called, "The Man."

She made a copy. It said, "Move the cocaine to the warehouse." She moved to his bank and stopped. She looked up, "I don't know his code. I'll have to wait until he opens it."

"Then we're out of here," Harriet said. "We'll find the bug and follow it."

"Maybe you had better start with his place of residence," Rose said. "I got this off his phone." She handed her the address.

"I thought he lived at the warehouse."

"Not recently, he has an address in Duarte. It could be a girlfriend's."

"We'll check it out," Harriet said. "Let's go gang."

"I appreciate you people bringing me in on this," Ramos said moving towards the door. "Please keep me informed." He did not want to know how they would be obtaining the information. It would be better to let them retrieve it and give it to him. He stepped into his car and drove off feeling more confident he was finally getting somewhere on the case.

The limousine pulled out behind him leaving Rose to herself. She locked the door and set the alarm. Then she went back to her computer and began working the information off the phones they had collected. Jose's phone had been turned-off, but she had already gotten all she could off of it. He had made frequent calls to someone he referred to as 'The Man'.

She moved that number through the Verizon database. She had a name, and a post office box. Next, she entered the tracking system. She went through several tracking grids until she located the man in downtown Los Angeles. Using a Los Angeles map, she located it at the Biltmore Hotel.

She picked up the phone, "I found 'The Man.' He's located in the Biltmore Hotel. I am sending the information to your computer in the limousine."

Moments later the tracking switched to Youngsu receiver.

The limousine parked a half block from the hotel. It was past ten. The streets had emptied out. The Man's phone was moving.

"See if you can place a bug," Harriet said. "He's our next rung."

Youngsu jumped from the limousine, ran up the half block. When he reached the door to the hotel, 'The Man' was coming out.

Youngsu, wearing his chauffeur uniform, stepped in front of the man, slipped an electronic bug in the man's coat pocket while asking, "Do you need a chauffeur, sir!"

"No," The Man' said. "I have my own car." A black car pulled up in front of the hotel.

Taking his keys, 'The Man' stepped into his car.

Youngsu memorized the license plate as the black car drove off. He walked quickly back to the limousine, wrote the license number down, and handed it to Harriet. He immediately began following the black car.

Harriet called Rose and gave her the license plate.

Ten minutes later Rose called back, "It's a rental car. I'll have to call you back on who rented it, but I suspect it will not be his real name."

"Okay, call us as soon as you find out," Harriet said.

The computer in the limousine had the bug's frequency. They could hear the noises of the car, and the dial tone of a phone.

Phone:

"Black here! We haven't got the money yet. Tell them we're leaving the merchandise in the ship containers for now."

Pause:

"We'll get the money! Tell them that!"

Pause:

"I said we didn't make delivery! That was the DEA being cute."

Pause:

"You can think anything you want. You can even take the merchandise back, or you can wait until the money surfaces."

Pause:

"Yeah, I know eight hundred million."

Pause:

"You're dealing with me, not Brown. Yeah, I'm on my way there." The phone went quiet.

Youngsu looked at the direction the car was going, "He go to airport, lose bug for sure now."

"We have the phone number," Harriet said. "We'll stay with him until we lose the bug in security."

"I say we pick his ass up, and haul him in," Mc Craw said.

"He would not stay for long," Harriet said. "We have no hard evidence, and we do not know how dependable the police are at this point."

The Man's phone rang. He opened it.

"Black Here!"

Pause:

"About time you called. Did you get McCraw and company?"

Pause:

"A dump-truck?"

Pause:

"We blew up a dump truck?" His voice went up an octave. "We spent a million and a half to blow up a dump truck."

Pause:

"Did you kill anyone?"

Pause:

"How about Hernandez?"

Pause:

"When you do know, call me!" The Man closed his phone, and muttered, "Gees, what am I dealing with?"

The phone comes alive again:

"Yes sir, I am heading there now."

Pause:

"You don't need to replace me sir."

Pause:

"The money? It will surface. We're checking the old man's bank accounts."

Pause:

"You want me to go to the Bahamas?"

Pause:

"I thought I was coming there."

Pause:

"Yes sir, the cartels want their money.

The phone clicked, and another dialed tone.

"Black here! Get me a flight on America Airlines going to the Bahamas."

Harriet dialed the Office:

"Rose, a Mr. Black is trying to find a reservation to the Bahamas immediately. Make sure he doesn't get one for at least two hours."

Pause:

"Good!

Next Harriet punched in Ramos' phone number:

"Detective Ramos we need your help. A Mr. Black is going to board a plane to the Bahamas on America Airlines. He doesn't have a reservation. Rose is presently preventing him from boarding a flight. We need access to his lap top and his phone a few moments."

Pause:

"His full name? Give me a sec."

She hung up, called Rose:

"I need his first name."

Pause:

"A Jed Black is trying to find a reservation. That has to be the one. Stay with him. We need to delay him, but we want him going to the American Airlines."

Pause:

"Good!"

She dialed Ramos again:

"Got it! Jed Black! Now can we pull him off to the side and inspect his bags. We need to download his computer and phone."

"I'll work on it," Ramos said, "I'm on my way there."

He hung up, and dialed Homeland Security:

"This is Detective Ramos of the Los Angeles Police Department badge number 466. There is a Mr. Jed Black attempting to board a flight to the Bahamas on American Air Lines. I have reason to believe he has ties with the cartels and may be dangerous. I am on my way there. Just detain him until I arrive."

Pause:

"Yes, I said dangerous. He's implicated in a car bomb attempt." Ramos closed his phone.

The black car entered the airport and drove into the rental location. The Limousine went directly to the American Airlines terminal.

Harriet made a quick copy of Jed Black's phone conversation. She stepped out, "Mc Craw with me, Youngsu, park the limo, and come inside. You're our backup."

"Yes, Miss Brown."

Harriet walked into the terminal, dialed Rose:

"Did he get a reservation?"

"Yes, the plane leaves in one hour," Rose said, "He has to go to the desk to pick up his tickets. You can intersect him there."

"Thank you, Rose."

Harriet closed her phone, moved on inside, and looked around. She saw the line to the American Airlines and stood to one side of it. She knew the man was wearing a black suit.

She called Ramos:

"We're waiting for him to show, I could send Mc Craw looking for Home Land Security."

Pause:

"You're asking: do we have enough for an arrest?"

Pause:

"I have him confessing to the murder attempt on Hernandez and blowing up the dump truck. He is carrying the next step up the ladder, and he is leaving town."

Pause:

"Okay, I'll have Mc Craw find Home Land Security. You'll be here in thirty minutes."

She closed the phone, turned to Mc Craw, "Better get Home Land Security, Ramos is on his way."

"Where do you want to take him?"

"When he goes through security," Harriet said.

Mc Craw nodded and left her at the front counter.

Harriet moved around trying to find their man. Fortunately, not many people were wearing suits. Thirty minutes later, she saw a man in a black suit come into the line. She immediately stepped in behind him. When the man's turn came, he walked to the counter. She did not see more dark suits. She moved in closer to hear his name.

"Jed Black to pick up tickets."

Pause:

"Going to the Bahamas."

Harriet immediately left the line. She had her man. She walked down to the security line slowly. She stopped to look at the electronic scheduling board. This allowed Jed Black to pass her as he stepped into the line. She moved in behind him holding her hand in her open purse where she carried her Colt 45 revolver.

Mc Craw was at the turnstile. She saw Ramos walk in. "They should have allowed Home Land Security to do this," she thought.

The Man in the black suit saw them. Something did not feel right. He started to turn out from the aisle when he found the barrel of a 45-pistol sticking in his ribs.

"I would keep going if I were you," Harriet said.

The man did not turn around but kept moving toward Ramos and Mc Craw.

Ramos reached in, placed his handcuffs on the man, and moved him away from the crowd.

Harriet lifted her phone. "Youngsu come in now."

Youngsu had already parked the Limousine. He was waiting by the door for the call.

They hauled Jed Black to a side room separating him from his phone and laptop. Youngsu quickly downloaded both as Ramos walked from the side room.

Harriet handed him a thumb drive of the previous conversations on Jed's phone.

Taking it, Ramos said, "This had better be good. He's already threatened to take my badge."

"There is probable cause if nothing else," Harriet said. "Now we have more information to take this further."

"He's a very dangerous man."

"He's already tried to kill me twice," Harriet said. "What do I have to lose?"

"I see your point." Ramos said going back into the side room with the computer and phone.

Ten minutes later a police car pulled up outside the American Airlines terminal. Harriet watched them place the man inside the police car. His phone and laptop went with them.

Ramos came out of the terminal and walked up to Harriet.

Harriet watching the police car drive away, asked, "Why did you allow the police to take his phone and laptop?"

"That was my instructions. I had no way of transporting, and they wanted the evidence to go with the prisoner."

Police Car

Jed Black sitting in the back seat knew he had made one mistake too many. Los Angeles was now wide open. The money missing, the wasted drone hit on a dump truck, and the leaks. "No, he is not going to survive." When the accident happened, it did not surprise him.

The truck bashed in the side of the police car on the freeway. Then he felt something strike his head. He dimly saw someone reach in, take his laptop and phone before he became unconscious and died.

The two police officers remained alive, but barely. The man driving the truck disappeared in another car that had stopped to help. Traffic backed up ten miles. An hour later, the two police officers, and Mr. Black arrived at the hospital. They pronounced Mr. Black dead. Witnesses quickly moved on down the road.

9 Drug King

Harriet planned to meet Ramos at an outside café on Colorado Boulevard in Pasadena and go over the evidence they had gathered. He had called her at her office a few blocks away.

She felt a little apprehensive at first because of the recent events. She did not think they would be seeking revenge this soon after the death of the man in black. They probably will be scrambling to see who would take over his position.

She had Youngsu driving the limousine, just him, and her this time. She spotted Ramos sitting by himself at the café. His face seemed relaxed.

Youngsu pulled the limousine up into the empty space in front of the café and Ramos.

She liked him. Maybe this would be more than a business date.

Youngsu opened the door and helped Harriet out of the limousine. She smiled walking towards Ramos carrying her purse.

Ramos stood, pulled a chair out for her, "You do travel in style."

"It's inconvenient at times, but I am getting used to it," Harriet said taking the chair offered.

"I ordered a cup of coffee for you. I hope that is okay."

"Yes, thank you," Harriet said. "Now tell me about the evidence."

"There is no evidence. It seems whoever smashed into the police vehicle took the evidence with them. You have the only copy."

"How did they know about the evidence, or for that matter we had even captured Jed Black?"

"I don't know," Ramos said. "That's why we are meeting out here. We did find a bug on him."

"That was Youngsu's bug. You may have a leak in the police department. Did you follow it out to see where the message went?"

"Yes, it went through several hands, and finally ended up with Chief Morales. He gave the order to send the patrol car."

"What about the evidence? Who told you to give it to the patrol car?"

"That's standard procedure to avoid contamination of the evidence," Ramos said. "Having said that, I also agree with you, we have somebody in the police department giving out critical information."

"Then we will continue to amass information," Harriet said.

"Are you going to give me a copy?"

"If you can keep it out of the police department," Harriet said. "You will be our second source. Remember, we don't want someone compromising our data."

"I think I can do that," Ramos said.

"Now, how about some clothes," Harriet asked. "All of mine are locked up tight in my house."

"I'll check it out. Maybe we can arrange for you to remove your belongings."

"Thank you, a girl likes to wear more than one outfit."

Harriet sat facing the on-coming traffic. Her eyes saw a black car suddenly speed up. Two gun barrels came out of the windows. On her feet, running for the limousine, her hand slipped into her purse, and clasped her Colt 45 revolver. Her purse fell to the ground as she flipped the safety off.

The two rapid-fire guns sent bullets into the crowd. One bullet struck a little girl of ten hitting her in the stomach. Another one struck her mother standing beside her in the leg. Another man took a bullet in the arm as he ducked behind the tables.

Ramos flung himself out towards the limousine tucking his head against the concrete. He could not believe Harriet. She stood behind the limousine as the bullets came whizzing by him.

Bullets struck the limousine, bounced off the bullet-proof glass and doors, sending pieces of the bullets back into the speeding car.

Harriet had her cannon in both hands and leveled on the roof of the limousine. She lined up on the driver and pulled the trigger. Her arms flung upward as the large bullet shattered the back window, piercing the driver in the right shoulder. It threw him against the wheel turning it hard to the left. The black car crashed into two parked cars across the street.

Youngsu, out of the limousine immediately, ran to the damaged black car. The two shooters were not wearing seat belts. The one in the front slammed into the dashboard, and temporarily became incapacitated.

The one in the back seat hit the cushion front seat. Still dazed when Youngsu arrived, he struggled to get out of the black car with his gun pointing outward. Timing it, Youngsu grabbed the gun away from man, slammed the butt of it into the man's face breaking his nose and left zygomatic arch (facial bone). The man fell to the pavement unconscious.

The second man coming out of the front seat suddenly found himself pulled from the car with his feet still hanging inside. He fell face down to the pavement as Youngsu came down with his elbow breaking three ribs above the man's heart.

Youngsu kicked the guns away and leaped up on the car. Dropping to the other side of it, he pulled the driver with the busted right arm to the ground. The man screamed in pain.

Ramos managed to collect himself. He ran out behind Youngsu. The action done, he picked up the rapid-fire weapons carefully as Youngsu took the wallet and phone from the driver.

Youngsu's gloved hand quickly went through the wallet taking pictures of the identity cards with his phone. Finished he returned the wallet to Ramos. He kept the phone and took a picture of the license plate of the black car. The other two did not have any identification, but one of them had a phone. Ramos retrieved it and threw it to Youngsu.

In the background the sirens could be heard from the police, and the ambulance arriving.

Youngsu recognized the driver to be Jose Morales. He also noticed him bleeding out. He took Jose's belt, and tied a tourniquet over the bronchial artery to stop the bleeding.

Harriet came off the top of the limousine with her hands shaking. It took her a moment to set the safety on her gun and find her purse. She could not talk. She just wanted to go home.

Ramos sent her on her way. He did not want another attempt on her life. The little girl and her mother left in the ambulance first. The second ambulance took Jose Morales. The man with the bullet in the arm said he would see his own doctor, and left, but not before Ramos took his name and address from his identification.

The police collected the other two men without identification and transported them to the police station. Ramos followed in his car. Impressed how well Harriet and Youngsu worked together. He's ducking his head, while she's fighting back with her cannon.

The interrogation at the Pasadena Police Station only revealed they were nationals here without a visa from Columbia. They did not speak English. He knew they would-be transferred to Los Angeles FBI, or Home Land Security. He would not get another chance to interrogate them.

Harriet, still shaking, entered her Detective Office in Pasadena. She took a chair immediately.

Youngsu gave Rose the phones, Jose Morales's address and social security number. Finally, he said, "Miss Brown survive drive-by shooting. Three people shot, one small girl. It was Jose Morales."

"We need to get to Jose's residence before they do a sweep of the place," Harriet mumbled out staring at the door. Then she continued, "Someone ordered that shooting. We need to find them before they try again."

Mc Craw walked in, "Did anyone hear about the shooting on Colorado?"

"They were shooting at us," Harriet said. "We need to reinforce this office. This could be their next target."

"I already did after our last attack here," Rose said. "The glass is bulletproof, and the door locks like a bank vault. We also have an escape hole in the bathroom that leads to the outside behind the trash bucket. We can survive."

"We need a place to stay that is more protected. I think we should all stay together until this is over," Harriet said.

"That limo is like a beacon right to us," Mc Craw said.

"Not if we are staying at a hotel where limousines are expected."

"I like it, but can we afford it?" Mc Craw asked.

"For a while, meaning we have to move faster on this," Harriet said. Feeling better, she looked at Youngsu, continuing, "You better go for Jose's apartment saying he gave the correct address on his license this time."

"Let me look," Rose said, bringing the address up on the screen. They could see the structure, and the ground around it. She saw the black car with the license number of the drive-by car sitting next to the building.

"That's it!" Youngsu said, "Only one camera on street." He left the office running.

"Mc Craw, go with him for back up," Harriet said. "We may not be in time."

He nodded and followed Youngsu out the door.

"Okay, let's get to work, and figure out who ordered the drive-by," Harriet said. "The shooters only had the one phone between them."

Rose opened the phone, looked at it, "It's clean except for this one phone number. It must be the one who ordered the shooting."

She ran the phone number through her computer program and came up with an address. "This is where the call originated, but now to find a name to go with it." Continuing, she said, "The person's moving." She went to the map board, stuck a pin on the street the call came from.

She looked at it a moment, "The Biltmore hotel is right here. I bet he is staying at the hotel." She switched to her hotel logarithm program, "Let's see who recently checked in the last day or so." The logarithm worked a moment, then stopped.

It had ten names. She quickly removed eight from the list because they had checked out. Leaving two, one was an older woman with her dog, and the other one a man named Herman Schmidt. "That's him," Rose said.

"Probably an alias, but it's a start."

"Room number?" Harriet asked.

"Number 1704," Rose said.

"Good, book us a room close to him," Harriet said.

"How about 1706, next to him. That just became vacant."

"That'll work," Harriet said.

Rose began placing a room reservation with the electronic hotel machine. In a few minutes she said, "I have it, but it will cost you four hundred dollars a night."

Jose Morales Apartment

Youngsu drove the long limousine down the alley towards Jose's apartment. Mc Craw began asking questions about the drive-by shooting.

"You mean she stood right up there popping the back window out with her cannon?" Mc Craw asked.

"Yes sir, she pay no attention to the flying bullets, and sent cannon loose, hit Morales's car, Miss Brown very brave."

"Where was Ramos all this time?"

"On sidewalk with head down," Youngsu said smiling. He pulled the limousine to the side of the alley, "Limo stop here." Above them, he could see a slightly open window. "Mc Craw stay with limo for fast get away."

Youngsu jumped out of the limousine and opened the trunk. He retrieved his bag whispering, "Be few minutes," and leaped up on the roof of the limousine. He took three suction cups from his bag. He placed two on his feet, and one on his left hand. Jumping to the wall, he shoved his feet into it. Immediately the suction cups took hold. He quickly worked his way up the wall and opened the window with his right hand.

Climbing inside, he began looking for Jose's computer. He found it under the bed mattress. Quickly removing it, he downloaded everything from the computer to his thumb drive.

He noticed a slip of paper on each side of the computer view screen. They appeared to be codes for getting into his internet and bank. He stuffed them into his pocket. Finished, he slipped the computer back under the mattress.

He went around the room quickly, checked the mail for anything other than the utilities, and stuffed them into his shirt.

Finished, he went back to the window, slipped on his suction cups, and quickly made his way down the wall after he closed the window. Once on the limousine, he removed the suction cups, put them in his bag, and jumped to the pavement.

Seconds later, he had the limousine moving out of the alley, and down the street. On the other street west of them, he heard a police car approaching. He turned quickly into another alley and came out the other side. In moments, on the freeway, he headed north.

Hospital Bed

Hospital nurses wheeled Jose Morales into his room. They moved him to his bed and set up all the tubes monitors while he came out of the anesthetic. His shoulder had one big bandage going down to his waist.

The doctor walked in, looked everything over. He noticed Morales was awake and staring at him.

"How bad is it," Jose asked.

"You're lucky to be alive," the doctor said. "Whoever placed that tourniquet on you probably saved your life. You almost bled-out."

"What about the little girl?"

"She'll make it, but she'll have a nasty scar the rest of her life."

"It wasn't my fault," Morales said. "They had a gun to my head."

"Your brother is here to see you," the doctor said to avoid the issue.

"I don't need to be seeing him."

"I would recommend it, if you are ever planning on leaving here a free man."

Captain Morales entered the room as the doctor left. He looked around, "It appears you are going to survive." Then he shook his head slowly, "How do you get into these messes?"

"It wasn't my fault this time."

"You got a police car involved again."

"These guys put a gun to my head and made me drive."

"Do you know who they were?"

"They were speaking Spanish, but my guess would be Columbia nationals. They don't like how we are handling things here."

"You mean the DEA?"

"Yeah, who else?"

"You're supposed to be out of there."

"Someone hasn't told them yet."

"The police car, I told you no more police cars."

"Yeah, they took my driver's license."

Captain Morales looked at him hard, "I don't know if I can fix this for you. You shot a little girl."

"I didn't shoot her. I'm the one that got shot."

"Yeah, and you're to stay away from those detective people. I don't want you near them. There's enough people after them."

"She put a slug through my shoulder."

"Yeah, and it was her man that saved your life. If it was me, it would have been easier to let you bleed out."

"They did that?" Jose asked. Then thinking a second, he asked, "What are my chances with the drug cartel?"

"I don't know. They are going to be blaming you for the failure. I understand they don't like failures. It might be safer to put you in protective custody."

"I rather take my chances on the outside."

Ramos called Harriet:

"Checking to see how you are doing?"

"I'm doing fine, but I am not going back to Nadine's house. I do not want to endanger her more."

"Where are you going?"

"I rather not say, but I am going to need some clothes. Can you let me into my house?"

"I can arrange that."

"Can you do it without telling everyone?"

"You don't think I can do that?"

"Look, somehow they knew I was having lunch with you. Have you checked to see how that came about?"

"I see your point! I'll be at the house in thirty minutes."

"Thank you," Harriet said. She did not tell him she was already at the gate waiting.

Youngsu had parked the limousine out of sight back from the front gate.

They waited fifteen minutes when a black car showed up.

Youngsu recognized the police license plate, "Police car, Miss Brown. You want Mr. Mc Craw and me to take out police?"

"Disarm them, then we will wait for Detective Ramos."

Youngsu and Mc Craw quickly moved down the dark street. They saw a man unlocking the gate in front of the black car in undercover clothes (Black Suits). Youngsu headed straight for him as Mc Craw came up thirty feet behind him.

When the second man opened the car door to level his gun, Mc Craw jerked the gun from his hand, and pulled him out of the car.

The man had unlocked the gate. When he turned back to the black car, he saw Mc Craw coming. He started to pull his revolver, when a foot struck him in the chest sending him back into the fence. The second kick sent his gun flying into the bushes.

Mc Craw pushed the man he pulled out of the car up against it. He immediately recognized him as Jed Black, "What in the hell are you two doing here?"

"The Chief said we are to escort Miss Brown into the house."

"How did you know we were coming here?"

"The Chief did, we are only following orders," Jed Black said.

"The next big question, how come you have the very same name as man running a drug cartel?"

"It's probably forged. Unfortunately, he used my name."

"Or maybe you're going to be his patsy when things went south."

"I wouldn't know. I have never met the man."

"You seem to be in too many places involving us," Mc Craw said.

"I go where they send me," Jed said.

"Yes, a little too often to be accidental selection."

Youngsu had moved the second man up against the car when Ramos showed up.

Ramos stepped out of his car, looked at the situation, "What's going on here?"

"I like the answer to that question myself," Mc Craw said.

"Chief Morales sent us," Jed Black yelled out. "We're to check everything she takes out of here."

"She's not here," Mc Craw said. "We're taking everything." He still had the two police officers up against the car, and continued, "You against that?"

Mc Craw saw Harriet approaching from the street. She had her cannon in her hands. She could hear the conversation in the still night air.

Suddenly Ramos pulled his gun, pointed it at Mc Craw, "Release them or take a bullet."

"I thought you were dirty," Mc Craw said. "I suppose you set up that drive-by too."

"I've been trying to keep her alive, but she is very hard to protect."

"The drive-by!" Mc Craw yelled. "That's why you were on the ground."

"I didn't know it was going to be a drive-by," Ramos said.

"Maybe you should think about dropping your weapon, and turning around very slowly," Mc Craw said in an even voice. "There's a forty-five pointed at your back. You know how big of a hole it makes."

Ramos glanced back slowly. He saw Harriet ten feet away with her weapon pointed at him. He knew she was not afraid to use it. "Dropping my weapon," Ramos said, and slowly placed his weapon on the ground.

Then Harriet became extremely angry yelling, "Who killed my father? Tell me in five seconds or I am going to start blasting one of you at a time."

"We don't know!" Jed yelled. "We're instructed where to go by the dispatcher, and we go. This is my first time here."

"Ramos?" Harriet asked. "I have yet to hear the truth from you."

"I was working on finding out who did, but I haven't found anyone. So, if you are going to shoot us, you might as well get started."

"Youngsu, take their handcuffs and cuff them. Remove their phones and ID while I think about who I am going to kill first. Mc Craw, bring me their guns."

Youngsu cuffed the three police officers and turned them towards Harriet as Mc Craw handed Harriet their revolvers.

"Youngsu, put Detective Ramos in the police car," Harriet said as she placed her weapon in her purse, and looked Jed's gun over. She stepped-up to him, pointed the gun at his head, yelling, "How did you know I was coming here? You only get one chance to tell me the truth."

"I got a call from the Chief saying to come here," Jed said.

The revolver became heavy in her extended arms as she moved the barrel back and forth. Finally, she pulled the trigger. The bullet passed his head and entered the tree beside the driveway.

"Now tell me your purpose for coming here?"

The man realized she had no qualms about shooting him.

"Were we to have an accident?" Harriet shouted. Her hand began to quiver again causing the end of the barrel to move back and forth across his eyes.

"You know too much," Jed said quickly.

"And!" Harriet yelled.

"We were to shoot you in the house."

"Detective Ramos?"

"All four of you."

"Who ordered it?"

"Morales, Chief Morales." He yelled. "The man's threatening my family. He shot my dog for god-sakes."

"And your buddy?"

"I don't know about him," he shouted.

"Youngsu, put him in the car."

Youngsu quickly placed Jed Black in the car beside Detective Ramos.

Mc Craw lined the other man up in front of Harriet, as she took his gun from her purse.

She aimed it at him, "It's your turn to tell the truth."

"I don't know anything the same as Jed."

"You get one chance," Harriet said. "What's your name, and how many people in the police department are dirty?"

The man visible shaking, timidly said, "Name's Hogan, Mike Hogan. You mean on the take or something else?"

"Those that help the drug cartel exist here?"

"I don't know, maybe four or five on the lower level, and maybe two or three on the higher levels."

"Who on the higher level?"

"All I know it goes very high."

"What level are you on?"

"Lower level, madam."

Harriet moved the barrel of the gun towards the tree and fired. The man almost fainted.

"How much did they pay you to be dirty?"

"Hundred thousand with promise of more."

"Were you going to leave our bodies at the house after you killed us?"

"That was our instructions."

"Who's instructions?"

"Chief Morales."

"Give me the name of another dirty cop, and I'll let you live," Harriet shouted.

"Cooper, Chris Cooper!"

"Another one! Now!"

"Anderson, George Anderson, I don't know anymore."

"Throw him in the car, Mc Craw."

The man dropped to one knee shaking as Mc Craw lifted and pushed him towards the car.

"Youngsu, take Detective Ramos from the car, and remove his handcuffs."

He looked at her a second.

She nodded.

A moment later Detective Ramos came out of the car with his handcuffs off.

"Nice acting Ramos!" Harriet said handing him the weapons. She gave the wallets and phones to Youngsu, "Please bring up the limousine."

Youngsu ran back to the limousine. Once inside the limousine, he downloaded the phones, and took photos of the bankcards, license, etc. He noticed the recording machine. It had been running. He flipped a switch and heard Detective Ramos on the phone. He smiled. He knew Harriet had placed a bug in her purse. He pushed the thumb drive into the machine and downloaded the confessions.

Harriet, while she was waiting for Ramos to finish his call, sent Mc Craw to dig out the bullets from the tree.

Finally, Ramos closed his phone, turned to Harriet, "I have a car coming to retrieve these two, and pick up Cooper and Johnson. Are you going to give me a copy of their confessions?"

"Youngsu is bringing it. Who are you giving it to?"

"It's evidence, otherwise I can't hold them. Even then it will not hold up in court. We will try and use it to reach higher, but that's the best we will get out of it."

Youngsu arrived with the limousine. He handed the thumb drive to Harriet. She gave it to Detective Ramos, "I still need to get some clothes if that is alright with you."

He waved her on, saying, "It will be at least twenty minutes before they get here."

She entered the limousine. Youngsu pressed the gate button in the limousine, the gate opened. He removed the yellow ribbon, drove the limousine up the long driveway, and parked in front of the house. Youngsu helped her out of the limousine. She walked up to the house.

Harriet unlocked the door, went inside, it was a mess. Someone had tipped the furniture over and torn them apart. The walls were ripped open and left exposed. The floors had deep holes in them.

Harriet worked her way around the mess and started up the stairs. She noticed blood on the steps. She knew whose it was. She stopped a moment. She did not know if she could do this. Taking a deep breathe, she pushed on up the stairs.

On the second floor, the same. Walls and floor spaces, torn open and exposed. When she reached her room, she found her bed upside down, and torn apart. Her clothes were scattered across the floor.

She found a suitcase and began collecting the clothes she would need. She threw in the few personal items that she could find scattered across the floor.

Finished, tears flowing, she could not stay longer. She felt her father's presence touch her. She quickly walked down the stairs by-passing the bloodstains and ran out the door.

Youngsu had the limousine door open as she ducked inside. He placed her suitcase in the trunk. Slowly he drove the limousine down the long driveway, "I can drive slower, Miss Brown."

She wiped the tears from her eyes, "I'm okay, let's go. They will pay."

Youngsu drove the limousine out the gate and stopped beside the police car. Mc Craw, finished retrieving the bullets, climbed into the back seat.

Harriet rolled the window down, "Do you want us to wait with you, Detective Ramos?"

"It's probably best you were not here when they arrive."

"Maybe you had better look inside my suitcase to ensure I did not take any money out of the house."

"If you think that will be necessary?"

"It was the reason for you meeting us here."

He nodded, "Okay, open the trunk please."

"Youngsu, please check Detective Ramos's car for a bug. If you find it, place it in the police car."

"Yes, Miss Brown," Youngsu said as he stepped from the car. He went to the trunk and removed his bag as he opened Harriet's suitcase for the detective.

Walking to the detective's car, he dropped his bag, and brought out a small scanning device to pick up frequencies. It picked up one immediately. He traced it to a small space under the dash. Reaching in, he removed it.

The size of a golf ball, the bug emitted a blue light. Large for a bug, but it gave a range of twenty miles. He placed another bug with a fifty-mile range in the detective's car. It was the same size.

He took the blinking blue light device to the police car, opened the front door, and placed it far up under the dash. Coming back, he picked up his bag, and placed it inside the limousine trunk beside the now closed suitcase.

Ramos came up to the window, looked inside, "Clean, you may go Miss Brown."

"Thank you, Detective Ramos," She pushed the button, the window closed.

Youngsu entered the limousine. In moments, he had them moving along the dark road.

Harriet leaned forward, "Let's go to ground now."

"Yes, Miss Brown." Youngsu said as the limousine headed for the freeway. She dialed her grandfather, Henry Brown.

Phone conversation:

"Yes, Harriet?"

"Papa, we're going to ground. I would recommend you find another address for a while."

"You're sounding more like a detective every day," Henry said. "So, what's got you so frightened that you need to go to ground."

"Another attempt on our lives by the police department for one," She said, and started to drop a tear, but taking a deep breath, she continued, "I don't know who to trust right now."

"Okay, okay, I know about the break in, but what else?"

"A drone was sent to blow up our limousine but blew up a dump truck instead. There's been a drive-by shooting. The only thing saving us was the bulletproof limousine. The shooters were nationals from Columbia, now this attempt to kill us at the house." She felt the tears coming.

"I agree, take everyone, and go to ground immediately."

Wiping her nose, she asked, "And you?"

"Don't worry about me but take Nadine with you.'

"They're planting bugs everywhere," Harriet said. "They may be listening to this conversation."

"I scan my place every day. I assume Youngsu had taken precautions."

"He's very good. Thank you for sending him."

"Okay, need to go, love you very much. Hide deep."

She heard the dial tone and closed her phone. She knew he said deep to throw off anyone listening. She thought about calling Nadine, but she did not know if she had a bug free phone.

She knew Rose's phone would be good and called her.

"Rose, pick up Nadine. We are going to ground now. There's been another attempt. They've been placing bugs everywhere. Be careful."

"I'm on my way."

Police Car

After the limousine pulled out, Detective Ramos waited another fifteen minutes before the police car arrived. It pulled up behind the other police car with a prisoner in the back seat.

A large burly police officer in front passenger seat stepped out, opened the back door, "I found Chris Cooper."

Reaching inside, he pulled Cooper, a thin man, out of the car, and directed him towards the other police car.

"What about George Anderson?" Detective Ramos asked. He had never met George.

"He's out on patrol," the police officer (George Anderson) said. "We thought it better to come here, and unload what we had first."

He shoved the handcuffed Cooper into the backseat of the police car forcing the other two to move over. It was crowded. The police Officer, (George) walked around to the driver's side, and climbed in. Leaning out the window, he asked. "Where do you want me to take them?"

"Downtown for more questioning."

"What about the evidence?"

"I'm taking their confessions with me." Detective Ramos said. "I'm following you in."

The police officer nodded ducking his head inside. He turned the police car around and headed out towards the freeway.

The other police car with only the one driver followed, and Detective Ramos followed him.

George Anderson, driving the police car with the prisoners, earlier had received the call to pick up Chris Cooper while his partner, Officer Peter Davis, a medium size black man was driving. He did not know Detective Ramos, but he knew the location of his former partner, Chris, and directed Davis to him.

They picked him up and headed for the estate trying to understand what had happened. Why would somebody want to find them? His mind worked on this as he headed for the freeway.

In the back-seat Jed yelled, "Anderson, how come you're driving the car?"

"I'm trying to figure out who fingered me."

"We had no choice man," Jed said.

"There's always choices." He looked into his rearview mirror. He saw Officer Davis's police car following with Ramos' car behind him.

He punched the #2 button on his phone, lifted it to his ear, "Ramos is in his car moving towards the 210 freeway."

Pause:

"Yes sir." Anderson said folding his phone. He placed it on his seat beside him.

"What gives, Anderson?" Jed asked.

"We're getting rid of evidence."

A man in a uniform placed his phone to his ear after he had placed the voice distorter, "Send it, but be sure it's the small one. We don't need to take out a dump truck this time."

"Yes sir, the small one," a slender man named Cal Chapman said.

In Chino Hills, a small drone took off from the dirt road. It headed towards Pasadena carrying a small missile in its nose. Once airborne, it headed west until it picked up the beeper, and moved quickly that direction. Moving over the 210 freeway, it found its target. It quickly dropped in elevation. Coming in low it passed the detective's car, the second police car, and centered on the first police car with the prisoners in the back seat.

The missile pierced the roof of the police car, found the box with the blue light, and exploded. All those inside died instantly sending body parts out the windows. The metal doors burst outward sending debris in all directions.

A piece of metal landed on the hood of Detective Ramos's car as he pulled to a stop.

Still in shock, Ramos stumbled out of his car. He looked at the burnt piece of metal as the fire consumed the police car. It looked like a phone still in one piece. He picked it up and placed it in his pocket. It was still hot, but he endured it.

He heard the fire truck in the distance. He backed his car up to allow it room to reach the burning car.

Officer Davis did the same. He had not seen the missile.

The local police arrived and began controlling traffic as the fire truck made its way to the burning car.

Ramos called Harriet, "A missile blew up the police car as we entered the 210 freeway. What's going on?"

"That missile was for you," Harriet said. "Youngsu found a box with a blue light up under your dash. He moved it to the police car thinking it was a large listening device. It appears now it was part of a guidance system directing the missile. Someone's trying to kill you."

Stunned, he stammered out, "I found a phone. It's been burnt, but maybe you can find something in it. It has to be the driver's."

"We need to get it," Harriet said.

"I would like to meet you, but I am a target now. It could endanger you."

"We've been endangered for a while, welcome to the club."

"What did they want from me?"

"Probably the confessions. You should still take it to the police department, and enter it as evidence," Harriet said. "It will take the pressure off of you."

"What about you?"

"They'll still use you to find us," Harriet said. "They will place a bug in your clothes, home, car, or your favorite places to eat and sit. To call me, you will have to use a new phone that is clean. If I call you, we make the conversation quick to avoid a trace. I will only call in an emergency."

"Okay, where do you want to pick up the phone?"

"Drive-by, drop it in the gutter, now." Harriet said.

"On my way in ten," Detective Ramos said closing his phone. He walked over to the local police officer, "Is there anything else you wanted to know?"

"Yeah, what happened?"

"A missile stuck the police car."

"Do you know where it came from, or who sent it?"

"We're looking into it."

"Your Partner said you were transporting prisoners, is that correct?"

"We were only bringing some people in for questioning. That's all I can tell you."

"Okay, if that's it. Do you have a card in case we have more questions?"

Ramos handed the police officer his card, "Call me anytime." He turned and walked back to his car. He had a rendezvous to keep.

His phone rang. He noticed it was Captain Morales calling. His heart skipped a beat as he opened his phone.

"Yes sir, Ramos here!"

"What in hell happened? I get more from the Channel Seven News than I do from my own men."

"Sorry sir, it's been quite a mess. We've been transporting prisoners as ordered. When we started to enter the freeway, a guided missile blew up the prisoners' car. It was one big ball of flames. Davis and I were trying to control things until the locals arrived."

"They're all dead?"

"No one survived, sir."

"You sure it was a missile?"

"Yes sir, like the dump truck."

"You come straight here."

"Yes sir, coming in."

The Channel Seven News team arrived as Detective Ramos pulled out. "Someone had placed a call saying a second missile had destroyed a police car carrying four officers."

The news people jumped from their van and began filming as the fire truck hosed down the flames. One of the news people found Officer Davis, shoved a mike into his face, "We heard a police car carrying four officers was struck by a drone missile."

"We know something blew up the car," Officer Davis said, "We don't know if it was a drone missile. The investigation has not been completed."

The overhead helicopter had the flames focused in as the reporter said, "This is the second drone missile to strike a vehicle. Who is attacking us? Is anyone safe driving the freeways? Where is our Home Land Security?"

Officer Davis received a call from an irritated Captain Morales, "You get your ass in here now. No more interviews, you trying to panic everyone?"

"Yes sir, on my way in."

Ramos pulled up in front of the outside closed café on Colorado Boulevard in Pasadena. He pulled into the parking slot in front of it, opened his door slightly, and slid the burnt phone to the curb. Then he pulled out, headed for the freeway, and the Los Angeles police station.

A slim man stepped out of the shadows, walked to the curb, and picked up the phone. He walked quickly into the alley and stepped into a limousine. Seconds later, the limousine left the alley, and headed for downtown Los Angeles.

Detective Ramos entered Captain Morales' office just ahead of Officer Davis. Morales seating behind his desk, nodded towards the chairs behind them. They both quietly took a seat.

Morales looked around the room a moment, then he asked, "Do you know who was just in here asking me questions I could not answer?"

Neither of them said a word.

"The head of Home Land Security for the west coast, Jeffery Adams himself! Do you know why he came in here?"

Neither of them said a word.

Then looking at them, he said, "He wanted to know why there are drone missiles flying around Los Angeles striking vehicles, and now killing four police officers. I did not even know what he was talking about because my officers did not bother to call in. Instead, they're giving the news media every little detail. Where did they get that information? Why from our own police department giving out information not based on fact. Does any of this sound familiar?"

"It was a missile, sir," Detective Ramos said. He had to be careful what he said. He remembered the confessions involving the Chief.

"What makes you so sure it was a missile?"

"One, I saw it strike the car. Two, it had the same crater marks as the dump truck, but this attack was very up close."

"From this point on, you do not answer anyone's question concerning the missile attack, and that especially means Home Land Security. Tell them to talk to me. We need to keep our information correct. You are to gather evidence and hand the evidence over to me. Is that understood?"

"Yes sir," they both said.

"Now, give me those confessions you are carrying. That's evidence."

Ramos removed the thumb drive from his pocket and handed it to Captain Morales. He knew Harriet had a copy of the confessions.

"Now, I want you to bring that detective bitch in. She's way out of control and take that damn gun away from her before she kills someone. That will be your assignment Ramos since you know her better than anyone-else.

Davis, you'll partner up with Ramos here since you lost your partner. No more of this on your own. I am moving you into the detective division. It will be teams until we get to the source of these missile attacks, any questions?"

"No sir," Ramos said.

"Now get the hell out of here!"

They both started to leave when Captain Morales said, "Davis, you wait a minute."

When Detective Ramos left the room, Morales looked at Davis, "You keep an eye on Ramos, tell me when he is out of line. I want to know everywhere he goes and sees?"

"Yes sir."

"Now out of here!"

"Yes sir," Davis said, and quickly ran after Ramos going out the second door.

Captain Morales smiled to himself, "Yes, you also need a leash. You're way out of control." He slipped the confession thumb drive into his computer and listened to the confessions. He smiled, "That is one lady I don't want mad at me."

10 Making the Mark

Rose arrived with Nadine to the Biltmore Hotel in Los Angeles. They had four bags between them. The valet took her car to the parking garage, and the hotel porter carried the four bags on his cart. Rose walked to the counter with Nadine beside her, "I have a reservation for Mrs. Jose Morales." She produced a credit card, and a driver's license with her name on it.

The hotel clerk ran the card. He gave her two card keys. The hotel porter followed them to their room on the top floor. He opened the door, set their luggage down, and showed them how things worked in the room.

The room had 910 square feet of living area with two large bedrooms, one with two queen size beds, and the other one with one king size bed and a roll-away. Most importantly, it had connecting doors to the suite beside them. Rose gave him a twenty-dollar tip.

He smiled, "If there is anything you need, do not hesitate to call."

The door closed. Rose smiled, "We're in, but we cannot stay long."

"How much is this costing us?" Nadine asked.

"It's on Jose Morales credit card," Rose said. "He's in the hospital so he will not be objecting." She began to unpack and set up her equipment.

The limousine pulled up to the Biltmore Hotel in Los Angeles. Youngsu stepped out of the limousine and opened the door for Harriet. Mc Craw opened the trunk, retrieved Harriet's bags, and followed her into the hotel.

Youngsu took the limousine to the garage. He parked it next to Rose's car out of sight in the corner.

A porter attempted to take Harriet's bags, but changed his mind when he saw Mc Craw pick them up. She already had her man. When they left the elevator, Mc Craw started to say something, when she placed her hand to her lips, and shook her head. She knew all too well how sound carried in the hallways.

They passed the target room. She knocked on the door to her room softly.

Nadine opened the door. She saw Harriet and gave her a big emotional hug. Finally, she pulled herself free, she started to say something when Harriet put her finger to her lips and shook her head.

Going into the room, Harriet looked around, "Guys in the double queen beds and us in the other one." The door closed as Mc Craw placed Harriet's luggage on the king bed.

They heard a small knock at the door. Nadine opened it revealing Youngsu.

He entered the suite, and immediately went to the doors connecting the rooms. He opened their side slowly. He looked at the locked on the other door and nodded. Then taking his stethoscope, he placed the cup on the door, and listened.

No sounds, he removed a heat-sensing device from his bag. He turned it on, moved it over the wall and the connecting door, no heat signatures. Finally, he said, "All Clear!"

He worked the lock with his picks, the door opened. He quickly entered and planted a few bugs in the room. He placed one in the hotel phone, came back quickly, and closed the door locking it again in the process.

Everyone breathed easier. Rose continued to set up her machines and computers.

"Okay everyone," Harriet said, "The goal is to acquire as much information as possible, then make a plan. Rose, we have acquired a number of phones. We need to see what numbers everyone has been calling.

We are trying to identify who is at the top of this. We're caught in the middle of a drug deal that has gone bad. They seem to have the drugs stashed somewhere, but the money to pay for them is missing. My father appears to be responsible for that. I am sure he left a code somewhere, but I am not in any hurry to find it."

She turned to Rose, "I think we should find another safe house. We may have to leave here in a hurry."

"Where do you want it to be?"

"Out of Los Angeles, and some place limousines are not rare. We should also have a route there that will not have any cameras on it. So, find a route without cameras.

Now, we want to get inside this man's phone and internet. Youngsu will place the bug into his cell phone tonight. We will be looking for the location of the drugs. It will have to be a fair size container or several smaller ones."

"What are you planning on doing with it, once you find the location?" Mc Craw asked.

"That depends on where the drugs are located. I want them to be missing like the money."

"That'll cause a drug war," Mc Craw said, "That may get a lot of innocent people dead."

"Then we will have to move fast once we have the information. That part of the plan, I have not thought out yet. Now, we just want information. Okay, any questions?"

"How about food?" Mc Craw asked. "Did anyone think about bringing any?"

"We'll send Youngsu for food. If anyone has any favorites, tell him. I don't want room service coming in here. Okay, let's get set up."

Rose had her scanners out. She placed them against the wall and went back to her computer. She hooked up the cable and pulled out the thumb drive from Jose Morales' computer.

Youngsu was taking orders. When he came to Rose, he asked, "Whose phone?"

"Jose Morales!"

"Look at these," Youngsu said, taking out the four folded pieces of paper with letters and numbers on them, "Found on computer."

Rose looked at it closely, "That's his E-mail address and code to get into his computer, and I think this is his bank ID and entry code."

Harriet came over to look and nodded for Youngsu to go after the food. It was going to be a long night.

Rose opened his bank account using the passwords, and downloaded the information going back three years. It showed large sums of money passing through. Presently he only had four hundred dollars sitting in his account. She downloaded his E-mails going back several years. His phone numbers included several calls to his brother, and Sid Black. Nothing seemed to go to anyone higher than Sid Black.

An hour later, Herman Schmidt with a woman on his arm, stepped onto the elevator ahead of Youngsu with the food. Drunk, he used the woman for support.

Youngsu remained in the elevator, when Schmidt and company stepped out. He took it all the way to the bottom floor and returned to the top floor. Long enough he thought to allow Schmidt to enter his room. He quickly walked down the hall and knocked softly on the door.

Harriet opened it, let him inside, and pointed to the wall.

Youngsu nodded and placed the food on the table.

They could hear noises coming from the next room. Youngsu placed his stethoscope to the wall, and whispered, "Sex!"

Ten minutes later the woman left the room. They could hear her walking down the hall still trying to put on one of her shoes.

They heard the shower going a few minutes, then a thumping noise when Schmidt fell on his bed. Five minutes later, they could hear loud snoring.

Youngsu slowly unlocked the door between the rooms and entered quietly. He easily found Schmidt's phone, removed the chip, and inserted the spyware. Next, he placed spyware in his laptop computer, and turned it on. Now they had full access to his phone and computer. It took five minutes. Done, he quickly moved back into their room, closed, and locked the door.

Rose immediately accessed his phone. She downloaded all of his phone numbers, and names. Going into his computer, she was able to read, and download all of his E-mails. One of them showed a Long Beach container storage facility.

Opening up the E-mail, she found a document indicating he had four container units. The four numbers listed, requested the containers be picked up. "I think I've found the cocaine," Rose said.

Harriet came over to read the document, "Can you get into the facility's computer?"

"Give me a minute I have to get through several walls." Rose began working her computer following the E-mail address back, thirty minutes later, she said, "Okay, I have it, now what?"

"Can we make it appear the containers have been picked up?"

"If I show the numbers were picked up, then change one number, but keep the location numbers intact, the containers can remain right where they are. Now, who do we want to pick them up?"

"What numbers has he been calling?"

Rose moved through his phone contact lists, "Do you recognize anyone here?"

"Let's go to his most recent incoming calls."

"There's only one recent local one," Rose said bringing it up on the computer.

"Let's check his recent outgoing calls."

"There's four here," Rose said, "I'll bring them up."

One of the numbers matched the Columbian's phone in the drive-by shooting. Pointing it out, Rose said, "He was your executioner." Then looking at the other numbers, one of them matched the incoming call. Checking the time, the incoming call was before any of the others. "I think we need to find out who this is. He may have given the order."

Rose began comparing it with the other listed numbers. It finally matched a Jeffery Adams. "There it is, Jeffery Adams called Schmidt, who called the Columbia assassin."

"Not so fast," Harriet said. "All we really know is this Jeffery Adams called before Schmidt sent out the assassin."

"Jeffery is on his speed dial."

"Then he's no one time caller."

Mc Craw stood in the background until he heard the name, Jeffery Adams. The name rang a bell, but he could not believe it was the same man. Finally, he said, "Give me that Colombian's phone. I have to make a call."

"You're going to be waking him up," Harriet said handing him the phone.

He dialed the number.

It rang six times, then an irritated voice answered the phone, saying, "Jeffery Adams, Homeland Security, this had better be good."

"Sorry wrong number," Mc Craw said closing his phone. He stood there a moment looking at Harriet.

"Well?" Harriet asked.

"Jeffery Adams Homeland Security," Mc Craw said in a low voice.

"There's a connection between Home Land Security and Schmidt?"

"That's what it appears."

"We don't know if Jeffery Adams is dirty from a few phone calls," Harriet said.

"He's in Schmidt's speed dial, meaning he calls him a lot."

"So, we have the drug cartel meeting with Homeland Security. Maybe Jeffery is waiting for some hard evidence."

"He answered as Homeland Security," Mc Craw said. "He's not trying to hide something. Therefore, he has to be working with him."

"How about we place the blame for the drug loss on Jeffery Adams," Harriet said. "He orders the shipment shipped."

"Our friend Schmidt would probably come unglued," Rose said.

"Exactly, he calls Adams yelling, and threatening him, but he does not have the drugs. Adams will defend himself allowing us to get everything recorded."

"Okay, the Long Beach Container company will send a notice to that effect via E-mail. I will use the same format the container company used naming Jeffery Adams as the one taking them." Rose looked around, "Do I send it?"

"Send!" Harriet said.

Rose sent it, "This is going to create a reaction."

"We need to find out who Adams calls after being accused of taking the drugs. Do you have an address on him?"

Rose goes through her data banks, came up with an address, "He has a house a block over from your former house in Brentwood."

"That figures," Harriet said. "We need to find out who he calls after he receives our friend's call."

"I go to house, mount transmitting dish," Youngsu said.

"Good, take Rose's car," Harriet said. "The limousine is too easily recognized. Then come back here, and place one on the roof. We may have to leave here in a hurry"

"Good idea, Miss Brown."

"Maybe I should go along, and make myself useful," Mc Craw said.

"No, we need you here to evacuate quickly," Harriet said. "Besides, things may get out of hand here."

Youngsu packed his bag and took one suitcase to carry his gear. He left quickly taking Rose's parking slip. Downstairs he handed the parking slip to the valet and waited five minutes. He tipped the valet five dollars and was on his way.

An hour later, he reached Jeffery Adams' house. He hid the car in the bushes camouflaging it. He took his bag with the dish and headed towards the house. He moved slowly to avoid the security system especially the cameras. He had them all located and turned to give him an escape route back out. When close enough, he mounted the dish, and extended the antenna. He camouflaged the dish and transmitter and left.

Coming back to the hotel, Youngsu checked the car back in. Taking his bag, he took the elevator to the top floor, found the stairs, and slipped a piece of paper into the lock.

Continuing up the stairs, he picked open the lock, and placed a piece of paper in the lock. He walked out on the roof of the building. Quickly finding the area over their mark, Schmidt, he set up the dish receiver and transmitter with the antenna. He did not try to camouflage it.

He turned it on and set the meltdown button. Now if the antenna moved without turning it off, the receiver would meltdown inside.

Done, Youngsu moved back through the doors, removing the paper allowing them to close, he entered the upper floor hallway. He lightly knocked on the door. It opened. He slipped inside. Most of the night was gone. "Might get five hours sleep," he thought heading for the bedroom.

At eight sharp Schmidt saw his phone blinking. He picked it up. A message from the Long Beach Container Company said, "The containers have been picked up."

At first, he did not realize what it said. Finally, realization set in, "The containers had been delivered." He quickly called the company, but all they could tell him that early in morning: a Jeffery Adams had picked them up.

He immediately pushed his speed dial to Jeffery Adams.

Adams came on the phone still not awake. He heard Schmidt yelling at him about the containers. Finally, awake, Adams yelled, "What containers?"

"The ones with the product!" Schmidt shouted. "Someone has taken delivery, and that someone is you!"

"It's not me Schmidt! This is the first I've heard of it!"

"I'm onto your scam! You promised money for the product until it was delivered, then you suddenly can't pay. Now you take our product. We can't absorb this loss! You have twelve hours to deliver the money."

"Look! I don't have the money, and I don't have your damn product," Jeffery Adams yelled back!"

"Twelve hours with the money or you're dead!"

"Let me see what happened. Sometimes the DEA boys do things on their own. I'll find your damn product."

"You've taken delivery of the damn product! We only want our money now. I've been patient enough, twelve hours, remember Jed Black!"

The phone cut off as Adams started to say something. Schmidt made another call out of country.

Phone: Speaking in Spanish:

"I need two hits. I need to teach some damn Yankees a lesson. He will find the car on level four at the Los Angeles airport, and on level two at the Dulles Airport. Use the clickers to find the cars. He will find what he needs is in the trunk. Yes, I know the amount. There's ten thousand in the glove compartments."

He closed his phone.

They could hear the man pacing inside the room.

Youngsu checked the recording device on the roof. Transmitting, their recorder was picking up everything.

The next call came up immediately from the receiver he had planted at Adams' house.

Phone:

"Morales, Adams here! We've got a problem. Some damn fool has taken the product, now Schmidt wants his money, or he's coming for me in twelve hours."

"Sorry sir, no one here has taken the product as far as I know. Have you checked with the DEA?"

"I'll give them a call."

"I'll keep my ears open here."

"Thanks." He hit his speed dial. A man answered the phone.

"Bryant Kelly here."

Listening, Mc Craw whispered to Harriet, "Head of the DEA."

"Adams here, what do you know about a product bust?"

"Usually that is kept quiet, a need to know basis."

"Look Kelly, someone has taken delivery of the whole damn product. It's either you or Morales. I'm thinking more you, since Morales is missing four men, and you would know how to disperse it."

"Jeffery, no one here took it. It's just them trying to pressure you for the money. If it is gone, they took it themselves. Don't play into it unless you have the money."

"I don't have the damn money. Brown hid it somewhere. I think his daughter is looking for it."

"Let her find it for you, unless you have a better idea."

"She won't find it in twelve hours," Adams said. "I'll be a dead man after that."

"Hide good!"

The phone hung up:

"Damn!" Adams said hitting his speed dial again.

A woman answered, "Yes sir."

"Mary, Adams here, send me a team of ten to my house immediately."

"Yes sir, expecting trouble?"

"Just get them here."

"Yes sir."

"Keep both recorders going on mike only," Harriet whispered. "It is time to be moving." They began gathering up their gear as Mc Craw removed the fingerprints.

Ten minutes later, Rose and Nadine came down the elevator with Mc Craw carrying their bags. Rose went to the desk to check out using Morale's card.

Youngsu went down to the garage, retrieved the limousine, and pulled it up in front of the hotel as Rose's car arrived from the garage.

Harriet, already in the lobby, walked out pulling her one bag. Youngsu retrieved her bag and placed it in the trunk. Then he opened the door for her. Going around to the other side, he climbed in as Rose's car arrived.

Harriet placed a call to Rose, "Mc Craw is to drive, and follow us. I want you in the limousine."

When Rose's car pulled up, she motioned for Mc Craw to drive, "You are to follow us." She took one suitcase from Mc Craw and climbed into the limousine.

The valet opened the door for Nadine. She climbed into the passenger side of Rose's car as Mc Craw tipped the man and stepped into the car.

Inside the limousine, Rose was putting in the route to the next safe house twenty miles north of Los Angeles.

Harriet checked the transmitters. They picked up the signal from both locations. The recorders came on automatically every time someone would speak in either of the locations.

"I need to call Ramos and warn him about the possible hits." Harriet said as she picked up her phone.

Phone:

"Ramos here,"

"Ramos just listen, there are two possible hits coming down, one a Bryant Kelly Head of DEA in Washington DC, and the other one Jeffery Adams Los Angeles Home Land

Security. It's going to happen in less than twelve hours." She closed her phone not giving Ramos a chance to ask questions or place a trace on the call.

Rose looked up, "I have a Hilton hotel south of Oxnard."

"Good," Harriet said.

Rose had the route, handed it to Youngsu.

"Don't use the GPS, they could cross triangle us," Harriet said.

"I use map, Miss Brown, should be there in twenty minutes."

"What credit card should we use?" Rose asked. "I have them on line."

Harriet thought a moment, then said, "Use yours! Youngsu, let one highway camera see us heading north, then pull off the freeway, and head back to my house using side streets."

"Your house?" Rose asked.

"The last place they would expect us to be, and the best place to hide the limousine," Harriet said. "As soon as you are off the freeway, pull over. I do not want to use the phones anymore."

"You figure they will see my credit card at the hotel."

"We have to be smart, but not too smart," Harriet said. "Detective Ramos will recognize your card eventually."

"One camera has spotted us," Youngsu said.

"Good, pull off the freeway."

Youngsu took the next ramp off the freeway. He pulled over on a side road. Rose's car pulled up behind them.

"Find us a route to the house, Rose," Harriet said stepping out of the limousine.

She walked back to Mc Craw who had rolled down the window. "We are going back to my house. There is a guesthouse behind it we can stay in, and a garage to hide the limousine and your car. You should follow us. We are trying to find a route back without cameras. Do not use your phone unless it is an emergency."

"Got it, we are to follow you," Mc Craw said.

Harriet nodded and walked back to the limousine.

Rose, working on the route, said, "I have it. It's going to take us an hour, but I don't see any cameras." She had her computer working though the street cameras in the route.

"Then let's go," Harriet said.

Police Station

Ramos, at the police station when he received the call, knew it was from Harriet. She probably picked up the information with one of her spywares. He had been trying to find her as ordered by Captain Morales. "She's an amateur and amateurs get killed."

He had been checking the hotels around Los Angeles. He suddenly found a Hilton Hotel had Rose's credit card on their reservations lists. He planned to meet her there. He did not tell Chief Morales.

"Who'd the call come from?" Peter Davis asked.

"I got a tip a hit has been placed on Bryant Kelly in DC, and Jeffery Adams here."

"You think it's serious?"

"Hard to say," Ramos said. "It could be someone trying to save a life, or it could be a crank call. Anyway, I got a lead on the Brown girl. Let's go!"

"Give me a minute," Davis said waking into the bathroom. Inside he dialed Chief Morales.

"Davis here, sir! He had a call come in saying there was going to be a hit on a Bryant Kelly, and a Jeffery Adams."

"How serious?"

"I don't know. He said it could be a crank call."

"That's it?"

"We have a lead on the Brown girl. We're going to follow it up."

"Keep me informed." The phone clicked.

Davis quickly walked out of the restroom.

Ramos, waiting for him, knew why he went to the bathroom, but he did not let on and led them from the station.

Harriet's House

The limousine with Rose's car following moved through the residential streets working their way to her house in Brentwood. Reaching the gate, Youngsu left the limousine, and removed the yellow tape going across the entrance. He entered the limousine, pushed the gate button on the overhead, the gate opened, he drove through.

After Rose's car came through, he replaced the yellow tape, and closed the gate. Driving up the long driveway, he took the limousine to the garage, pressed the door opener. The door opened, the two vehicles parked inside.

The huge door closed. Everyone climbed out taking the equipment and suitcases. Using her key, Harriet opened the guesthouse.

They quickly began setting up looking for places to store their luggage. The house, twenty-seven hundred square feet, had three bedrooms.

Youngsu secured the antenna on the roof to receive the transmissions from the phone bugs. Back inside, he asked, "Is it working?"

Rose already had her equipment up, "It's coming in good."

Mc Craw had checked the refrigerator, nothing. Then he checked the cupboards finding it full of dried foods. "Just add water," He said. "No beer."

"We need to keep the lights off," Harriet said.

Rose began working on the burnt phone Ramos had given them. She managed to remove the chip inside. An hour later, she retrieved the last call it had received. It was Chief Morales' phone number. She handed the number to Harriet, "This is who ordered the hit on Ramos' car."

"It only shows he called Morales before the drone hit," Harriet said. "It does not say he sent it, but let's keep the option open."

11 Death Squads

In the guest house behind the Brown mansion the people began to wake up. Mc Craw looked the kitchen over for more food when Harriet walked in. He turned when he heard her, "We need to send someone for food."

"No, every time we leave here, we run the risk of being spotted. This is supposed to be empty, but the main house has food. I will see what I can find."

Nadine walked in the kitchen hearing the conversation, "You're not going alone, I'm coming with you."

"Thank you, let's get it over with," Harriet said.

They both left the guesthouse, moved across the drive, and entered the mansion going through the kitchen door.

Harriet checked the refrigerator. It was full of produce, meat, and plastic containers full of left overs. The electricity was on meaning the food was still okay.

Nadine felt something and moved into the other room. She slowly walked towards the front door. Harriet noticed her leaving and followed her.

Christopher Charles

When Nadine reached the staircase, she stopped, took hold of the banister. She did not move. Her eyes closed as she entered a trans-like state:

Nadine's Vision

She sees a woman open the door. A man in a police uniform stands there.

"I am here to see Mr. Brown."

Mr. Brown coming down the stairs sees the police officer pull his revolver from behind his back. He starts to turn, and run up the stairs, but the bullets reached him first as he tumbles down the stairs.

The woman tries to run from the room. She makes four steps before a bullet stops her. The police officer walks into the kitchen, fires two shots into another woman trying to leave out the back door.

A limousine pulls up in front of the house.

The chauffeur jumps out of the car and runs towards the house. He makes it to the door when two more bullets stop him. The police officer walks up the stairs and comes back with a laptop computer under his arm. He steps over the chauffeur and leaves the house. The scene closed as Nadine dropped to the floor."

Harriet ran to Nadine lifting her head gently.

Slowly Nadine opened her eyes, "I saw him kill everyone."

"Who?" Harriet asked.

"A police officer, I don't know his name."

"Would you recognize him?"

"I could draw you his face," Nadine said as she tried to stand. Her body still weak as Harriet helped her up.

"Maybe Mc Craw would know him," Harriet said leading Nadine into the kitchen.

They took what they could from the refrigerator and left the mansion. They both were relieved to be out of there.

Reaching the guesthouse, Nadine began drawing the face of the police officer. When she finished, she handed it to Mc Craw, "Do you know him?"

Mc Craw looked at it a second, and slowly said, "Yeah, that's Chief Morales. That means he killed my wife, the same bullets were used." His face became very angry, as he said, "It all fits! He's been there all this time."

"It's not proof," Harriet said. "It's only a vision Nadine saw. It could still be someone who looks like him."

"It's him!" Mc Craw said. "Remember those other officers fingered him too."

Los Angeles Airport

A man in a dark suit left the terminal. He headed for the parking garage. He found the black car on the forth level using the clicker. The open trunk revealed a box with a scope rifle packed inside, and a car bomb.

He stepped into the car and checked the glove department. He saw the package of money, smiled, picked up the phone, and called Schmitt.

Biltmore Hotel

Schmitt, on the bed, was thinking his next course of action, when he received a call. He picked up the phone.

Phone, Voices in Spanish:

"This is Mr. Pieon. I am in Los Angeles. Who are the targets?"

"Bryant Kelly Head of DEA, Washington DC, and Jeffery Adams Los Angeles Home Land Security."

"You are to stay in your hotel until this is finished."

The phone clicked.

Christopher Charles

Schmitt knew Mr. Pieon was the hit man for the cartels. Was there another target?

Police Station

Chief Morales waited a couple of hours before he decided to call Bryant Kelly Head of DEA in Washington DC. He went through four recordings, and two secretaries before he finally reached him thirty minutes later.

Phone:

"This is Bryant Kelly what can I do for you Chief?"

"Chief Morales of the Los Angeles police department, sir. We had a tip you are a target for a hit today by the drug cartel."

"How real is this tip?"

"I do not know the source, but I thought it might be prudent if you took some precautions, sir."

"I appreciate your concern, Chief, but I am quite a ways from Los Angeles."

"Yes sir. It was just a tip." Morales said closing his phone.

He thought about calling Jeffery Adams, but he already knew about the possibility of a hit.

Jeffery Adams' House

Jeffery watched his team go to work. They had placed a perimeter around his house placing six guards in the yard, and four inside. He sent his family off to a safe house. He felt protected. He had a mansion with wide-open fields of grass surrounding the house. The only thing that could reach him was a drone, but he knew who controlled them.

His phone rang. He debated whether he should answer it until it stopped ringing. It rang again. This time he picked it up.

"Yes,"

"Bryant Kelly here, Is this Adams?"

"Yes sir, sorry sir, I am a little spooked."

"Why is your man Morales, calling, and threatening me with a hit?"

"I had no idea he called."

"How serious is this?"

"I told you I had to come up with the money in twelve hours. That was two hours ago, sir."

"How does that concern me?"

"I think you know, sir."

"You tell your man Morales to take care of this now. Use any means he feels is necessary."

"Yes sir, drones?"

"I said any means necessary."

"Yes sir."

The phone clicked, and Adams dialed Chief Morales:

"Morales here!" He immediately recognized the voice.

"Why in the hell are you threatening the head of the DEA with a hit?"

"I got a tip, sir. The tip also included you. Therefore, I assumed it was real."

"Take care of the problem immediately."

"Any restrictions?"

"Eliminate the problem using any method necessary."

"Yes sir."

Harriet had recorded the conversations coming from Jeffery Adams' house. She had proof now of the link between Captain Morales and the drug cartel.

Christopher Charles

The Assassin

Mr. Pieon found the addresses of his targets on his computer tablet. His first target was Jeffery Adams. He drove to his house and parked three blocks away hiding his car beside the road in some bushes.

He removed the small car bomb from the trunk and ran towards the house. He immediately picked up the black cars surrounding the house, and knew his target had protection.

He worked his way into the neighbor's yard moving from bush to bush. The sun had set giving him cover. He went over the fence and moved to the side garage door. He quickly worked the lock slipping inside. He saw the big black Mercedes Benz.

He crawled beneath it with the car bomb, taped it to place, and connected it to the ignition. Done, he worked himself out from under it, and slipped out the door. He pushed the lock in place. Going back over the fence, he worked his way to his car.

An hour later, he had returned his car to the Los Angeles Airport parking stall and boarded a plane for Washington DC. Six hours later, he checked into a hotel across from an apartment complex that Bryant Kelly occupied. He had his binoculars searching the windows, and balconies of the complex.

Bryant Kelly, still thinking about the threat on his life went over the possibilities. He limited his exposure to the Cartels by always working through Jeffery Adams. They did not really know him. They had no direct connection. They would not have his address. He set it up that way. Jeffery Adams became his fall guy.

He walked out on the balcony, leaned against the rail. He liked his life. He had a beautiful wife. They wanted kids, but the timing was not right. He pulled out a cigarette, lit it, and took in a deep breath.

It was his last breath as the bullet pierced his head. He fell forward over the rail landing on the cement pavement below. No one heard the shot above the night's noises. The silencer also helped.

Mr. Pieon quickly took his gun apart and slipped it into his case. Three minutes later, he walked out of the building. An hour later, he sat on a plane heading back to Los Angeles. He felt his coat inside pocket. It had twenty thousand dollars in it. He smiled, now to earn another ten grand.

Los Angeles

Jeffery Adams watched the news in his living room. His team had insisted he stay away from the windows. They secured his perimeter and sent his wife and kids away. Listening to the television, he heard them announce the death of Bryant Kelly the head of the DEA. His body laid on the cement at the bottom of his apartment complex. At first, they thought suicide until they saw the bullet hole in his head.

Jeffery immediately called Morales, yelling, "What the hell are you doing? They got Kelly already."

"I heard," Morales said. "Just sit tight, I am working on it."

"Not very good by the looks of it!"

"I'm on my way to see Schmidt now."

"To arrest him?"

"He's not the assassin, but I will try, and draw him in."

"Then what?"

"I thought a drone from Chino Hills might be effective."

"Let me know when it's done."

"You will know." Morales said clicking his phone.

Christopher Charles

Brown Mansion

Harriet listening to the conversation, said, "We have to get some help, and fast. Anyone have any suggestions?"

"I can send a drone warning to the FBI. They may not be contaminated yet." Rose said.

"Mc Craw, what's your opinion?"

"He's going to blow the top floor of the Biltmore hotel if we do nothing."

"Send the warning, Rose." Harriet said.

Rose opened her computer. She brought up the FBI emergency line and typed in: "Drone attack coming from the Chino Hills, intimate." She immediately closed off the site to avoid tracking.

The FBI field unit notified of the threat, swung into action. They were already aware of two other drone attacks, the last one killing four police officers. They had a break on this one. They sent four units to Chino Hills, and cross triangulate the area. They looked for any transmissions.

Special agent Steel, a tall thin man with glasses, stood in the command center. He looked at the map for possible sites the drones could come out of without someone noticing. He had three locations.

Biltmore Hotel

Captain Morales took the elevator up to the top floor. The desk clerk had given him Schmidt's room number. He knocked on the door. He heard the latch come off the door and pushed the door in hard as it started to open. It knocked Schmidt to the floor.

Schmitt moved backwards using his arms and legs. When he reached the bed, he looked up, "If you're going to kill me, get it over with. I'm dead anyway."

Morales closed the door. Looked down at the pathetic man on the floor, "It seems your man was very effective. He killed Bryant Kelly."

"You here to arrest me?"

"In due time!" Morales said. "I want your assassin."

"He's going to kill me. You have to arrest me."

While they were talking, Morales walked past Schmidt on the floor. He looked in some of the drawers. In one he placed a golf ball size object that had a pulsating blue light. He closed the drawer quietly as Schmitt worked himself up on the bed.

"What do you know about the Bryant Kelly assassination?"

"Nothing! He didn't confide in me!"

"Where is the assassin now?"

"I don't know."

"You sure he is going to kill you?"

"I'm not sure of anything," Schmitt said, "If you people had just given us the money."

"The money's gone, and the drugs are gone," Morales said. "Our side didn't take either."

"That is not the way our side sees it. We have proof Adams took delivery. Kelly probably took the money. I don't know where you fit in?"

"Old man Brown took the money. I made sure he paid for it. The product, I don't know yet. I'm thinking you."

Schmitt felt a glimmer of hope, "Maybe we can work something out,"

"Not with that assassin running loose."

"He's coming here after he completes his contract."

"Why would he do that?"

"I'm sure he has a contract on me."

"Maybe we can work something out," Morales said. "You have to delay him until I can get here."

"How long?"

"Five minutes should be sufficient."

"I'll delay him the five minutes."

"Good," Morales said leaving the room. He smiled walking down the hallway. He had his trap set, now to wait. Downstairs he walked over to the desk and told them to notify him if anyone asked for Schmitt's room.

He walked to the lobby, took a chair where he could see the door. He picked up a newspaper and read about the assassination of Bryant Kelly. He waited an hour before he saw a man dressed in a black suit come through the door.

The man walked to the desk, picked up a room number, and headed for the elevator.

Morales looked at the man at the desk.

He nodded.

Morales plugged his phone into his voice scrambler, pushed his speed dial, and raised his phone to his ear. A voice came on the other end.

"Send the small drone towards Los Angeles. It's marked." He closed his phone and waited.

Chino Hills

The FBI had checked out two likely spots and came up negative. Special Agent Steel began to think the E-mail might be a hoax, as he led the vans down the dirt road towards the third, and last possibility, a house near a small lake in the middle of Chino Hills.

As they approached, he saw a drone moving towards them on the dirt road. He flipped on his flashing red lights and siren. The other vans did the same as they raced down the road.

The drone took off barely missing the oncoming FBI cars. It climbed two hundred feet heading towards Los Angeles.

The man, Cal Chapman, at the house saw the flashing lights and ran for his motorcycle. He leaped on, kick started it, and, raced across the field going around the lake. One of the FBI vans took off around the lake to cut him off while another one tried to follow him.

The third and fourth cars pulled up fast to the small house. They jumped out of their vans and raced into the garage.

The equipment continued to run. They could see the drone on the screen. Steel worked the computer trying to turn the drone, but to no avail. It had already linked to the small golf ball in the Biltmore Hotel. The computer no longer controlled it. He flipped his phone open.

Steel's phone:

"We couldn't stop the drone. It is on its way into downtown Los Angeles. We are trying to apprehend the man who sent it off."

A voice at the other end asked, "What is the target?"

"It just has Los Angeles. It is being guided by something in the city. We should have the man soon."

"Call when you get a target."

"Yes sir."

Chapman's motorcycle hit a patch of mud sending him flying when the front wheel dropped into it. The FBI van pulled up beside him. Two men jumped out of the van and pulled him to his feet.

Looking up at them, he yelled, "I'm on your side! I'm on your side!" They had him up against the car placing the handcuffs.

Christopher Charles

"Look, this is a police action. Chief Morales ordered the drone out. I was only following orders."

"Where is it going?"

"He said to send it to Los Angeles. It picks up a locator when it's within twenty miles of it, and hones in. It's very precise. This is not the first time he asked me to send one. Ask him, you'll see."

Steel opened his phone.

"It's heading for Los Angeles. It is being directed by Chief Morales of the Los Angeles police department."

"What the hell? What's going on here? Bring the man in for questioning and pick up Chief Morales."

"Yes sir."

Biltmore Hotel

Mr. Pieon knocked at Schmitt's room.

"The door's opened," Schmitt said backing up behind the bed.

The door opened slowly. Mr. Pieon entered. He closed the door, turned, and looked at Schmitt. "I guess you know why I am here."

"You were paid," Schmitt said.

"Yes, but now I want my bonus."

"I didn't take the money or the product."

"That is not my problem," Mr. Pieon said. "I think they want new management."

"Can we talk about this?"

Mr. Pieon withdrew his pistol. He began placing the silencer on the end of it while Schmitt watched.

"This is not necessary," Schmitt said looking for a place to hide.

Detective Harriet Brown One The Mystery

Mr. Pieon pointed his pistol and pulled the trigger. The bullet struck Schmitt between the eyes as the drone came through the window. It found the pulsating blue ball in the drawer, exploded, sent what remained of the window outward, and blew out the walls of the adjourning rooms. The whole hotel shook. The transmitter on the roof, blown off its spot, and began to melt.

Jeffery Adams' House

The seven o'clock news channel showed the blown-out section of the Biltmore Hotel. It reported two people in the room killed, and only slight injuries reported elsewhere. Mr. Schmitt seemed to be one of the victims, but the identity of the other one remained unknown.

Adams stepped back from the TV and smiled.

Phone rang:

"Adams here."

"Morales sir, I think you are safe now."

"I saw the news, a little dramatic, Morales, but thanks for getting him."

"I may need your help sir, the FBI have taken me in for questioning, seems they didn't like the drone."

"I'll see what I can do." He closed his phone thinking it was time to get back to the office. He began sending his armed guards away. An hour later, he walked out to his garage. He stepped into his Mercedes Benz, pushed the button to open the garage door.

He turned the key to start the car. The ignition sent a spark to the car bomb. The explosion blew outward demolishing the entire car and garage. The neighbors called 911. The fire department came out along with the police. They managed to put the fire out before it reached the house, but the man in the car was part of the debris.

Christopher Charles

The Harriet's transmitter, blown from its position, landed on the ground where it immediately began to melt down.

12 The Fall Out

Brown Mansion

"That's it." Rose said. "We're shut down from both sources. Something loud blew them away. I'm guessing a drone at the hotel and something similar at the Adams' house."

"Then let's download our evidence to the FBI, and give a copy to Ramos' E-mail," Harriet said.

"Can we trust the FBI?" Mc Craw asked.

"What would you suggest?" Harriet asked.

"Let's get a bug inside."

"That's not going to be easy. Any ideas, Youngsu?"

"I need to place the transmitter somewhere."

"There's the KB Homes building next to the FBI building," Rose said. "You should be able to get to the roof easier. There are also some light poles across the street from the building to place your receivers."

"Okay, who places the bugs inside the building?" Mc Craw asked.

"That will have to be me," Harriet said. "I'll need some practice in manipulating the bugs."

"Practice tonight, you should be going in tomorrow morning," Mc Craw said. He knew they probably would be questioning Chief Morales then.

"Okay then it is a go," Harriet said. "We have a lot to do before then."

"I would like to plant a location bug under your skin for a while," Rose said, "Also under Youngsu's skin. The back of the neck just under the hair is the best spot."

"Do Youngsu's first," Harriet said. "He has to get going."

Rose took a sterile locator bug and placed it under the skin where his hair touched his neck. She used a sterile blade to make the small incision and placed a bandage when she finished.

Rose tested it and sent Youngsu on his way. She placed another bug under Harriet's skin. It hurt a second as she made the cut.

Youngsu, using Rose's car, headed downtown. He entered the KB Homes building carrying a briefcase. He walked to the elevator following a group of men wearing suits. At the top floor, he entered the staircase, placed his pieces of paper over the latch, and quickly moved to the roof. He secured his transmitter to a high structure then made his way back out of the building. The whole process took less than fifteen minutes.

He went back to his car a block away, changed his shirt to a city worker's uniform. He quickly walked to the light pole across from the FBI building. Unfolding his long extension rod, he placed the receiver on the end of it and pushed it up the pole. When he reached the top flat portion of the light, he flipped the receiver over. It landed on the top of the light. The magnet held it tight.

You would not see the receiver from the sidewalk, but you could if you used binoculars from the FBI building, and knew where to look. Then it would appear as small bump on top of it.

He went to the other light poles doing the same until he had the building surrounded. Finished, he walked back to his car, and returned to the Brentwood Mansion. Coming into the guesthouse, he said, "Done, now your turn."

The next morning, Harriet dressed, and removed the small bandage from the back of her neck. She had Rose replace the buttons on her coat with the bugs inside of them. She could pull them off her coat, push the button inward, and the bug would pop out into her hand. Then she could return the magnetic button to her coat.

She would have liked to get into his phone, but that would be too risky. They would have to wait until they were sure he was dirty.

Rose handed her the thumb drive with the evidence, "There is a bug in the drive. The only way you can tell is by the lack of storage. I was still able to place all of the conversations on the drive portion."

"Once they have the drive, they will probably transfer it to another drive," Harriet said.

"At least we will know what their reactions are to the first exposure," Rose said.

Harriet, ready, had Youngsu drive her to the FBI building in downtown Los Angeles. He agreed to pick her up out of camera range a block away. She walked into the FBI building, went through the security check, and entered the elevator that took her to the 17th floor. She left her gun with Youngsu.

She knew Assistant Director James Clark had his office on this floor. She also knew Rose was tracking her at the guesthouse.

She walked to the counter, "I would like to see Assistant Director Clark. It is an urgent matter of national security."

"Do you have an appointment?"

"No, but this cannot wait. Time is of the essence."

"Assistant Director Clark has someone in his office at the moment," the woman behind the desk said. "Perhaps we could have Special Agent Steel talk with you."

"No, it will have to be Assistant Director Clark. This is a life and death situation," Harriet said as she placed a bug under the counter. She replaced the button on her coat.

"Special Agent Steel can handle anything you might have."

"No, it has to be Assistant Director Clark," Harriet said. "There have been four attempts on my life." She had tears coming. It was not difficult. She has been close to tears for many days now.

"Very well take a seat. I will see if he can see you."

Harriet took a seat opposite the counter and looked at the woman as she made a call. The bug picked it up.

"Sir, she says she will only see you."

Pause:

"Yes sir, there's been four attempts on her life. She does not trust anyone else."

Rose smiled. The transmission was coming in loud and clear.

A moment later, a tall man with broad shoulders, and wavy brown hair came out of the office, "I am Assistant Director James Clark. What can I do for you?"

Harriet stood. She had her tears flowing and ran into his arms. Her left-hand fingers went below the inside hem of his coat pocket where she squeezed a bug into place. "They've been trying to kill me," she said through her tears."

"Easy, there young lady," Clark said. "Maybe we had better go to my office."

She dried her tears as Clark led her to the inner office. She already had another bug loose from her coat. Entering the large office, she walked on around the desk following the Assistant Director. When he turned around, she was right behind him. Her hand had already squeezed another bug to place beneath the lip of the desk.

Her tears still flowing, he moved her to the chair n front of his desk. She managed to release another bug from her coat button. As she sat down she inserted it into the chair.

She took her coat off replacing the button at the same time. She turned and sat in the chair with her coat on her lap.

Settled, Assistant Director Clark looked at her, "First, what is your name, and then tell me what this is all about?"

"My name is Harriet Brown. It is about the murder of my father, Mr. George Brown, and his staff, the bombing death of Jeffery Adams, Home Land Security, the shooting of Bryant Kelly head of the DEA, the murder of four police office, and two drug cartel deaths with drone missiles, and four attempts on my life."

Assistant Director Clark sat there a moment unable to speak, then he said, "I need to bring Special Agent Steel in on this. Can you wait a minute?"

"I prefer to talk only with you," Harriet said.

"He's the lead agent on the drone killings. He will have to know about this information eventually." He lifted his cell phone, "Steel, come to my office please. I have something very interesting here."

Harriet already had another bug out of her coat button.

When Special Agent Steel entered the room, she stood, and started to walk back to shake his hand. Her right foot caught her left foot sending her flying towards him. She flung out her arms. He stepped forward to catch her as she squeezed a bug into the inside seam of his suit pocket.

Slowly she regained her feet, "Sorry sir, I am very nervous."

He helped her to her chair and took a position beside the desk with his left leg up on it. Harriet immediately noticed how comfortable Steel felt in the office. She became more nervous and apprehensive.

They waited until she situated herself in the chair and appeared composed. Then Clark asked, "Now tell me again what brought you in here, and who is trying to kill you?"

"Chief Morales has tried to kill me four times," Harriet said. "Only the grace of God has prevented it."

"How do you know Chief Morales?"

"I have never met him," Harriet said. "I've tried very hard to avoid him. He wants me dead!"

"Why would he want you dead?" Steel asked.

"Because I know he murdered my father, and everyone in our household. I only survived because I was not there at the time."

"Who was your father?" Steel asked.

"George Brown!"

"You are his daughter?"

"Yes," Harriet said softly. "Chief Morales also accidently murdered four police officers when he tried to kill Detective Ramos with a drone. Then he sent a drone into the Biltmore hotel to kill the two men responsible for the death of Jeffery Adams head of the Home Land Security and Bryant Kelly head of the DEA. He tried to murder me with one too, but he only blew up a dump truck."

Steel swallowed hard. He knew about the three drones. Very few people knew a drone took out a dump truck. He looked at Clark.

"That's why I brought you in here," Clark said.

Special Agent Steel returned to Harriet, "What evidence do you have?"

She reached into her pocket, took out the thumb drive, "It is all in here." She placed it on the desk in front of Clark.

"Do you have any more copies?"

"Should I have made one?" Harriet asked in a quiet voice.

"We need to hear this," Clark said as he stood. Taking the thumb drive, he continued, "You can wait here. We will want to ask you some questions after we hear this."

Harriet watched them go. Another agent came into the room. He remained by the door. She suddenly realized they were not going to let her go. Becoming nervous, she stood, and walked towards the Agent.

The agent put his hand up, "Sorry ma'am, but you are to remain here."

"I need to go to the bathroom," Harriet said in a soft voice. "I need to go now. My stomach hurts something awful."

The agent looked around for some help. Then he said, "Follow me." He took her to the bathroom and stood outside.

Harriet walked inside. When she realized he was not going to follow her, she turned her coat inside out revealing a light pink material with flowers. She had a reversible coat. Then she quickly put her hair up into a ponytail. Two women came into the bathroom. She continued to play with her hair.

One of the women finished and walked up beside Harriet to wash her hands and fix her hair.

"This is my first day here," Harriet said. "It's all very intimating,"

"It's like any other job," the woman said. Turning, she continued, "Don't think of it as the FBI."

"Assistant Director Clark looks very interesting."

"He's a workaholic, you don't want him hon, many have tried only to be hurt."

Harriet looked at her watch, becoming nervous, she said, "I need to get back."

Christopher Charles

"Come on, I'll walk with you," the woman said leading Harriet out of the bathroom.

Harriet turned her head slightly to the right as she continued to talk with the woman.

When she reached the elevator, she thanked the woman, and stepped into it. She pushed the button, the elevator descended to the ground floor. She walked past the security station, and out the door.

She continued to walk quickly across the street, and down the block. She opened her phone, pressed the speed dial to Youngsu. When she heard his voice, she said, "I'll be there in two minutes. We need to leave immediately. This may have been a bad idea."

She was almost running when she reached Rose's car. Her heart was beating fast. She quickly stepped inside, "Let's go!"

Youngsu immediately moved the car out into the traffic. He began picking streets that did not have a camera. They had worked the route out earlier.

Guest House

Rose picked-up on the bugs Harriet had planted. The first one to come alive was the bug in Agent Steel's coat. He had placed a call.

Phone:

"Morales, Steel here, we've got a young lady here claiming you are trying to kill her. Her name's Harriet Brown."

Pause:

"That's her. She has a thumb drive with evidence of you trying to kill her and several other people. Clark and I are going to hear it now."

Pause:

"I can't stop him from hearing it."

Pause:

"I have to go. I'll call you afterwards."

Pause:

"I don't know if I can destroy it."

Pause:

"She said it was the only copy."

Pause:

"I've got to go. She's still in the office. Okay, I'll call when she leaves. Gotta go!"

Rose called Harriet on her phone:

"Where are you?"

"On my way back there," Harriet said.

"Good, someone by the name of Steel just called Morales. I don't think they intended for you to come out alive. He's also going to try and destroy the thumb drive."

"What about Clark?"

"So far so good, his bug is still working."

"We should be there shortly." Harriet said pushing the 'End' button.

Next, she placed a call to Ramos, "Where are you?"

"Waiting in the lobby of the hotel you are supposed to be at."

"Are you by yourself?"

"I am now, seems Davis got a call. He took off with my car and left me here."

"I gave a thumb drive to the FBI. Agent Steel called Morales immediately after I gave it to them."

"You think that is why my watch dog left me here."

Christopher Charles

"Morales' needs the drive. It tells it all."

"I have to get back there."

"You will be too late. You might call Assistant Director Clark and warn him about Steel."

"You think he will believe me?"

"He is dead if he doesn't." Harriet said closing her phone.

She had already been on the phone longer than she wanted to be. Youngsu made some more turns making their direction more confusing.

FBI Building

James Clark had the thumb drive working when Steel walked in. "Where have you been?"

"I had to make a pit stop. What's on the drive?"

"Listen!" Clark said.

A half hour later, Clark sat back, and looked up at the ceiling. He had heard the whole thumb drive, "That is the most incredible piece of detective work I have ever heard. We've got organized drug conspiracies going the full length of the government. I never knew the drug cartel had that much power here."

He thought a moment, "We've got to protect that girl, and get Morales back in here."

"Yes sir," Steel said. "You want me to put the drive in the evidence room?"

"No, I'm keeping this with me." Clark said. "Let's go question that girl."

They both left the room. Walking back to the Clark's office, they saw the agent who was supposed to be guarding her standing by the bathroom.

"Where is she?" Steel asked.

"She's in there," the agent said.

"How long has she been in there?"

"She went in right after you left, sir."

Steel pushed open the door and began checking the stalls. He caught one female agent in one of them. There was a scream, and the slamming of a door.

Coming back out, he said, "She's not in there."

The woman came out of the bathroom, glared at Steel as she marched on down the hall.

"Maybe she went back to the office?" Clark said walking fast. When he reached the room, he found it empty, yelling, "Check the cameras!"

Steel left the office, went to the computer room, and brought up the cameras. Six screens revealed different sections of the building. He took the camera back twenty minutes. Two of them revealed a young woman with her hair up and wearing a pink coat walking out of the building.

"Is that her?" Clark asked.

"That's the lady that came out of the bathroom," the agent said.

"Switch to outside cameras, maybe we can get a license plate," Clark said.

"There she is walking across the street," Steel said, "Now she's gone."

"Gee's, at least we still have the drive," Clark said. "Steel, see what you can get on the girl, and bring in Morales for questioning."

"Yes sir," Steel said. "Don't forget your meeting with the mayor in fifteen minutes. He wants to know the progress on the Biltmore drone hit."

"Cancel it," Clark said.

"That may not be a good move, sir" Steel said. "I can have Morales here when you get back."

"You may be right," Clark said thinking. "You pick up Morales."

"Yes sir." Steel said and smiled. He watched Clark enter the elevator. He pressed his speed dial, placed his phone to his ear.

Phone:

"He's coming out now. You take him out, I'll get the drive."

Pause:

"I said I will get the drive!

Call ended:

Rose recorded the conversation at the guesthouse. She called Harriet, who immediately called Ramos.

Ramos called Clark in the elevator:

"Who are you?"

Pause:

"Look detective are you trying to say your Chief of Police is going to try, and kill me?"

Pause:

"When and where?"

Pause:

"Now! How do you know?"

Pause:

"Agent Steel placed the call to Morales? I don't believe you."

Pause:

"Hey! Damn he hung up."

The elevator opened. He debated whether he should take the threat seriously. Steel was a friend as well as his officer. He would trust him with his life.

Then the detective had no reason to discredit him. He sounded very positive. His mind flashed to the recent death of Jeffery Adams and Bryant Kelly. He felt a quiver run down his back. He turned, walked to the weapons room, and placed a bulletproof vest under his shirt. He could not close his suit coat allowing it to hang open.

Feeling better, he walked to the front of the building, out the door, and towards the waiting car. When he was half way down the steps a Mercedes coup pulled up in front of the building and shot four rounds. A second later, it sped around the corner.

The first round grazed Clark's shoulder. The other three rounds struck his vest knocking him to the granite steps. His head struck the hard surface knocking him unconscious.

Steel came running out of the building and dropped to his knees beside his boss. He saw the blood flowing from the arm wound, and the three holes in his chest. His hand went into Clark's pocket withdrawing the thumb drive as other agents began coming out of the building. Steel stood, and yelled, "He's been shot. Someone call 911."

Slowly Clark began to regain consciousness as the other agents gathered around him. He looked at his shoulder wound and checked the back of his head. It was sore. He looked up at the startled Agent Steel, "Arrest that agent!"

Two agents quickly took Steel into custody and removed his gun as Clark stood.

Clark walked over to Steel, looked him hard in the eyes, as he reached into Steel's coat pocket to remove the thumb drive, "Arrest him for attempted murder! Then pick up Chief Morales for questioning and take his gun for evidence."

The two agents took Steel away as the ambulance pulled up. Clark picked two agents, "You two come with me."

Christopher Charles

The three of them climbed into the ambulance. It sped towards the Keck hospital.

Sitting back on the stretcher, Clark pushed the button on his phone that had his last incoming call. He heard the man's voice on the other end.

Phone:

"Detective Ramos?"

Pause:

"Your tip paid off. I took three bullets in the vest, and one in the arm. Thanks for the warning. When can we meet? We have some serious things to talk about."

Pause:

"Okay, I'll have an agent come, and get you."

Pause:

"You prefer to find your own transportation."

Pause:

"I don't blame you."

Pause:

"I will see you in an hour. I have to get my arm patched up."

Hilton Hotel

Detective Ramos waited in the hotel lobby for Davis to return. He had already figured out Davis had made an attempt on the Assistant Director's life. He preferred to arrest him in the hotel with plenty of witnesses.

Twenty minutes later Davis arrived. He parked Ramos' Mercedes in front of the hotel and stepped out. He knew Ramos would be yelling at him for taking his car, but he only followed orders.

He also knew Ramos would not be making it back to the station. He began thinking where he would do the deed as he came through the doors. Still in a high from killing the Assistant Director, he put on a big smile approaching Ramos coming to his feet.

Suddenly he found himself facing the wall with handcuffs going over his wrist. "What are you doing Ramos?"

"I am arresting you!" Ramos said. "What does it look like?" He took him out to his Mercedes, shoved him into the passenger seat, "You have the right to remain silent. Anything you say can be used against you in a court of law."

"Wait a minute Ramos? Let's talk about this."

Ramos pulled the seat belt tight clicking it in. Davis had to sit on his hands.

Going to the trunk, Ramos opened it to find an assassin short rifle, "I bet this is what shot the Assistant Director." He came back around. Climbing into the car, he started it and moved out of the hotel driveway.

"You can't prove nothing," Davis yelled.

"What makes you so sure?" Ramos said driving back toward Los Angeles.

"Morales is why. You're as good as dead."

"Right now, Morales has his own problems."

"You have no idea who you are dealing with."

"And what is that?"

"You will see."

"We have plenty on Morales."

"None of it is going to stick."

"You know Morales killed your four buddies with his drone missile?"

"That was a mistake."

"He doesn't make mistakes. If he survives the FBI, you will be the first one he will eliminate."

"He's not going to kill me."

"You know too much."

"Then you have to protect me."

"Me? You were going to kill me a minute ago."

"That was only orders from Morales."

"I don't know. You sent four bullets into the body of the Assistant Director of the FBI."

"That was all Morales. He wanted him killed."

"What's Morales' got that's going to save his ass?"

"He's got long legal arms if you know what I mean?"

"I know what you mean, but it's not going to do you any good unless I hear a name."

"Judge Bracket for one, Morales has him in his pocket. I've seen them eating together."

"What's he got on him?"

"I don't know. I only know he's got something on him."

"Not helping much. I need more to save your life."

"I can't give you more. You gotta save me."

"I'll take you to the FBI. Maybe you can cut a deal, but you're going to need more than this."

Guesthouse

Harriet and company listened to the bug Youngsu had placed in Ramos's car earlier. It had a fifty-mile range. Rose had picked up and recorded Davis' confession. Ramos seemed to know he had the bug in his car.

An hour later FBI Office

Chief Morales sat in the "A" interrogation room with his lawyer. Special Agent Steel sat in "B" interrogation room without a lawyer. Assistant Director Clark waited in his office for Chief of Detective Ramos to arrive.

Ramos entered the FBI building with Davis in handcuffs. He took him directly to the Assistant Director's office and placed him in the chair facing the desk.

Clark looked at him a moment, "It isn't very often one gets to look at his assassin."

"You're still alive? I shot four bullets into you." Davis said.

"You going to tell me who ordered it? You should know everything you say here will be recorded."

"I…. I told Ramos it was Morales."

"You mean Chief Morales?"

"Yes."

"Why?"

"Something to do with a thumb drive I think. I am only guessing here. He didn't say."

"You usually kill someone especially a FBI Director on the word of one man."

"He has connections like I told Ramos."

"What kind of connections?"

"There's some guy in the DEA, and there's another guy in Home Land Security. I don't know who, but I know there is someone there very powerful."

"That's old information. What else do you have?"

"He has a couple of Judges."

"Names?"

"Judge Bracket for one."

"Another?"

"A…A Judge Lawyin, I think she is the other one."

"Both superior court judges."

Clark pushed his intercom, "Send in the Marshals." Then looking up at Davis, he said, "I'm going to have the marshals take you into protective custody. I do not need to tell you if you escape from them, you will probably be dead within twenty-four hours."

"I know my position, sir."

"Good! I hope you stay alive."

The Marshals came in and took Davis away.

After he left, Clark turned to Ramos standing, "Please take a seat."

Ramos seated himself, looked at Clark, "I am glad to see you are still alive, sir."

"I am relieved as well. It seems I am in your debt here."

"Not mine, sir."

Clark looked back at him, "Who?"

"I am not at liberty to say at the moment sir without losing a valuable asset."

Clark smiled, "You can thank her for me."

"Yes sir."

"Now we have a problem," Clark said. "We have Chief Morales and Special Agent Steel downstairs waiting to be interrogated. They both are very familiar with the procedure, and Morales has brought his lawyer.

I don't know if we can make our charges strong enough against Morales to prevent bail especially if our friend is correct. This place's Miss Brown in extreme danger. He will need to remove her before his trial comes up. He has enormous resources I am told."

"What would you suggest?"

"Put her into protective custody with the Marshals?"

"I don't think she would trust the Marshals, sir. She's had four near misses already. I think you spooked her when she came in here."

"Sorry to hear that, but it's still her best option. I cannot protect her otherwise. The thumb drive recording is very good, but it is not very strong without her testimony."

"She will have to make that decision, sir."

Clark's intercom came alive, "Police Commissioner Harold Jobs is here, sir."

"Good! Send him in."

Jobs, a gray hair short wiry man, came through the door in a very irritated mood. He walked straight towards the desk as the two men stood. He shook hands with Clark, ignored Ramos standing in front of the desk, "What's this I hear you have Chief Morales in the interrogation room downstairs?"

"He's in here on murder charges," Assistant Director said.

"Those had better be damn good charges because you are ruining a man's career by just making the accusations," Jobs said.

"I have something for you to hear. Follow me," Clark said. The three of them walked down the hall. Clark stepped into the computer room with them following. Once inside, he closed the door, and pushed the thumb drive into the computer as they each took a chair. Immediately the speaker came alive revealing all the details on the drive.

The Police Commissioner was in shock. Detective Ramos swallowed hard, "I had no idea."

"That is some fine detective work," Police Commissioner Jobs said. "You may go ahead and prove your case."

"Thank you," Clark said. "I have made several copies. You may have this one." He handed him the original thumb drive and kept the copy in his machine.

Jobs took the thumb drive, looked at Chief of Detectives Ramos, "You will temporarily take over the Chief's duties until this can be proven one way or another. Do you have any questions?"

"No sir."

"Then you may leave, I want to talk with the Assistant Director a few minutes."

"Yes sir, I will start immediately."

Jobs nodded as Ramos stood, and left. He turned back to the Assistant Director, "Does Chief Morales have to be locked up James?"

The Assistant Director looked him hard in the eye. Then in an even voice, "He tried to have me killed! No, the man remains locked up for as long as I can keep him there."

"I didn't hear that on the tape," Jobs said.

"No, that just happened. That's why he's in my interrogation room. I took three slugs in the chest, and one in the arm. Lucky, I was wearing a vest, or I would not be here talking about it."

The Police Commissioner squirmed in his chair, "Then it is a good thing you arrested him." He stood and worked his way out of the office. He went downstairs to the interrogation room where Chief Morales and his lawyer, Charles Johnson, were waiting.

He handed the lawyer the thumb drive, "This is what they have on him plus an attempted murder charge." Shaking his head, he turned to leave, "Why did you try to kill the Assistant Director? I don't see how you are going to get out of this one."

"Thank you for the drive," Johnson said. "At least we know what they have."

The Commissioner nodded and left. He did not look at the Chief.

Ramos entered the elevator and took it to the bottom floor. He walked out of the building remembering they were keeping his car for evidence in the attempted murder on the Assistant Director.

He heard a horn, looked up, it was the black limousine waiting for him. The door opened. He climbed inside and sat beside Harriet. Rose sat in the seat in front of him, and Youngsu drove.

"I thought we would give you lift." Harriet said.

"I'm going to the police station," Ramos said.

"Would you rather hide out with us?"

"That sounds inviting, but I probably can do more good at the police station. I am the temporary Chief of Police."

"Congratulations!" Harriet said.

"It's no favor!" Ramos said. "You should take the Marshals safety net yourself and go into hiding."

"I don't think I will be any safer with them, than here." Harriet said. "At least we will not have to fear a missile hit."

"That's a plus, but you are the number one on his hit list."

"And you," Harriet said. "Therefore, you need a tracking device. It will allow us to track you."

"Me?"

"We'll place a bug in your phone. If you can get someone to talk, we will record it for you."

She gave him a new belt with a hidden satellite transmitter inside with a twenty-mile range.

He gave Rose his phone as he put the new belt on. She replaced the tracking device with the spyware and handed it back.

"I think that will do it," Rose said.

The limousine stopped in front of the Los Angeles Police Station. Ramos looked around, "Anything else?"

"If you could get us the name, and address of Morales' lawyer, that would be helpful, Chief," Harriet said.

Ramos smiled, "Okay, I am out of here," He stepped out of the limousine. It drove away as he climbed the steps. He felt deserted, and a little apprehensive. He knew what he had to do. He went through security and walked to the office passing people at their desks.

The FBI already had their people there. The agents coming out of Morales' office carried his files. He spotted another agent coming from the evidence room carrying the expended bullets from the Brown massacre.

In the midst of all of the confusion Ramos stopped at the desk of Morales' secretary, "Maybe I should make the Chief's lawyer aware the FBI is here. Do you have his name and number?"

The secretary's whole body shook. She looked up at him, "Did they really arrest Chief Morales for murder?"

"I think they did. Do you have his name and phone?"

"Yes, yes," She said looking in her desk drawer. She came up with a card, "I think this is it."

Ramos placed the card in his coat pocket as an FBI Agent came over to ask her questions. He entered his office, and read the card aloud giving Rose in the limousine the information. The bug in the belt worked.

13 The Legal Process

Interrogation Room A

Chief Morales sat with his attorney, Charles Johnson, a tall man with dark piercing eyes in the interrogation room. He received the thumb drive from Commissioner Jobs. He was anxious to hear it. He did not like his client being questioned without this knowledge.

He also heard they were holding his client for the Brown massacre, and the attempted murder of the Director Assistant James Clark.

He leaned over to Morales, "What do they have on you concerning the Brown Massacre?"

"Nothing!"

"Anything in the evidence locker?"

"I said nothing! The bullets will not match my gun."

"The Director Assistant?"

"Nothing they can prove."

"Okay, we will see what they have."

Christopher Charles

Interrogation Room B

Special Agent Ted Steel sat in the room waiting for the Director Assistant to arrive. He began debating whether he should call a lawyer. Maybe he could cut a deal here.

Director Assistant Clark entered the room. Steel started to stand when the handcuffs held him to the table.

Clark took the chair across from him, looked at him hard, "I thought we were friends. It was not until the bullets actually cut into my body did I believe you would kill me."

"It wasn't personal. You've got to believe me. It's the damn thumb drive. I had to get it before anybody was aware of it."

"Did you plan on killing the young lady as well?"

"That's obvious."

"I can see why she ran. So why are you protecting Morales?"

"If he folds, a lot of important people are going to come down with him including me."

"He's folding, so what are you willing to do?"

"I can give you his connection with the drug cartel."

"You mean Herman Schmidt, he's dead. You heard the thumb drive."

"He got some judges. You want those?"

"Judge Lawyin and Judge Bracket, I have those. What else do you have?"

"I can testify he ordered the hit," Steel said.

"That is your only saving grace, but you should know I already have that covered. If that's it, I need to see Morales."

Standing, the Assistant Director Clark, said, "If you think of anything else we can use on Morales, let me know. All I can say now is that you are a cooperative witness."

As he walked out of the interrogation room, he nodded to the officer outside, "Keep him in there awhile longer. We'll see if he remembers anything else."

In the limousine, Rose had recorded the conversation from the bugs planted on Steel and Clark.

Interrogation Room A

Assistant Director Clark walked into the interrogation room. He looked at Charles Johnson, Morales' attorney sitting beside him, "I guess you have advised him of his rights."

"We haven't heard what is on this drive so any questions pertaining to it will not be answered."

"The information on the drive does not need any cross examination. It says it all. It does not have the recent attempt on my life. That's what we will be talking about."

"My client was in his office when that attempt was made," Johnson said.

"Yes, and I have witnesses stating Chief Morales placed a hit on me to retrieve the thumb drive you have in your hand."

"I suppose there is another thumb drive," Johnson said.

"You have the thumb drive that incriminates him in a number of murders in the city. What I want now is the rest of the conspiracy."

"My client will not answer any questions in that area."

"Very well, we have him for attempted murder of a federal officer, and perhaps with the help of the thumb drive the massacre of the brown family, the use of drones to kill four police officers and two men in the Biltmore hotel."

"Those are serious accusations. If you do not prove your case, my client will sue the FBI for defamation of character. You have ruined his career as a police officer."

Christopher Charles

"He is going down, and all those connected with him are going down. Maybe you should consider that," Clark said. He was becoming very irritated. He had to leave before he said anything else that might weaken his case. He stood, walked to the door, "Put him back in his cell."

Attorney Charles Johnson's Home

Rose had found Charles Johnson home address in Beverly Hills, the corner townhouse in a small complex. The limousine stopped a block away. Youngsu stepped out of the car with a transmitter in his bag leaving the others in the limousine.

Rose had her receiver working as Youngsu walked quickly to the complex. He noticed two light poles were pointing to the upper story townhouse giving a front and side view. Using the same technique as before, he placed a receiver on the top of each light pole. He used the telephone pole in the middle of the block to place his transmitter. Going up the pole, he strapped it into place. Done, he quickly returned to the limousine.

Rose already had the address to Johnson's office located two miles from his townhouse on the top floor of a twenty-story business complex that occupied one square block.

The limousine moved that direction. Youngsu parked the limousine in a parking garage next to the business complex. Rose handed him a vase of flowers with a hidden bug inside. She placed a card on it thanking Attorney Charles Johnson. He took the vase, and his briefcase with him as he walked quickly to the building.

They did not have any security allowing him to take the elevator to the top floor. He entered the attorney's office and handed the receptionist the vase of flowers.

She thanked him as he quickly left the office. The receptionist took the vase back to Johnson's office. She placed it on his desk.

Youngsu went to the stairs, climbed to the roof where he placed the transmitter and receiver. He placed the receiver right over the Attorney Johnson's office using the chip in the vase below to line it up. It only had to penetrate four feet to be in his office.

Finished, he left the roof, and took the stairs down to the nineteenth floor. He entered the elevator, took it to the ground floor, and left the building.

Reaching the limousine, he stepped inside, and headed out of the garage. Rose already had Judge Judy Lawyin's home located in Brentwood, a small house located in an expensive neighborhood.

She had a large German Sheppard dog guarding the house. They parked a block away after they drove by slowly. Ten minutes later, Youngsu, wearing maintenance clothes, placed the receivers on two light poles. He used the telephone pole at the corner to place the transmitter.

Done, they had one more. Rose was running out of hardware. They had material spread out over the city. She had some more hidden at the office, but they would not be going that direction.

Reaching Judge Bracket's house, they found him home at his Brentwood house. He lived on a corner lot. It had only one light pole, but it was directly in front of his house.

Already dark, Youngsu saw his target, a large tree on the side of the house where the light from the pole did not hit.

Youngsu worked his way up the tree placing his receiver onto a branch with a thumbtack. He placed two to be sure it would stay. He camouflaged it the best he could, and quickly descended the tree. He found a telephone pole to place his transmitter.

Finally done, they headed back to the Brown Mansion. Youngsu used the streets without cameras. Halfway home they received their first ping. It came in from the thumb drive Attorney Johnson had taken.

Christopher Charles

Attorney Johnson's Car

Johnson was holding the thumb drive in one hand as he drove his Mercedes from the FBI office. He needed legal help. How damaging was the thumb drive? He placed it in his pocket and made a call.

Phone conversation:

"Judge Bracket, Charles Johnson here. We have a serious problem. Chief Morales has been arrested on murder charges. We need to meet."

"Tonight?" The Judge asked.

"Now, at my home in Beverly Hills."

"I know where it is."

"Twenty minutes!"

"I'll be there."

Johnson flipped his phone closed, thought a moment, then opening it. He speeds dialed another number.

The phone responded:

"Judge Judy Lawyin this is Charles Johnson. We have an emergency. Chief Morales has been arrested for murder. How soon can you be at my townhouse?"

"That's very irregular, Mr. Johnson, especially if I end up residing over his case."

"Just be there. You are not residing now, so there is nothing irregular about it."

"You have a point. I'll be there in twenty minutes. You're still in Beverly Hills?"

"Yes." Johnson said flipping his phone closed.

He felt better. He had the legal arm working for him. Now was the time to call in the favors they owed him.

Rose had picked up the conversations from the bug in the thumb drive. It had a range of ten miles. The limousine immediately turned around heading back towards the attorney's townhouse. They wanted a clear reception. They parked in a shopping mall parking lot a mile away. They did not need to be closer.

Twenty minutes later the judges began arriving. Johnson barely had time to open up his townhouse. Judge Judy Lawyin arrived first. She had been there before. She did not have to use her GPS.

Johnson opened the door inviting her inside. He had her seated with a glass of wine when the doorbell rang again.

Judge Bracket entered. Surprised to see Judge Lawyin, he asked, "Did you need to see the both of us?"

Johnson held up the thumb drive, "I wanted you to listen to this to check the legality of it."

"Okay, if I can have a glass of your wine," Judge Bracket said noticing Judge Lawyin had a glass.

Johnson poured another glass, "I have not heard what is on this tape, but it was enough to have Chief Morales arrested. I want to know if we can get him out on bail." He opened his computer, and slipped the thumb drive in. He poured himself a glass of wine as the thumb drive worked in the computer.

After twenty minutes the drive stopped. All three sat there not saying a word a few minutes. Finally, Johnson said, "Well, can we get him out on bail?"

"Is that all they have?" Judge Bracket asked.

"He's also being held for putting a hit on the Assistant Director of the FBI?"

They both swallowed.

"Was he successful?" Judge Bracket asked.

"The Director had a bullet proof vest. He took three bullets in the chest, and one in the left arm."

Christopher Charles

"I could have given you bail on the thumb drive because it is circumstantial if he was really involved in the drones. Someone else could have given the instructions, but the Assistant Director is another matter."

"What does he have that points to the Chief?" Judge Lawyin asked.

"He has the accomplice, and the man who did the actual shooting."

"There's no way I can give him bail?" Judge Lawyin said. "He's going to try and kill those people, and he will certainly try for the people who made this drive."

"I agree with Judge Lawyin," Judge Bracket said, "He will have to stay in jail."

"I don't think you understand what I am asking," Johnson said, "You are to give him bail."

"Under what grounds?" Judge Bracket asked. "I can't think of any."

"How about so he can find evidence to defend himself in court," Johnson said. "He needs a fair trial, and he needs to prepare for it. He can't do that in jail."

"But to set him loose?" Judge Lawyin asked.

"He will improve his position," Johnson said.

"The bail will have to be high," Judge Bracket said. "How much can he afford?"

"Maybe two hundred thousand dollars."

"It will need to be more to make it look somewhat legal," Judge Lawyin said.

"Will a million dollars do?"

"That's more like it." Judge Bracket said.

"Good, now what do we have to do to improve our case?" Johnson asked.

"You already said; the witnesses are your greatest problem. They seem very solid. You need to weaken that up a bit," Judge Bracket said.

"Is there any hard evidence other than the drive that he shot Mr. Brown and his people?" Judge Lawyin asked.

"Chief Morales said no. I don't think there is any evidence connecting his gun to the bullets that penetrated Brown."

"Then we are back to the thumb drive," Judge Lawyin said. "It's the witness's word against your client's as to who is on the drive. You need to weaken that as you already know."

"The drones are a weakness," Judge Bracket said. "Can they prove a connection?"

"The operator at the site is a problem. He will say he took orders from the Chief."

"Then you already know the problem there," Judge Bracket said. "I can see why you need our Chief out on bail."

"I think that covers it," Johnson said standing. "I will seek bail in the morning. We have a lot of work to do to pull us out of this one. Just remember if he goes down, we all go. I expect one of you to get this case."

"We know our responsibilities," Judge Lawyin said putting her glass down, and standing. She did not like the pressure Johnson placed on her. She also knew she would be setting a man loose who would be murdering innocent people to protect himself. How did she get herself into this position? She left quickly.

Judge Bracket remained. He sat with Johnson taking another glass of wine. They did some small talk until finally he asked, "Why do we keep Chief Morales alive? The papers are going to have the story by tomorrow. His value to anyone is over. A quick bullet solves everyone's problems. All of the mess in the thumb drive will have nowhere to go. If he starts killing people, it will create even a bigger mess taking us all into it. The simplest solution is to do away with the problem."

Attorney Johnson sat there a few seconds analyzing what the Judge had said. Finally, he said, "I never thought of it that way. I was thinking of trying to save the man, and not look after my own position. You do present an interesting case. One bullet, and all of the problems go away."

"It's the most logical position," Judge Bracket said. "One bullet, everything remains intact."

"Okay, you give us bail tomorrow. I will see about the bullet."

Judge Bracket smiled, "I am pleased you see the logic in this." Standing, he emptied his glass of wine, "We still have a good team if we keep it intact. The Chief has taken things too far. The Cartels are not going to deal with him when he has all of this baggage. I am surprised they have not sent one of their assassins."

Johnson patted him on the shoulder, "You make a very good argument Judge. Can we drop that bail to two-hundred thousand? We need to get him out of jail first."

"Sure, why not," Judge Bracket said leaving. He felt good the problem would-be solved. When he reached his home a half-hour later, his thoughts turned to the previous conversation. Maybe he was setting himself up. Could he trust the attorney? He picked up his phone and dialed a number in Columbia.

"Senor Paniagua, this is Judge Bracket in Los Angeles."

Pause:

"Yes, I know things are a mess."

Pause:

"Look, the man responsible for this is Chief Morales. He killed your men at the Biltmore Hotel, and he is about to expose every connection you have in Southern California including myself. He is a cancer that needs getting rid of quickly."

Pause:

"You heard right, he's in jail, but I am setting him loose on bail tomorrow at 10 AM. The rest will be up to you."

Pause:

"You'll take care of it."

Pause:

"Good, I would like to reestablish our relationship."

Pause:

"The money and the product were under Morales's control. He lost control of both."

Pause:

"I have no idea where they are, but I will find out for you."

Pause:

"Thank you, I knew we could come to an understanding."

The phone goes quiet.

The team in the limousine heard and recorded both conversations.

Harriet knew she would have to take the thumb drive to the Assistant Director.

She placed a call to Detective Ramos, "Judge Bracket is releasing Chief Morales tomorrow at 10 AM. He's arranged for the cartels to kill him."

"The Chief is not that easy to kill," Ramos said. "He has deep connections in the Cartel, but I will tell the Assistant Director they are setting bail tomorrow and give him the warning."

"Thanks!"

"When he makes bail, he will be coming after your crew with a vengeance."

"I know," Harriet said. She closed her phone, turned to Youngsu, "We need to place a bug in Chief Morales' home tonight."

Already after twelve midnight, Rose had his address on file, the limousine moved out once again. He had two houses, a townhouse in Beverly Hills within a block of Attorney Charles Johnson's townhouse, and a beach house in Newport Beach.

They approached the Beverly Hills townhouse first, a two-story townhouse with the garage occupying half of the bottom floor. A corner building, it had a light pole on each side allowing him to place two receivers. He placed the transmitter on a nearby telephone pole.

In Newport they found his house among a string of one-story houses side by side forty-foot-wide going back a hundred feet to the beach, a walkway, then sand before the surf became the back yard. With no light poles facing the house, he had to go to the roof.

Using the fence next to the end house, he leaped to the roof. He knew the homes were usually empty as he made his way over the roofs. Locating Morales's house, he placed his receivers and transmitter. He quickly worked his way to the limousine and headed back to Brentwood.

Harriet placed a copy of the conversations on a thumb drive. "Let's deliver this to Ramos," She said. "You have him on your tracker." It was already early morning.

"He will be leaving for work shortly," Rose said.

"Let's intercept him," Harriet said.

The limousine pulled up in front of Ramos' apartment as he was coming out. He saw the limousine and walked over.

Harriet rolled down the window, "You need to hear this, and pass it on, but don't give away your source."

"What is it?"

"An assassin plot on Morales. I was debating about passing it on. Now it is in your hands."

Ramos took the drive, nodded, "Thanks, I think."

The limousine pulled out of the parking lot moving onto the busy street.

Going inside, Ramos placed the drive in his computer, and listened to the hit plans. He decided he would call the Assistant Director Clark and allow his conscience to work.

At 10 AM Chief Morales came before Judge Bracket with his attorney. Assistant Director Clark, already present, planned to stop the petition. They all took a seat in front of the judge as he looked at the petition.

After a few minutes, Judge Bracket looked up, "I do not see any flight possibility here."

The Assistant Director stood, "He is a risk to himself and others. The safest place for him to be is in protective custody."

Attorney Johnson stood, "Chief Morales needs to prepare for the allegations he has been accused of. He cannot do that in Jail."

"If you allow him bail, you place many people at risk," Assistant Director Clark said.

"Anything else?" Judge Bracket asked. No one said anything. "Then I set the bail at 200,000 dollars. You may see the bondsman." He stood and walked back to his chambers.

Assistant Director Clark could not believe his ears. He knew immediately the Judge was tainted. His phone beeped. He opened it. Irritated, Clark said, "Yes!"

"Ramos here, the judge and Morales' Attorney Johnson are planning on killing Morales when he leaves the courtroom. They've sent an assassin loose."

"You sure of this?"

"You know my source."

Clark looked up at Morales leaving the court. He started to go after him when he heard the sound of a gunshot coming from the judge's chambers. Keeping his phone in one hand, he pulled his gun, and ran to the chamber. Judge Bracket on the floor had blood oozing out of a head wound. Going to the opened side window, Clark saw a car pulling out of the alley.

Coming back, he lifted the phone, "There's been a hit, but it was Judge Bracket not Morales."

"Really, Johnson must have switched sides."

"Do you have any evidence?"

"I have a thumb drive planning the hit. I want to deliver it personally. There's too many lives at stake here."

"I won't be passing it around," Clark said. "We need the information to keep coming."

"Thank you, sir. The system has set loose one very dangerous man."

"I've placed several tails on him. That should slow him up a bit."

Attorney Johnson's car

The thumb drive still in Johnson's pocket allowed Harriet and company to hear the conversation between him and Morales. They remained within two blocks of the car.

Morales stretched out in the car, smiled, "I bet our Judge was surprised when the assassin showed up in his chambers."

"I thought it was rather poetic," Johnson said, "Him thinking the assassin is going for you when it is him being taken out."

"I owe you one, Johnson. Now we have a mess to take care of. That Brown bitch and her company are the first on the list. She needs to be stopped, but first I want to hear what's on that drive."

"My house or yours?"

"Mine, I want to take a shower."

When they reached his Beverly Hills home, they walked up the steps, and stopped. Morales checked the door. He had left a piece of thread across the door. Still intact, they went inside.

Morales took a shower as Johnson placed a call to Senor Paniagua.

Phone:

"Johnson here."

Pause:

"Your man did well, thanks."

Pause:

"I told you we will have your money in two weeks."

Pause:

"I know that's why Morales is alive."

Pause:

"And me?"

Pause:

"Look, we get you your money, and its business as usual."

Pause:

"Yes, there's going to be trial, but the opposition will be gone, and we expect the judge to cooperate."

Pause:

"The trial is in a month."

Pause:

"You don't have to threaten me, sir." He closed his phone.

Morales came out of his shower, "Who was that?"

"Our friends from Columbia, I was reassuring them."

Christopher Charles

"How much time do we have?"

"Two weeks to find the money," Johnson said.

"We're going to need longer," Morales said. "We don't have the resources."

"Maybe our FBI friends can be of help. They have the resources to find the money."

"Once they find it, how do we get it?"

"One thing at a time, first we need to make them want to find it."

"How are you going to do that?"

"Let me think about it."

"Okay, let's hear what they have," Morales said going to his computer. He pushed the drive in.

Twenty minutes later, the drive completed, Morales did not say a word for a moment, then he said, "It didn't sound like she had all that much on me. She sure nailed the others."

"If she cannot testify against you, the material on the drive can be dismissed as hearsay. Who recorded it? It could be someone else. I didn't hear your name mentioned."

"I see your point, eliminating her people makes the information useless."

"Too bad you don't have your drones anymore."

"Yeah, they had there uses. What about the drone man, Chapman?"

"He's a problem. We don't know where he is."

"Can you find him?" Morales asked.

"Maybe closer to the trial date I can demand the right to question him. That will give you an opportunity for him to have an accident."

"Okay what's next?"

"They took the evidence from the police locker. I suspect they have the bullets that killed Brown and his staff."

"They probably do, but the bullets do not fit my gun."

"You saw to that?"

"What do you think?"

"Okay that leaves the attempted murder of the Assistant Director?"

"I didn't pull the trigger," Morales said. "One of my officers went crazy and made the attempt. He was only supposed to acquire the thumb drive from the Assistant Director for my inspection. I certainly did not tell him to kill him. He was to pick up the drive from Agent Steel. Steel by the way was only protecting the thumb drive when he removed it from the supposed dead body of the Assistant Director."

"It would be better to eliminate your officer before the trial." Johnson said. "Then it is all supposition."

"Okay, the money, any ideas yet?"

"Let's shift everything to the cartels," Johnson said. "Get the FBI involved. Let's tell them about the money, and the lost product. We'll be cooperative. They will check out all the sources for us. Ramos has a tie with them. Maybe we could lean on him for the information."

"You mean admit to our association with the cartels?"

"Admit to your investigation of the Cartels. Bring Ramos up to date. Have him pursue the money. He'll bring in the FBI and their resources. We don't have to recover the money only find it to take the pressure off our backs. Once it's out in the open, they'll know we didn't take it."

"Okay, I like it. Now we need soldiers."

"I would think about now the drug supply on the streets is about dried up," Johnson said, "There should be many willing soldiers just waiting for the call."

Morales smiled, "Yeah, I know a few who could do some recruiting for us."

"Our first target should be the Brown group. They can do us the most damage. It should not be that hard to locate them.

She drives a black limousine. That should be easy to spot."

Limousine

Harriet had them move the limousine. They could pick-up on the conversation now that Morales was home. "Let's find Ramos and give him a copy of the recording." Harriet said. She was beginning to get an uneasy feeling in her stomach.

"I have him close to the FBI building," Rose said.

"That's where he is going." Harriet said. "Let's go."

They could see Ramos parking his car and walking towards the FBI building. Harriet raised her phone, "Ramos, if you could slow down a bit, I have another thumb drive to give you."

Ramos stopped walking, looked around. He saw a long black limousine coming around the corner. It pulled to a stop beside him. The window rolled down, a hand held out a thumb drive. He took it as the hand retreated quickly. The limousine sped off around the corner.

"We need to find another location. Let's be thinking where that might be." When they arrived at the guesthouse, Harriet held a meeting with everyone.

"Okay, where can we go to be unseen for a while?"

"I don't know anywhere with the limousine," Rose said. "It stands out too much."

"Maybe if we use the cars only," Nadine said. "I have my car here."

"It would give us more options," Mc Craw said.

"According to the recording, we are Morales' number one target," Harriet said. "We need a place where we can still pick up our transmitters, and yet be somewhat isolated to avoid anyone else becoming involved."

"Morales' resources are limited in locating us because he will not have access to the credit card companies," Rose said.

"He will have people looking for us especially the street people needing drugs," Harriet said.

"Then we stay away from the downtown area," Rose said.

"We need to move the limousine immediately," Harriet said. "He'll have his people looking for it within the hour. If we are going to move it, it will have to be now. Then it will have to stay put until this is finished."

"It carries equipment," Youngsu said.

"It will have to be transferred to the cars saying we are using Nadine's car," Harriet said. "It will be Rose and me with Youngsu driving in one car, and Nadine and Mc Craw in the other car. The immediate equipment to monitor and record will be in our car. The rest of the equipment will be in Nadine's car. I don't think we have a great deal in that department since most of the receivers and transmitters are already out."

"Have one pair left," Youngsu said.

"Let's put it up here," Harriet said. "Somebody may come looking here. It would be good to know. The equipment in the limousine should continue to record all of the present sites as a backup in case our portable one is jeopardized."

"I know where to hide the limousine," Nadine said.

They all turned her direction.

"We rent a hangar at the Chino Airport. They hold small planes. The limousine should be no problem. Rent it under my name. Few people know of our connection."

"Does anyone have a better idea?" Harriet asked.

No one said a word.

Christopher Charles

"Okay, we rent a hanger. Rose, can you set that up?"

Rose immediately begins to work her computer to find a space.

"Next, where do we hide out?" Harriet asked.

"Rent house to place antenna," Youngsu said.

"Where?" Harriet asked. "It should be a house people will not notice someone moving in."

"Santa Monica Beach," Mc Craw said. "People move in and out of there all the time. No one pays attention to someone coming in. They are used to renting to people for a short periods-of-time. They usually will not require a contract. It's relatively close to the downtown, but the scum will not be going there. Besides, I like the beach."

"Anybody with a better idea," Harriet asked. She looked around. "Okay Rose, find us a beach house."

"It's going to be expensive," Rose said, "The reason the scum as Mr. Mc Craw calls them are not there." Seeing that did not register, she asked, "Who's card do you want me to use?"

"Nadine?"

"I'm already in way over my head," Nadine said. "What's a lot more?"

"Okay, we need to move the Limousine first before the traffic becomes heavy, and Morales' people come looking for it," Harriet said. She kept taking deep breathes quietly trying to keep herself calm. She could feel a huge emotional wave working its way over her. They needed to leave.

"I have us a house," Rose said, "Three thousand a month. It's a bargain. I think we should take it."

"Will they take cash?"

"I think they prefer it." Rose said.

"What was the hanger cost?"

"Rose looked at her computer, "A little under 2,000 dollars. They wanted first and last month rent. I told them it was a small plane."

"That's my limit," Nadine said. "My ability to pay is zero since I lost my job."

"I still have some money," Harriet said. "I can reimburse you."

"We'll wait until this is over," Nadine said. "I am sure we will have more expenses."

"Okay, let's clean up here. Nadine and Youngsu will take the limousine, and her car to the Chino Airport. Youngsu, make sure the recorder is working before you leave. Mc Craw, Rose, and myself will rent the beach house, and set up there. Rose, give them the address and direction, any questions?" She looked around. "Okay, let's get moving. Make it look like we were never here."

FBI Building

Ramos walked into the FBI building. They checked him through security and sent him on his way. Going to the seventeenth floor, he approached the secretary, "Chief Ramos to see the Assistant Director."

"He is expecting you, give me a second." She pushed the intercom, "Chief Ramos is here, sir."

"Send him in!"

Ramos walked into the Director's office. They shook hands.

"It's good you could make it."

Ramos handed him the two drives, "She just gave me the second drive, sir. I think it has their present plans on it."

"Let's go listen to it," Clark said standing. "I want to make a copy."

"We cannot act on the information, sir, without exposing the source."

"Let's hear what's on it," Clark said walking down the hallway.

In the computer room, Clark placed the thumb drive into the computer. He pointed to the two chairs in the room. They both sat back and relaxed as the drive played.

When it was finished, Clark said, "He just gets in deeper every time we set him loose. Too bad we cannot arrest someone for talking about killing someone."

"It is very sensitive material, sir. They will know they are being bugged if we act on this information. She's playing a risky business. I don't know how much longer she can do this?"

"We need information to know how to proceed," Clark said. "We set a ticking bomb loose, and we have very limited information on him."

"You will see here, they planned to take out Morales, but evidently that changed, and the judge took the hit."

"They play a very deadly game."

"The question is; how many more assets does he have?"

"He has the cartel that is not all that solid at the moment," Clark said. "He has one judge we know of that is still with him, but I don't see her killing anyone."

"He's bringing in the street gangs. They want drugs," Ramos said. "They will stop at nothing to find her."

"She needs to come in immediately. We can protect her."

"You will lose your source, and you will also locate his target for him."

"It sounds like he made a promise to the cartel that he is depending upon us to deliver for him. That is an opportunity. We should take advantage of it. Maybe drive him in deeper, and make an arrest, or allow the cartel to take care of the problem."

"You mean find the money for him?"

"Not actually, but make it appear we have."

"Why would you want to help out Morales? If we do nothing, the cartel solves our problem."

"I want the cartel out of here for good," Clark said. "If we use Morales right, we might catch the whole ring here."

"I think the ring has already been cut down severely," Ramos said. "You will only be catching the scraps and bringing in more cartel people from the outside to handle things here."

"Let's just see what our net will bring in?"

14 Payback

Home of Chief Morales

He had been on the phone for two hours. Finally, Morales had his six-man hit team together. He turned to Attorney Charles Johnson, "Where do we send them?"

"I've been thinking," Johnson said. "Where would I go to hide a large black Limousine? That is their one mistake. It does not blend in well anywhere except a hotel, but even there the limousine is still exceptional, and easily remembered."

"You going to keep me in suspense? Where?"

"Why at her father's home," Johnson said. "A very natural place to keep it, and the last place anyone would think to look."

Morales picked up his phone, punched in some numbers. He waited a few seconds. Finally, someone answered:

Phone:

"Joel, Chief Morales here, make the hit at the old Brown Mansion in Brentwood."

Pause:

"Look it up, George Brown in Brentwood, take out all of them. I want no mistakes."

Pause:

"When the job's done."

He closed his phone.

"What did you promise him?" Johnson asked.

"Twenty thousand in cocaine."

"Where are you getting that?"

"I have it here."

"You keep cocaine here?"

"For an emergency like this one, I thought about giving him a bullet." Morales said with some undertones.

Johnson could already see he made a mistake in not taking Judge Bracket's advice. "He's drowning," he thought. "He could see no way out. Not only is the man dangerous, he'll never be given his position back. There's just too much against him for that. He's only surviving, and not doing all that well. He was frightened too. Morales would kill him if he smelled even the slightest disloyalty."

Guest House

Harriet, Rose, and Mc Craw had left first for Santa Monica beach to acquire their new lodgings. Youngsu and Nadine followed with Youngsu driving the limousine behind Nadine in her car. He closed the gate behind him and reset the yellow tape. They headed for the Chino Airport to hide the limousine in a small hanger.

No one had been listening to the recording coming in from Morales's house, and the impending hit at the mansion.

Once away from the house, Harriet felt better. She would listen to the recordings once they settled in their new lodgings. The Condo laid back off the grass parkway overlooking the ocean with the pier a block away. They would be hiding in the crowd. She paid the one-month rent. They brought the suitcases and equipment inside.

They set up quickly. Rose had the recordings working. They had been off line two hours. When they tuned into Morales house, they pick up the hit on the mansion.

Harriet immediately called Nadine, but no answer. They left right after them, she thought. They should be on their way here.

She turned to Rose, "Check Youngsu's tracking bug?"

She brought up the navigator program (GPS) in the computer, punched in Youngsu's number, and immediately a dot appeared on the map.

Harriet looked at it closely, "He's back at the house!"

"Why did he go back there?"

"I don't know, but that's where the hit team is going," Rose said.

"See what is being recorded at the guesthouse?"

"Nothing," Rose said. "That means they are in the big house."

Harriet looked up at Mc Craw, "Let's go, the hit team already has them. Rose, stay here and monitor the recordings for anything we could use, of course if we don't make it back, take everything to Ramos, but always keep a copy hidden somewhere."

Rose gave Harriet a hug, "Be careful." She turned to Mc Craw, "You keep her from getting killed."

Mc Craw nodded, "Let' go!"

Mc Craw drove Rose's car. Harriet sat in the seat beside him, "You're breaking your parole."

"I'm keeping us alive," Mc Craw said. "You are not our best driver."

Harriet tried to smile when her phone rang. She looked at Mc Craw, "It's Nadine."

"Buy us some time," Mc Craw said.

Harriet answered the phone, "Yes."

"We have car trouble, you will have to come, and get us."

"What wrong with the car?"

"I don't know. It could be out of gas."

"Where are you?"

"We're at the mansion. The gate is open."

"Why did you go back to the mansion?"

"I forgot my suitcase," Nadine said.

"We're an hour and half from there."

"Please hurry."

"We're on our way," Harriet said. "I'll call you back when I am ten minutes away."

She hung up her phone, looked at Mc Craw, "There, I bought us some time."

She received another call from Rose.

"Yes"

"I am picking up something from the guesthouse. I think our hit team has moved into it."

"Good, keep us up to date on their plans. We should be there in twenty minutes."

Harriet closed the phone, looked over at Mc Craw, "Any ideas on how we are going to do this?"

"Depends on what they are going to do," Mc Craw said. "If we go head on, someone is going to get killed. We have to take out one at a time. Besides, we are limited on fire power."

"We could call Ramos in on this?" Harriet said.

"Then you have a hostage situation where those inside will certainly be killed. This is a hit team whose mission is to kill us."

"How good are they?"

"Probably not that good, but they will have automatic weapons to our one lone pistol."

"I see your point. Maybe we should call in Ramos."

"Your call."

"Let's have him coming twenty minutes behind us," Harriet said. "That will give us time to work our way to the guest house."

"They have the guns."

Fifteen minutes later, they drove up the dark road towards the mansion when Rose called in, "Listen." She had connected her phone to the computer to pick up the recording in the guesthouse.

Harriet placed her phone on speaker as they pulled up behind some bushes a hundred feet from the mansion's gate.

Inside the Guesthouse

Joel, a tall man, dark eyes and eyebrows, had Youngsu bounded, gagged, and thrown to the floor next to the back door.

One of the hit team, a big man with a small beard, asked, "Joel how much are we getting from Morales?"

"Twenty thousand in cocaine," Joel said, "We can double that by tomorrow night."

"You mean after we take some for ourselves," the man laughed.

Ignoring him, Joel pointed to the man next to him, and yelled, "You take him, go to the gate. Let them in, but don't let them out. You got that?" The door opened and closed.

Rose came on the speaker, "You heard, two men are walking to the gate now."

Harriet looked at Mc Craw, and said into the phone, "We need to go." She pushed Ramos' speed-dial.

Phone:

"Ramos here."

"Morales sent a hit team of six men to the guesthouse at the mansion. They have Youngsu and Nadine inside. They are alive at the moment, but that may not last long."

Ramos took all of this in. He did not say a word until she was finished, then he said, "Don't make a move to the house. If they get you, all of you will be-killed. I am sending a swat team now. They will be there in twenty minutes."

"Thank you," Harriet said. She closed her phone, looked at Mc Craw, "What do we do?"

"Let' take out the two coming to us first, and go from there," Mc Craw said stepping out of the car, "That'll give us some weapons."

Harriet nodded as she watched him move into the bushes on the other side of the open gate and torn yellow ribbon. He motioned for Harriet to take the other side. She ran to the bushes and worked her way into them.

The drive curved as it left the gate keeping them concealed. The two assassins appeared. The bigger of the two men motioned for the smaller man to take the right side of the gate as he moved into the bushes on the left side.

The smaller man stepped into the bushes. He met a hard fist to the face. It knocked him back out on to the drive, but his automatic weapon remained in Mc Craw's hands.

The larger man turned at the noise. He saw Mc Craw coming out of the bushes, but he stopped instantly when he felt the cold muzzle of Harriet's colt 45 on his neck.

"I wouldn't make any big moves," Harriet said. "This gun makes a very big hole."

The big man slowly lowered his automatic weapon. Finally, he allowed it to fall to the ground as Mc Craw came across the driveway.

Mc Craw came up fast striking him hard with the butt of the automatic rifle. The big man fell to the ground instantly with a bleeding forehead. Using Youngsu method of securing prisoners, he removed their belts, and shirts. He tied their hands with their belts, dropped their pants to their ankles, and used their shirts to gag them. Then he dragged each one to the trunk of the car depositing them inside. Finished, he said, "That should hold them until Ramos' gets here."

"Where to now," Harriet asked.

"Let's work our way to the back of the house," Mc Craw said. "I want to come in from that direction." He picked up the automatic weapons, looked at Harriet, "You want one of these?"

She shook her head, "I've never shot one. I'll stick to my revolver."

"Probably a good idea," Mc Craw said. "This is no time to be learning." He strapped one to his shoulder and carried the other one in his right hand. He nodded towards the house.

"Go ahead, I'll follow you."

Mc Craw took the lead moving them up the tree line staying in the trees or bushes. The sun had already set leaving only shadows.

Inside the house, Joel looked at his watch, "She should be calling in a few minutes." He shoved Nadine over next to Youngsu on the floor. He planned to kill them after he received the call.

They had left the lights off in the house leaving shadows. Youngsu on the floor had already worked the ropes off his wrist. He left the rope around them making it appear the rope still held him. When their attention shifted away from him, he worked on his feet. Joel threw Nadine on top of him as he slipped the last of the knot off.

Harriet and Mc Craw had worked their way around the house.

When they reached the back door, Mc Craw whispered, "Make the call." Harriet pushed the speed dial. Nadine's phone rang.

Joel walked over and pulled Nadine to her feet. He handed her the phone when the lights came on.

Youngsu jumped to his feet coming after Joel. He went into the air, sent his foot into Joel's face sending him to the floor.

Before the other three could react, Mc Craw stepped into the room, and lowered his automatic weapon. He sent a burst of metal into the floor in front of the three men. They immediately dropped their weapons and raised their hands. In the distance, they could hear the police sirens.

Joel, coming to his feet slowly, suddenly grabbed Nadine next to him as he pulled a knife from his boot. His left arm held Nadine close. His right hand placed the knife on her throat.

Mc Craw continued to hold his automatic weapon on the other three. He wanted to move it to Joel, but the other three would pick up their weapons.

Harriet stepped into the room pointing her Colt 45 at Joel as he moved towards the door.

"I'll kill her!" He shouted.

"Nadine, faint!" Harriet yelled holding her pistol with both hands as it moved back and forth.

Nadine suddenly dropped her weight onto Joel's left arm forcing him to go with her or cut her throat.

Joel could already feel the knife penetrating as his exposed right shoulder exploded. He heard the shot, but his arm went limp as he flung backward against the door. The knife fell lifeless to the floor beside Nadine. Her neck bled from where the knife had cut her.

The police, coming up the driveway, heard the shot as they pulled to a stop in front of the house. Armed men jumped from the vehicles and began surrounding the house.

Harriet flipped her phone open, pressed Ramos' speed dial. When he answered, she said, "Call off your army, we have things under control here."

"I thought I told you not to go inside."

"They had our people," Harriet said, and closed her phone.

Harriet helped Nadine to her feet. She placed a napkin on her neck to stop the bleeding. Looking at it closer, she said, "You may need some stitches."

"I thought you were going to shoot me the way your gun was moving around. I really fainted."

Harriet gave her a hug. Then she turned her pistol on the prisoners, "Mc Craw, kick the guns over here including yours."

He looked at her a moment, then realizing what she was doing, he threw his automatic weapon to the floor near Harriet's feet. He did the same with the other three weapons as Ramos and the police entered the house.

The police quickly took charge handcuffing the three assassins. Ramos, seeing the wounded man on the floor called an ambulance as he watched Youngsu place a tourniquet on Joel's arm to stop the bleeding. They needed this man.

"There's two more in the trunk down on the road," Mc Craw said as he threw Ramos' the keys.

Ramos handed them to one of the other police officers, "Go pick them up." Then he turned to Harriet, "I am glad you are alright."

"Are you going to arrest Morales? If you are not, then I am, enough is enough!" Tears were coming to her eyes.

"Can you tie these men in with Morales?"

"I can!" Then pointing to Joel, she said, "If you keep that man alive, you will have a witness Morales hired him."

They could hear the ambulance in the distance.

"I'll make the arrest and cut his leash." Ramos said.

"Arrest his attorney along with him!" She was almost shouting. "He's certainly guilty of conspiracy in this murder attempt."

"Anything else?"

"No, I need to get Nadine to the hospital for some sutures," She said quietly. "I will meet you at the Assistant Director Clark's office tomorrow at ten with all the evidence you will need."

Ramos looked around, "Okay, tomorrow." He turned to his men, "Let's get them out of here!"

They moved the prisoners out the door, but they waited for the ambulance before they moved Joel.

Harriet called Rose, "I guess you heard all of it?"

"Yes, when are you coming back here?"

"I'm sending Mc craw and Youngsu now. I need to take Nadine to the hospital somewhere to check her neck where she was cut."

"Just a minute," Rose said. "Here, I have an Urgent-Care a mile from you." Rose gave her the address.

"Okay, I am on my way," Harriet said, "By the way, Ramos is arresting Morales tonight."

"I heard, get back here, and we will hear it on the computer."

"I have to go. I will see you later." She closed her phone and led Nadine to her car, "I suppose you are not out of gas."

"No, but I am going to drive, cut neck or not."

Harriet smiled, "You don't think I can drive either."

"So far, I only have a cut neck," Nadine said.

At the Urgent-Care Nadine did not require sutures. They drew the tissue together with small stripped Band-Aids. Harriet also had her sutures removed.

The healing on her arm and side where she had taken bullets earlier had healed. Nadine drove them to the beach.

Morales' House

Already after eight, Morales began tapping his right foot on the floor. He had removed a hidden panel and taken out the twenty-thousand stash of cocaine. He had it on the table ready for delivery. He stood and walked around the room.

Johnson calmly watched him thinking, "Maybe he should make a deal with the FBI."

"I don't like this waiting around," Morales said. "Probably should have done this myself."

"Are they coming here?"

"Hell no, I'm meeting them downtown after they finished the job."

"We know they have two of them," Johnson said. "Maybe you should give them another call."

A knock at the door, Morales looked at Johnson, "They weren't supposed to come here." He went to the door, "Who is it?"

"Ramos, sir."

Morales looked back at Johnson whispering, "What's he doing here?"

Johnson shrugged his shoulders.

Morales looked at the bags of cocaine on the table, "Give me a minute." He quickly picked the cocaine off the table and slid it into his hidden wall compartment. Finished, he nodded to Johnson to open the door.

Johnson walked slowly to the door. He opened it to face Ramos with five police officers.

Ramos quickly entered the townhouse apartment, "Morales, you, and your attorney are under arrest for attempted murder."

The police coming in behind Ramos quickly began placing Morales and Johnson in handcuffs.

"You have no grounds for this," Yelled Morales. 'Tell him Johnson."

Ramos received a phone call. He opened his phone and heard Harriet's voice.

Phone:

"He has twenty-thousand in cocaine somewhere there to pay the hit men."

Ramos did not say anything closing his phone.

He did a quick look around. He did not see the cocaine he knew was there. He placed a call to the DEA division, and asked for a cocaine-sniffing dog.

"What are you looking for, Ramos?" Morales shouted.

"Why are you arresting me?" Attorney Johnson asked as the handcuffs clicked into place.

Ramos ignored them both, "Take them downtown, and book them for attempted murder. Anything you say can and will-be-used in a court of law. Get them out of here!'

Three police officers moved them out the door, and to the waiting police cars below. Ramos waited another half hour with two other police officers for the dog team to arrive. He wanted plenty of witness when they found the cocaine. It took the dog thirty seconds to find it.

Downtown the police officers booked, and confined Morales and Johnson. They allowed them one phone call apiece.

Johnson called a fellow attorney to bail him out of jail. He needed to separate himself from Morales to survive. He would-be held for 48 hours for the evidence to arrive. Morales would not be given bail again.

15 Pretrial

Harriet had compiled all of the recordings including the conversations at Morales' house. She had Mc Craw drop her off at the FBI Building. He found a parking spot and waited. They had coverage on the building. He knew Rose would call him if he needed to go inside.

She walked inside without her Colt 45 pistol, passed security, and entered the elevator. She stepped off at the seventh floor, walked to the Director Assistant James Clark's office, and stopped at his secretary's desk, "I'm here to see Mr. Clark."

"Is he expecting you?"

"Please tell him Harriet is here to see him."

"Please have a seat," the secretary said. "I'll let him know." She pushed her intercom, "Miss Harriet is here to see you, sir."

Pause:

"Yes sir, right away sir." She hung up the phone, smiled, "You may go in. He is expecting you."

Harriet looked around apprehensively as she stood and walked towards the door. She still did not trust the FBI. The last time she was here, they wanted to kill her. Other people in the office looked at her."

She opened the door, entered, and saw Ramos already there. She felt better. The Director Assistant walked towards her. He had a different coat on.

She worked another bug from her coat button. When he reached to shake her hand, she placed her foot sideways, and stumbled. She flung herself out. Assistant Clark quickly reached forward and caught her as the finger in her right hand pressed the bug to place on the edge of the inside lining of the upper left pocket.

He helped her to a chair in front of his desk as she managed another bug in the lining of the inside right-hand pocket.

"Sorry sir, I am very nervous. I just wanted to drop this thumb drive off and leave. I do not feel very safe here."

"You're safe now with Chief Ramos, and myself here," Clark said.

Ramos had regained his chair and smiled towards her.

Going behind his desk, Clark said, "I want to thank you for saving my life."

"It was really Chief Ramos, sir."

"Humm, you are a very clever young lady. One should not underestimate you."

"I have only been trying to stay alive, sir. There's been five attempts on my life. It needs to stop." She was almost in tears. "I don't understand you people. You knew he would try and kill me as soon as you set him loose."

"We have Morales in custody now," Clark said. "He will not be coming out of jail, if that is any relief for you."

She worked the tears back, "I…I brought you another thumb drive of the conversations implicating Mr. Morales in this last attempt on my life."

"Will you testify against Chief Morales?"

"If that will put him away, yes," Harriet said.

"I would like to put you in a safe house until the trial."

"I would rather trust my own people, sir," Harrier said. "There still could be moles in your organization."

"I understand your apprehension, but I think we may have everyone."

"I believe it still goes very deep, sir," Harriet said. "But I think we have most of them."

"Will you wait until I have listened to this thumb drive?"

"I rather not stay here any longer than necessary. The drive is self-explanatory."

"Why didn't you send it by mail?"

"I wanted to be sure you received it for one, and I wanted you to know it was from me."

"Fair enough, then I will see you at the briefing after the indictment of Chief Morales. The District Attorney Williams will want to ask you some questions."

"Have Detective Ramos call me with the date and time," Harriet said as she stood, and moved towards the door.

Clark debated whether he should stop her, but he did not want to jeopardize the District Attorney's meeting. She would show. He could ask his questions then. He smiled, 'Please be careful. Your testimony is very important in this case."

"Yes sir, I plan on staying alive." She turned, and quickly walked out the door. She took the elevator to the ground floor and left the building.

Clark, in the computer room with Ramos, looked at the screens. He watched her leave the building and walk quickly down the block out of camera range. Sitting back in his chair, he turned to Ramos, "There goes one brave young lady." He placed a call to the District Attorney's office:

Christopher Charles

Phone:

"William, Clark here, "I have another thumb drive you should hear."

Pause:

"I'll wait for you," Clark said closing off his phone.

Going into the computer room, he slipped the drive in, and made two copies. One, he put in his pocket, the other one he placed in the evidence basket. Relaxed, he sat back to listen to the drive.

"Are we going to listen to the drive before the District Attorney arrives," Ramos asked.

"It's going to take her thirty minutes," Clark said. "I think we should hear what is on it before she does." He pushed the drive in and listened.

Clark could not believe what he had heard, "The man sent a death squad to kill Harriet and her crew. No wonder she's frightened. I wouldn't trust us either."

When the District Attorney Jennifer Williams, a woman in her late forties, slim, hard bearing, arrived, he presented all the information from the thumb drives, and the reports Ramos has made on all of the murder attempts. She sat listening to the drives, and the two of them for an hour.

Finally, she said, "We have a good case to prosecute. I will want to interview all of the witness, and especially the young lady, Harriet Brown. She is your key witness here."

"Yes madam, she said she would be willing to testify."

"Good, I will set the arraignment for Friday. This will probably end his career as a police officer."

Arraignment

Friday, Police Chief Morales and his attorney Charles Johnson walked into the courtroom and sat in front of the District Attorney Williams. Assistant Director Clark along with

Chief of Detective Ramos and the Police Commissioner Harold Jobs sat across from them facing the attorney.

The District Attorney looked at the folder in front of her, "There appears to be sufficient evidence to proceed with a trial for both of you. Do you have anything to say, Mr. Johnson?"

Attorney Charles Johnson stood slowly, "Most of the evidence was obtained by the illegal use of spyware. Neither Chief Morales or myself agreed to its use making the information obtained to be unlawful, and therefore it cannot be used in a court of law."

"That is one interpretation of the law, but in cases of intimate harm and unlawful proceeding, it does not require consent."

"There was no court order obtained to place the spyware. More importantly it was not an agency of the court that placed the spyware," Johnson said.

"We have sufficient evidence to proceed with the case without the evidence that was obtained by the spyware. You may take up the legitimacy of the spyware then."

"You will be ruining Chief Morales' career by continuing this indictment."

"I am aware of the position this will leave Chief Morales in, but for the safely of others, this case will proceed to court a month from today at 9 AM in this courtroom. Are there any questions?"

She waited a few seconds, "I will see you in court." She closed up the folder, motioned for Assistant Director Clark, and Ramos to come forward as they took Chief Morales and Charles Johnson from the court.

When they reached the bench, she said, "Let's meet this afternoon at three. We will need Miss Brown and company. Mr. Johnson made a very good point. How legal are we here?"

Christopher Charles

"I will call her," Ramos said.

"Good, then this afternoon it is," Williams said. "This is a big case, and it will set some legal parameters. We had better be prepared."

"Yes madam," Clark said. "I have to agree with you. Do you know who the judge will be?"

"That has not been decided yet. It falls to Judge Lawyin, but Miss Brown's recordings says she may not be appropriate for this case."

"Will the recording be admissible?" Clark asked.

"That will be decided by the Judge," Williams said. "Let's go into this at three when everyone is here."

They both nodded as Jennifer Williams left the bench.

District Attorney Jennifer Williams' Office

Harriet brought her crew including Youngsu, Rose, and Mc Craw. They found chairs in the room. They brought two more chairs in to accommodate Chief of Police Ramos, and Assistant Director Clark.

When everyone was seated, Williams looked around, "Is everyone here?"

"The three witnesses, Special Agent Steel, Officer Peter Davis, and a Cal Chapman are in protective custody," Clark said.

"We will interview them later," Williams said. "Right now, we need to look into the legality of the recordings taken from the spyware." She looked at Harriet, "I want all of your spyware off the buildings they are presently on. There is no longer a need, and the longer they are on the weaker our case becomes."

"We will remove them all this afternoon," Harriet said. "The spyware saved my life and my crew repeatedly, saved Chief Ramos life twice, and the Assistant Director's life once.

None of us would be here this afternoon if the spyware had not been placed."

"I realized the value of the spyware, but it is the weakest link in this case. We will minimize it, and the defense will maximize it. We need to be ready for the tough questions."

"How much of the recordings do you want to reveal," Harriet asked.

"How much does the defense have?"

"They have what pertains to Chief Morales, but the recording involving Mr. Schmidt, and the late Homeland Security officer Jeffery Adams, and the late head of the DEA, Bryant Kelly are still in my possession."

"Is there any connection to Morales in these recordings?"

"It makes a good case for taking out Mr. Schmidt."

"That would help the defense," Williams said, "But we should be prepared in case they subpoena them."

"Do we have to give all of them?"

"Yes, tampering will negate the legitimacy of the recordings," Williams said, "I would like a copy to review before we go to court, and the defense will want a copy of all of them too." Then looking at Clark, she asked, "Did you check the bullets from Mr. Brown's body?"

"Yes, but Morales' gun did not match the bullets."

"It still could have been a cartel assassin that committed the murders," Williams said. "We will not be bringing them to court unless the defense calls for them. Is there any thing else that will tie Morales to those killings?"

"He could have used another gun," Clark said.

"Yes, but where is it?" She looked at Harriet, "Sorry, you are going to have to settle for the attempted murders, and the accidental killings of the police officers."

"He killed Mr. Schmidt, and the assassin, with a drone, and the accidental death of Jed Black was not accidental,"

Harriet said. "The truck deliberately crashed into the police car."

"Proving the death of Mr. Schmidt, the assassin, and Jed Black is not going to help our case. These were bad people. The jury will probably praise him for seeing to their demise. The best we are going to get is the attempted murders on you people here. The four police officers were accidental, so that will be a manslaughter charge. None of this will give him more than twenty years at the outside. We have to be satisfied with that."

"But he is bad," Harriet said. "How is it any different when a person tries to kill you receives a lesser sentence than if he is successful in the killing you. It doesn't make sense."

"That is the law," Williams said. Turning to Clark, she asked, "How reliable is your witness for the attempted murder against you?"

"Davis will move any direction that will give him the best deal," Clark said. "If he believes Morales might win his case, he will lie to protect himself. Otherwise, his fear of Morales will keep him in line. Agent Steel will be a more creditable witness. He is willing to make a deal. He knows he will go to prison, and his chances in there are not good."

"Then we should probably start with your attempted murder," Williams said. "Let them cross examine your witness while they are still not sure how the trial will go." She turned to Ramos, "Your testimony on your interrogation of Davis in your car will be important."

"We have a recording of that conversation," Harriet whispered.

"Good, we use that to keep Mr. Davis honest," Williams said, "That's saying the recording will be allowed."

"What do we have on the attempt on your life, Chief Ramos?"

"There have been three attempts," Ramos said, "One at the Brown house, one when the four police men took the drone hit met for me, and Davis was supposed to take me out."

"Let's go over those," Williams said.

"At the Brown house Morales sent two police officers to kill Harriet's people, and myself," Ramos said. "They were to leave us dead in the mansion. Unfortunately, the two were killed when the drone hit their car."

"I have a recording of the conversation," Harriet said, but it may not be admissible in court."

"Why is that?"

"It was taken under duress."

"And?"

"I shot a bullet by their head with their revolver," Harriet said. "I wanted results, and I also wanted a bullet from their revolver to see if it matched the one that killed my father."

Williams cleared her throat, "Was there any link to Morales?"

"Jed Black said he sent them to kill us."

"I cannot see where this is going to help our case since the officers involved are dead," Williams said.

"That drone was met for me," Ramos said.

"Then how did it take out the police car?"

"I had Youngsu check Chief Ramos' car for bugs," Harriet said. "If he found one, he was instructed to remove, and place it in the police car. We had no idea it was a drone guidance bug."

Williams turned to Youngsu, "It there anything else you want to add?"

"It large for bug. It also pulsates-a-blue light. I take from Detective Ramos car, place in policeman's car."

"How big was the bug?" William's asked.

"Size of golf ball."

"If we can link the drones to Morales, then we have a connection to the attempted murder of Ramos that resulted in the deaths of the four police officers. The best we will get here is a manslaughter charge, and an attempted murder charge." Then looking at Ramos, she asked, "Is there anything else?"

"No madam."

"Okay, we are to you Miss Brown," Williams said. "Let's go through these attempted murders on you."

"There have been several attempts," Harriet said. She proceeded to go through all of the attempts including Chief's Morales' brother breaking into her office, the firing range where the assassin dried to kill her, and at her Brentwood estate where the two detectives were sent to kill her and Detective Ramos, then later the drone hit killing the four police officers.

"Quite a story," Williams said. "It shows a link to Morales, but the link was established under threats, and the witnesses are all dead. At best, we can show a connection between the drones, and Chief Morales."

"There's more," Harriet said.

"Let's hear it all," Williams said. "She could already see her case falling apart. She needed something stronger.

"We have a recording of Chief Morales and Charles Johnson sending the hit team of six to kill us at the mansion. He was going to pay them off with twenty-thousand dollars-worth of cocaine that Detective Ramos later found in his house. You have the hit team in custody. That seems to be together.

We also have the recording of Chief Morales and Mr. Schmidt at the hotel making a deal to take out the cartel's hit man. That should connect him to the drones.

We have a recording of Johnson and Judge Bracket's attempt to place a hit on Morales that failed and took out

Judge Bracket instead. Then another recording in Johnson's car of Johnson and Morales discussing the hit on Judge Bracket."

"You were a busy girl," Williams said, and smiled. "I will not ask you how you managed to acquire this information, but I think we have a case. Give me all of your recordings immediately. Then we will see what the defense will want. I will meet again just before we go to court next month. I will want to interview all three of our witness before then.

Clark, you can take me to them or you can bring them here, whichever way is safest for them. Okay, I would continue to stay in hiding Miss Brown until the trial. If you come across something important, you may call Chief Ramos, and he can reach me. Okay, that about does it. I will see you all in court."

16 The Trial

Interviews – Three Weeks Later

Director Assistant Clark brought Peter Davis into the interrogation room 'A.' Special Agent Ted Steel was already in interrogation room 'B.' He returned to his office where the District Attorney Jennifer Williams was waiting to interview Cal Chapman regarding the drones. His two marshals stood outside the door.

Cal looked around the office. He had been in protective custody for the last three weeks. They kept him away from the newspapers, and anything that might contain the up-coming trial. They did not want to prejudice his testimony. When the Assistant Director Clark arrived, and sat behind his desk, he began to breathe easier. Finally, someone would hear him.

Clark had already met Williams earlier. This was going to be a long day. They decided to grill their witness to see where he might go in the trial. Clark nodded to Williams.

District Attorney Williams stood, and walked around Chapman. Coming back to the front, she asked, "Who ordered you to send the drones?"

"Well…A…Chief Morales ordered the drones."

"Did he set you up in Chino?"

"No, the drones were already there when I arrived six months ago. It was easy duty. It allowed me to take on-line college classes."

"How were you contacted for the drone duty?"

"I answered an ad wanting someone with computer experience, and willing to be away from their family for long periods of time. I thought it was for some overseas duty, but I found myself in Chino Hills. All done over the computer, I never met anyone. I found the drones as per the instruction. They had a manual on how to operate them. It was easy. I already had experience in building model planes."

"Was that a requirement of the internet interview?"

"Come to think about it, I did mention I had been in the model airplane club for ten years and operated my own planes in my resume."

"Did you know your boss was Chief Morales?"

"No and yes," Chapman said. "I knew it was some government agency. I didn't know which one at first, but I am good at my job. Working my way back through the ad on the computer, I soon learned it was the Los Angeles Police Department. I called different people in the department using pay phones until I heard twenty different voices.

Then when Chief Morales called for a hit, I knew who was calling for it. You don't go sending drones for just anyone. It could have been a terrorist organization calling for the hit. I was working for the Los Angeles Police Department."

"There's no mistake, you recognized Chief Morales' voice?" She turned to Clark, "Play the recording."

Clark pressed the button, and Morales' voice came alive talking with Detective Ramos.

"Was that the voice?" Williams asked.

"Yes madam, I would know that voice anywhere."

"Good," Williams said, and motioned for the marshals."

"Is that all?" Chapman asked.

"If you answer the questions as you have here, that will be all."

"Thank you," Chapman said. "I'm going back with the marshals?"

"Yes, they will protect you until we go to trial next week."

"I thought I would be free to go now."

"They are only protecting you, Mr. Chapman. After the trial we will look into you going home. People have been killed from those drones. We need to put those responsible away. You say it was Chief Morales. We are going to try and prove this with your help."

"Where do I stand in this?"

"We are not after you, Mr. Chapman. Your cooperation in this will stand you in good stead later."

"But I am innocent! I was only following orders."

"Yes, but even you suspected something was not right when you did not know who you were working for."

"I told you, I found out who it was, and I was relieved to learn it was Chief Morales. This was before I fired one drone. I wanted to make sure, you know."

"Yes, that will stand in your favor, and your testimony will also. I told you we are making a case for Chief Morales at the moment. Now you may be excused, Mr. Chapman."

The marshals came in and took out the nervous Cal Chapman.

Williams watched him leave, then turned to the Assistant Director Clark, "He is not a strong witness. He may fold under pressure, and his connection to Morales is a voice recognition that could have been contrived."

"I have the other two in the interrogation rooms," Clark said.

"Then let's go see if we can improve our position."

"Which one first?"

"Let's not keep Mr. Davis waiting," Williams said leading Clark out of the room.

Interrogation Room 'A

A few minutes later, they entered Interrogation room 'A.' Mr. Davis was sitting at the table and stood when they entered. He watched the marshals close the door. He suddenly felt depressed. He was not going to get out of this.

Clark motioned for him to sit down as he and District Attorney Williams sat down across from him.

"Have the marshals been treating you well, Mr. Davis?" Williams asked.

"It's alright, but you could improve on the food."

"Your safe, Mr. Davis," Williams said, "I think that is the most important thing."

"When is this trial?"

"It is scheduled for next week. I thought we would have a little talk before the trial."

"You gonna make a deal?"

"You shot the Assistant Director, Mr. Davis," Williams said. "Through no fault of your own, he is still alive."

"I still want a deal if you want me testifying against Chief Morales."

"We really don't need your testimony to prove our case against Chief Morales, Mr. Davis. We only wanted to make it tighter."

"What am I getting out of it?"

"You will get our recommendation you helped in prosecuting Chief Morales. That will allow some lenience with the judge when your trial comes up."

"I think I should have a lawyer before I say anymore."

"What lawyer will that be?"

"I will have Charles Johnson."

"I believe he is in jail at the moment for assisting in plotting to commit murder."

"Then I want his lawyer," Davis said.

"Very well, Mr. Davis," Williams said motioning for agents outside the door to come in. "Take him back to his cell. We will wait for his lawyer before we interview him."

Mr. Davis left the interrogation room as Williams and Clark watched. Then Williams said, "We may have lost him. If the other side gets him, his testimony could really change."

"Maybe we should have given him something," Clark said.

"He's an out-and-out killer with no remorse. He needs to be in prison away from people."

"I see your point, but this weakens our case against Morales."

"Yes, let's see if we can improve things," Williams said standing.

Interrogation Room 'B

A few minutes later, they walked into the interrogation room 'B.' Special Agent Ted Steel was sitting at the desk waiting for them. He looked up as they entered, but he remained sitting as they took the chairs opposite him.

"This is the District Attorney Williams," Clark said. "She wants to ask you a few questions."

Steel nodded, "I will try to be cooperative."

"You know we want Chief Morales," Williams said. "We already have a very tight case against him. Those around him are going down with him."

"Where does that place me?"

"Cooperating will show you do not want to be part of his demise."

"What kind of deal will you make with me?"

"You set your Assistant Director up to be killed," Williams said. "You gave the time, and place for his execution."

"I know what I did, but what kind of deal will you make?"

"You are going to jail. How long that is will be determined by your cooperation. We want Chief Morales."

"I see thirty to life here," Steel said. "What can you offer?"

"That will be up to the Judge, but as I said, your cooperation will help in that decision."

"I think I need a lawyer before I say anymore."

"Do you want a court appointed lawyer?"

"No, I already have my lawyer," Steel said. "I am ready to go back to my cell." He motioned for the agents by the door as he stood.

After he left, Clark looked at Williams, "I bet his lawyer is Charles Johnson."

"Yes, we are going to have a fight on our hands," Williams said. "We have the bullets from Davis' rifle. They match. We have Ramos' testimony, and the recording in his car. We also have the testimony Davis gave in here. That may be enough."

Courtroom

Charles Johnson stood in front of Judge Lawyin. Two plainclothes police officers stood beside him. The Prosecuting District Attorney Williams, and Assistant Director Clark stood to the right side of them.

Judge Lawyin studied a document in front of her. Finally, she looked up at Charles Johnson, "It appears here you are asking to be set free on bail to prepare for your court hearing. Is that correct?"

"Yes madam," Johnson said. "I am not a risk. I have no intention of fleeing, but I need the opportunity to prepare for Chief Morales, Peter Davis, Cal Chapman, Ted steel, and my own defense."

"You are representing all of them?"

"Yes madam."

She turned to Williams, "Does the prosecution have any objection?"

"His Client, Chief Morales, was given bail. He used the opportunity to make an attempt on Miss Brown's life. How many times are we going to subject Miss Brown to the possibility of being murdered?"

"Mr. Johnson was not on bail at the time, only Chief Morales."

"Yes, but the recordings will show Mr. Johnson along with Chief Morales plotted to take her life."

"I have yet to decide on the recordings," Judge Lawyin said.

"I would also like to subpoena all of the recordings since the prosecution will be entering them in as evidence," Charles Johnson said.

"We are not going to enter all of the recordings for evidence because a large portion of them do not pertain to this case," District Attorney Williams said.

"It may not pertain to the prosecution's case, but it may pertain to my clients' defenses," Johnson said.

"If we are going to enter the recordings in as evidence, it will have to be satisfactory for both sides," Judge Lawyin said.

"We will only accept them if we can have access to all of them," Mr. Johnson said.

Judge Lawyin looked at Williams, "Is that satisfactory?"

"Yes, your honor," Williams said. "I will provide the defense with all of the recordings."

"Then the recordings will be allowed in court. One side will see to it the other side does not tamper with them. Mr. Johnson may be set free on bail to prepare his cases something he cannot do in jail for this to be a fair hearing. Bail will be set for 200,000 dollars, see the bailiff."

Mr. Johnson smiled, "Please send all of the recordings to my office. I assume there will not be any more illegal recordings."

"You will have all of the recordings this afternoon," Williams said.

"My clients have been instructed not to answer questions unless I am present."

"Do any of them want to make a deal?" Williams asked.

"The deal time is over," Johnson said. "We are going for an acquittal." He turned and left.

"What do you think he meant by that?" Clark asked.

"He has all of our key witnesses testifying for the defense," Williams said. "That does not put us in a good position. We will have to concentrate on the murder attempts against Miss Brown. The recordings will definitely play a role in that, and they've been allowed. That may be his one mistake."

"He didn't sound like that was going to be a mistake," Clark said following Williams out of the courtroom.

"He doesn't know what is on the other ones. We'll see what he says after he is through listening to them."

Courtroom One Week Later

9 AM Friday morning the court opened the case between Chief Don Morales' people, and the State of California. Harriet Brown and Assistant Director James Clark had the front row. The Police Commissioner Jobs, Mr. Brown and his crew sat behind them. Jennifer Williams and her staff occupied the desk on the right side of the floor in front of the Judge.

On the other side, Charles Johnson and Chief Don Morales sat behind a desk on the left side of the court floor. He had the recordings set on the speakers. He had an expert witness on 'tapering with voice recordings' sitting behind him.

Judge Judy Lawyin, presiding, felt apprehensive. Charles Johnson did not try to contact her or make any indirect threats. She expected it, but it did not happen. She would like to see the lot of them go to jail and remove the weight around her neck. Maybe she will come out of this. She knew District Attorney Williams was good.

It had taken three weeks to select a jury. Neither side willing to give an inch ending up with an impartial jury. Lawyin knew many cases were lost in poor jury selection. Satisfied, she walked into court.

"All rise! The honorable Judy Lawyin is presiding."

Everyone stood until the judge took her seat. Then they all sat down.

When everyone settled, Judge Lawyin said, "This case is between Chief Don Morales and the State of California. In conjunction, the cases of Attorney Charles Johnson, Officer Peter Davis, Cal Chapman, Joel Garnell, and FBI Agent Ted Steel will run concurrently since they all have the same attorney. The prosecution may make their beginning statement."

District Attorney Williams stood, walked over to the jury, and said, "The state will prove Chief Don Morales used his position as the Los Angeles Chief of police to consort with the

Columbia drug cartel to make two attempts on the lives of Chief of Detectives Paul Ramos. One attempt on the life of Assistant Director James Clark, and four attempts on Miss Harriet Brown's life.

He was not successful in any of these cases because of the spyware Miss Brown had used to obtain the recordings giving her knowledge of the imminent danger to their lives. She has lived in fear for the past few months. Whom can you trust when the Chief of Police is trying to assassinate you? The system needs to work for her as it does for others in high places." She turned and walked back to her seat. They allowed the recordings. She was going to make the most of them.

Charles Johnson stood, walked slowly towards the jury with his head down. When he reached the bar in front of them, he raised his head, looked straight at them, "We will prove the charges against Chief Morales are false. That he was framed by a conspiracy to remove him from his office, and to acquire eight hundred million dollars.

The recordings, fabricated in parts, to make it appear Chief Morales was a willing participant in these attempted murders. He has an unblemished record of twenty years with the Los Angeles Police Department. He has served his community well. He does not deserve these accusations that have ruined his career as a police officer.

We will also show this conspiracy has led to the deaths of Bryant Kelly Head of DEA, and Jeffery Adams head of the Los Angeles Home land security. These men had families. They did not deserve to die. We will show Chief Morales tried to prevent this, but the process was already moving."

His body shook as he said, "We are trying the wrong people." He waved his hand towards Harriet and her people, yelling, "You must stop this miscarriage of justice!" He turned and walked slowly back to his desk.

The courtroom, stunned a moment until Judge Lawyin quietly said, "The prosecution may present their first witness."

District Attorney Williams stood slowly, "I will have Cal Chapman come to the stand."

Two Marshals brought Cal in from a back room, one on each side of him. He looked around at the people as he stumbled towards the stand. Obviously nervous, he placed his hand on the bible, and said he would tell the truth. He took his seat. He could feel everyone watching him. He did not want to be here.

Williams waited a moment for Cal to settle in, then she asked, "What is your name?"

"Cal Chapman."

"Cal what have you been doing the last six months?"

"I have been maintaining drones for the Los Angeles Police Department."

"How were you hired?"

"Through the internet, I answered an ad, gave them my resume, and they hired me."

"Did you ever meet anyone?"

"No, I was given a location, and told what to do via the internet."

"How are you paid?"

"Money was transferred to my account once a month for five thousand dollars."

"Then you did not know who was paying you?"

"I know it came from the Los Angeles Police Department."

"How do you know this?"

"I checked it out," Cal said, "I am good with computers. I followed the instructions back through the computer. I found where it came from. It was the Los Angeles Police Department."

"Your job was to await instructions to launch a drone missile when the call came in?"

"I didn't just take any call," Cal said. "I checked that out too. I looked up all of the top people in the police department and began calling them on pay phones until I could recognize their voices. Then when the call came in to send out a drone, I would recognize their voice, and know who it was. These drones are dangerous! I didn't want to be working for a terrorist group."

"Did you know those drones killed four police officers, took out a downtown hotel room killing two people inside, and one for God knows why took out a dump truck."

"I didn't program the targets," Cal said. "I just got them in the air and heading towards Los Angeles. The drones then picked up the targets and moved that direction."

"How did they find their targets?" Williams asked.

"A directional bug was placed at the site. It directed the drone to it."

"So, someone had to place the directional bug?"

"Yes, I had no idea where the drone was going," Cal said. "It just homed in on the bug."

"How big was this directional bug?"

"The size of a golf ball."

"How did a directional bug get into dump truck?' Williams asked.

"I rather not say," Cal said.

"I think you need to tell the court. We will find out anyway."

"I... I placed a phone chip code into the drone," Cal said quietly.

"You mean there is another way to direct the drones?"

"Yes, but I only did it once. I didn't kill anyone. I told him I wouldn't do it again. I wasn't into killing people."

"Who were you talking to?"

"Chief Morales." Cal said quietly.

"Louder please," Williams said.

"Chief Morales!"

District Attorney Williams turned, "Your witness!" She walked back to her seat.

Defense Attorney Johnson walked slowly to Cal Chapman. He carried a recording device with him. When he was up beside Cal, he pushed the button. Chief Morales' voice said, "Hello Cal, I am sorry you have to be here." Then looking hard at Cal, he asked, "Is this Chief Morales'?"

Cal looked at him, "You know it isn't."

Johnson pointed to Chief Morales at the table, "That is Chief Morales."

Then turning to the Jury, he said, "This is the recording the prosecution has allowed to be place in evidence. Let me play the prior sequence before the drone killed the four police officers."

The recording device started:

"Captain Morales sent us," a man's voice said, "We are to check everything she takes out of here."

"She's not here," a rough man's voice said. "We're taking everything. You against that?"

"Release them or take a bullet." A man said.

"I thought you were dirty," the rough man's voice said. "I suppose you set up that drive-by too."

"I've been trying to keep her alive, but she is very hard to protect." The man's voice said.

"The drive-by!" the rough voice yelled. "That's why you were on the ground."

"I didn't know it was going to be a drive-by."

"Maybe you should think about dropping your weapon and turning around very slowly. There's a forty-five pointed at your back. You know how big of a hole it makes."

"Dropping my weapon," man's voice said.

Extremely angry female voice yelled, "Who killed my father? Tell me in five seconds or I am going to start blasting one of you at a time."

"We don't know!" a man yelled. "We're instructed where to go by the dispatcher, and we go. This is my first time here."

"Ramos?" the female voice asked. "I have yet to hear the truth from you."

"I was working on finding out who did, but I haven't found anyone. So, if you are going to shoot us, you might as well get started," A man's voice said.

"Youngsu, take their handcuffs, and cuff them. Remove their phones and ID while I think about who I am going to kill first. Mc Craw, bring me their guns."

Pause:

"How did you know I was coming here?" the female voice asked. "You only get one chance to tell me the truth."

"I got a call from the Chief saying you were coming here," a man's voice said.

"Bang!" A loud gunshot.

Recording stopped:

Johnson turned the machine off, turned back to Cal Chapman on the witness stand, "Did you hear his voice?"

"Yes," Cal said, "It's the one the female voice called Ramos."

"You are sure that is the voice that ordered the drone hits?"

"Yes, that is the voice," Cal said. "I heard it many times."

"That will be all," Johnson said walking back to his seat.

Christopher Charles

"Would you like to cross examine," Judge Lawyin asked.

"I certainly would," Williams said. "Let's hear all of the recording." She picked up the recording device that was actually a small computer that sent the voice to speakers mounted in the courtroom. She pressed the button, and the voice started up again after the gunshot.

Recording:

"Now tell me your purpose of coming here?" The female voice asked. "Were we to have an accident?" The voice shouted.

"You know too much," the man's voice said quickly.

"And!" the female voice yelled.

"We were to shoot you in the house," the man's voice said.

"Detective Ramos?"

"All four of you."

"Who ordered it?"

"Morales, Chief Morales." The man yelled. "The man's threatening my family. He shot my dog for god sakes."

"And your buddy?"

"I don't know about him." The man was shouting.

"Youngsu, put him in the car." The female voice said.

There is a moment delay, and some noises.

"It's your turn to tell the truth." The female voice said.

"I don't know anything the same as Jed." The man's voice said.

"You get one chance," the female voice said. "What's your name, and how many people in the police department are dirty?"

"Name's Hogan," a shaking man's voice said. "Mike Hogan. You mean on the take or something else?"

"Those that help the drug cartel exist here?"

"I don't know, maybe four or five on the lower level, and maybe two or three on the higher levels."

"Who on the higher level?"

"All I know it goes very high."

"What level are you on?"

"Lower level, madam."

A gunshot.

"How much did they pay you to be dirty?" the female voice asked.

"Hundred thousand with promise of more."

"Were you going to leave our bodies at the house after you killed us?"

"That was our instructions."

"Who's instructions?

"Chief Morales."

"Give me the name of another dirty cop, and I'll let you live," the female voice shouted.

"Cooper, Chris Cooper!"

"Another one! Now!"

"Anderson, George Anderson, I don't know anymore."

"Throw him in the car, Mc Craw."

Some noises

"Youngsu, take Detective Ramos from the car, and remove his handcuffs."

Pause:

"Nice acting Ramos!" a female voice said.

Pause:

"Please bring up the limousine."

A few minutes of noise, and voices, then, "I have a car coming to retrieve these two and pick up Cooper and Johnson. Are you going to give me a copy of their confessions?"

"Youngsu is bringing it," the female voice said. "Who are you giving it to?"

"It's evidence, otherwise I can't hold them. Even then it will not hold up in court. We will try, and use it to reach higher, but that's the best we will get out of it."

Recording stopped:

District Attorney Williams turned to Cal, "Is it possible for someone to know you are checking their voices, and contrive Ramos' voice?"

"I made over twenty calls."

"It is reasonable to think the police department would become aware someone was checking on them after twenty crank calls, especially when the crank did not answer them. It would make them suspicious enough to consider the reason for the calls. If the one who hired you didn't want you to know who he was, would he be careless enough to use his own voice? Wouldn't it be reasonable he would use someone else's voice?"

"That seems reasonable. It is not all that difficult to do."

"Thank you, Mr. Chapman that will be all."

"Does the defense have any questions?" Judge Lawyin asked.

Johnson stood, "Yes, the last part of the recording could have been contrived to have the dead men respond to the questions asked, and I believe she had a gun to their heads. I heard a gun go off twice. She obviously was threatening them. I think I would say anything she wanted to hear to avoid getting a bullet between my eyes. Wouldn't that be how you would feel Mr. Chapman?"

"Yes sir, that's what I would do."

"No more questions," Johnson said.

"You may step down Mr. Chapman," Judge Lawyin said, "Call your next witness."

District Attorney Williams stepped aside as Cal Chapman left the courtroom with his marshals. Turning back to the judge, she said, "I will call Officer Peter Davis to the stand."

Two FBI Agents brought Davis out of the back. He left the agents and walked to the stand. He took the bible and promised to tell the truth.

When he settled, she asked, "What is your full name?"

"Detective Peter Davis."

"Mr. Davis, you told the Assistant Director of the FBI that you shot him three times in the chest, and once in the arm per the instructions of Chief Morales. Is that correct?"

"No, I was told by Chief Detective Ramos to kill the Assistant Director while he waited for me at the Hilton hotel. He even let me use his car."

"Then I would like you to hear this recording taken when Detective Ramos questioned you while he was transporting you to the FBI for questioning.

Recording:

"You have the right to remain silent. Anything you say can be used against you in a court of law.

"Wait a minute Ramos? Let's talk about this."

There is a minute of noise.

"I bet this is what shot the Assistant Director."

"You can't prove nothing," a man's voice said.

"What makes you so sure?"

"Morales is why. You're as good as dead." The man's voice said.

"Right now, Morales has his own problems."

"You have no idea who you are dealing with."

"And what is that?"

"You will see."

"We have plenty on Morales."

"None of it is going to stick," the man said.

"You know Morales killed your four buddies with his drone missile?"

"That was a mistake."

"He doesn't make mistakes. If he survives the FBI, you will be the first one he will eliminate."

"He's not going to kill me."

"You know too much."

"Then you have to protect me."

"Me? You were going to kill me a minute ago."

"That was only orders from Morales."

"I don't know. You sent four bullets into the chest of the Assistant Director of the FBI."

"That was all Morales. He wanted him killed."

"What's Morales' got that going to save his ass?"

"He's got long legal arms if you know what I mean?"

"I know what you mean, but it's not going to do you any good unless I hear a name."

"Judge Bracket for one, Morales has him in his pocket. I've seen them eating together."

"What's he got on him?"

"I don't know. I only know he's got something on him."

"Not helping much. I need more to save your life."

"I can't give you more. You gotta save me."

"I'll take you to the FBI. Maybe you can cut a deal, but you're going to need more than this."

Recording Stopped:

"Now we will hear your interrogation at the FBI office," District Attorney Williams said.

Recording:

"It isn't very often one gets to look at his assassin." A man's voice said.

"You're still alive? I shot four bullets into you." A man's voice said.

"You going to tell me who ordered it? You should know everything you say here will be recorded."

"I.... I told Ramos it was Morales."

"You mean Chief Morales?"

"Yes."

"Why?"

"Something to do with a thumb drive I think. I am only guessing here. He didn't say."

"You usually kill someone especially a FBI Director on the word of one man."

"He has connections like I told Ramos."

"What kind of connections?"

"There's some guy in the DEA, and there's another guy in Home Land Security. I don't know who, but I know there is someone there very powerful."

"That's old information. What else do you have?"

"He has a couple of Judges."

"Names?"

"Judge Bracket for one."

"Another?"

"A…A Judge Lawyin, I think she is the other one."

"Both superior court judges," A man's voice said. "Send in the marshals. I'm going to have the marshals take you into protective custody. I do not need to tell you if you escape from them, you will probably be dead within twenty-four hours."

"I know my position, sir."

"Good! I hope you stay alive."

Recording Stopped:

District Attorney Williams turned the machine off, "Was that your voice?"

"I don't know if it was or not," Davis said.

"I can have the Assistant Director of the FBI testify this was your statement."

"Yes, it was my statements," Davis said quietly.

"No more questions," District Attorney Williams said.

Defense Attorney Charles Johnson stood, walked to the witness stand, looked at Davis and said in an even voice, "Let's hear the truth of that day. Who really sent you to kill the Assistant Director of the FBI? You are not under any duress here. Detective Ramos cannot do you any harm."

"Detective Ramos threatened me. You don't hear that on the recording. He was going to drop me off in the bushes somewhere if I didn't follow his script."

"Meaning?"

"He was gonna kill me!"

"And at the FBI office?"

"He already had me confessing on his recording. He had me for murder. He sent me to kill the Assistant Director for god sake. He was standing right there watching me. I didn't dare say anything different. My life was in his hands. I have been waiting to tell someone the truth."

"Thank you, no further questions," Johnson said.

"Redirect?" Judge Lawyin asked. She was hoping the District Attorney had something. She heard her name mentioned on the recording.

District Attorney Williams walked slowly to the stand, and asked, "Who is your attorney, Officer Davis?"

"A... A Charles Johnson, but he didn't make me say anything that wasn't true."

"And whose attorney is Chief Morales?"

"Well a…A…Charles Johnson."

"Then it is in your interest to protect Chief Morales, is that correct? It certainly is in Charles Johnson's interest."

"I don't know, I guess you could say that."

"You shot the Assistant Director with the intend to kill him," Williams said. "There is no escaping that. That's life without parole at the very least, and more than likely be the death penalty. Cooperation with the prosecution and telling the truth will help in that sentencing."

Charles Johnson stood shouting, "She's threatening the witness!"

"Objection sustained, you will not threaten the witness here. Bargaining should have been done before this court hearing."

"Do you want to change your testimony?"

"No!" Davis said, "I know what I am doing."

"I have no further questions your Honor."

"Cross examination?" Judge Lawyin asked.

"That will not be necessary," Johnson said, and smiled quietly to himself.

"You may step down Officer Davis."

Davis walked slowly back to the FBI agent waiting for him.

Williams watched him a moment, then she said, "I would like to call my next witness, Assistant Director Clark to the stand."

Clark stood, worked his way to the stand, seated himself and looked out at the court.

When he settled, District Attorney Williams asked, "Your name please."

"James Clark, Assistant Director of the FBI."

"How come you are not dead after Officer Davis pumped four bullets into you."

"That is because Chief of Detective Ramos called me while I was in the elevator to warn me of an immediate attempt on my life. Taking him seriously, I went to the equipment locker, and retrieved a bulletproof vest.

When I walked outside, I saw this small Mercedes come around the corner. It stopped in front of me. A short barrel rifle came out the window. I felt this enormous pressure suddenly hitting me in chest. I fell back hitting the concrete with my head knocking me unconscious for a moment.

When I regained consciousness, my left arm was bleeding profusely. Then I felt Special Agent Steel reaching into my pocket and take out the thumb drive with all of these recordings on it."

"Why would Special Agent Steel be taking the thumb drive from you?"

"It was him who gave the assassin the place, and time to kill me. You can hear him giving the information to Chief Morales on the recordings. I didn't want to believe it, but here he was taking the thumb drive."

"Officer Davis was just heard giving a completely different interpretation of the events."

"Yes, he moves very easy to whatever side he believes will help him the most. The bullets matched the rifle found in the trunk of the car he was driving. He confessed to the attempted murder in my office, and he was informed it would be recorded."

"Again, who warned you of the assassination attempt?"

"It was Chief Detective Ramos," Clark said, "I would not be alive today if he hadn't warned me."

"Would it seem reasonable a man would be sending an assassin to kill you, and then warn you that he is coming?"

Johnson stood shouting, "She is leading the witness!"

"Sustained!" Judge Lawyin said.

"Detective Ramos did not send Officer Davis to kill me. That I am very sure of."

"No further questions."

"Cross examination?"

Charles Johnson stood, and walked over to the Assistant Director. He stood in front of him a few seconds, then he asked, "Is it a possibility Detective Ramos had changed his mind at the last second, and warned you when he could not reach Officer Davis?"

"What would be the reason?"

"He knew what was on the thumb drive, is that correct?"

"I am sure he knew some of its contents," Clark said.

"Especially the parts incriminating him," Johnson said.

"I was not aware of parts incriminating him," Clark said.

"No one has asked how the thumb drive came to be in your hands with all of this beautiful human drama on it. Would you like to enlighten us?"

"It came from the Brown Detective Agency. Miss Harriet Brown presented me with the thumb drive at my office. I was very impressed by the comprehensive detail it gave."

"Yes, Harriet Brown, the daughter of the man the cartels had killed for stealing eight hundred million dollars."

District Attorney Williams quickly stood, "He is leading the witness along lines that have not been established."

"Sustained," Judge Lawyin said.

"Then I would like to call this witness back after this has been established. No further questions at the moment."

"Witness may step down," Judge Lawyin said.

The Assistant Director Clark stepped down from the witness stand and walked back to sit beside Harriet.

Harriet leaned over, "I need to talk to you privately before she puts me on the witness stand. It's very important."

Clark nodded. He thought a moment, then he took out a piece of paper and pen, wrote a brief note. He handed it to District Attorney's secretary sitting at the table in front of them.

She looked at the note and nodded.

The District Attorney Williams turned to the judge, "I would like to call my next witness, Special Agent Steel."

Steel came out of the back room with an FBI agent on each side of him. When he entered the court area, the agents remained by the door. He took the witness stand and faced the District Attorney Williams.

"What is your name?" Williams asked.

"Special agent Ted Steel."

"You worked very close with the Assistant Director Clark?"

"Yes, we were friends."

"What were you doing after the thumb drive was received from Harriet Brown?"

"I was merely informing Chief Morales the thumb drive existed. I did not intend for anyone to get killed, especially my friend, James Clark."

"Allow me to refresh your memory with a recording of the conversation," Williams said.

Recording:

"Morales, Steel here, we've got a young lady here claiming you are trying to kill her. Her name's Harriet Brown."

Pause:

"That's her. She has a thumb drive with evidence of you trying to kill her, and several other people. Clark and I are going to hear it now."

Pause:

"I can't stop him from hearing it."

Pause:

"I have to go. I'll call you afterwards."

Pause:

"I don't know if I can destroy it."

Pause:

"She said it was the only copy."

Pause:

"I've got to go. She's still in the office. Okay, I'll call when she leaves. Gotta go!"

Recording Stopped:

After the recording stopped District Attorney Williams asked, "Is that your voice?"

"I will take the fifth amendment."

"Very well, we will go on, and see if your voice matches up again." Williams said.

Recording:

"Where have you been?" A man's voice said.

"I had to make a pit stop. What's on the drive?"

"Listen!" The man said.

Pause:

"That is the most incredible piece of detective work I have ever heard. We've got organize drug conspiracies going the full length of the government. I never knew the drug cartel had that much power here."

Pause:

"We've got to protect that girl and get Morales in here."

"Yes sir," A man said. "You want me to put the drive in the evidence room?"

"No, I'm keeping this with me." The other man said. "Let's go question that girl."

Pause:

"Where is she?" A man asked.

"She's in there," another man said.

"How long has she been in there?"

"She went in right after you left, sir."

Pause:

"She not in there."

"Maybe she went back to the office. Check the cameras," a man ordered.

Pause:

"Is that her?" A man asked.

"That's the lady that came out of the bathroom," another man said.

"Switch to outside cameras; maybe we can get a license plate."

"There she is walking across the street. Now she's gone."

"Gee's, at least we still have the drive," a man said. "Steel, see what you can get on the girl, and bring in Morales for questioning."

Recording stopped:

"There, Agent Steel, I think that identifies your voice on the recording a second time. We now know which voice is yours. Let's continue:"

Recording:

"Yes sir. Don't forget your meeting with the mayor in fifteen minutes. He wants to know the progress on the Biltmore drone hit."

"Cancel it," a man said.

"That may not be a good move," the other voice said. "I can have Morales here when you get back."

"You may be right," the man said, "You pick up Morales."

"Yes sir."

Pause:

"He's coming out now. You take him out, I'll get the drive."

Pause:

"I said I will get the drive!"

Recording stopped:

After the recording stopped, Williams turned to Steel, and continued, "This is what was said in the elevator that Assistant Director Clark was taking down to the first floor."

Recording:

"Who are you?"

Pause:

"Look detective are you trying to say your Captain is going to try, and kill me?"

Pause:

"When and where?"

Pause:

"Now! How do you know?"

Pause:

"Agent Steel placed the call to Morales? I don't believe you."

Pause:

"Hey! Damn he hung up."

The sound of the elevator opening.

Recording Stopped:

The District Attorney Williams looked at Steel, "Do you still want to deny that is your voice."

"I am not going to incriminate myself."

"The recording shows you gave the assassin a time, and the place to take out the Assistant Director. Is that how you treat your friend?"

"I didn't know the police officer was going to kill him," Steel said. "He was supposed to delay him long enough for me to retrieve the thumb drive. There was no need for Ramos to kill him."

"I thought I heard the name Morales in the recording not Detective Ramos. It also appears you knew Chief Morales very well. He did not question your voice. When your boss told you to pick up Chief Morales, you instead set up a hit."

"Leading the Witness!" Charles Johnson shouted.

"Sustained," Judge Lawyin said. "You will not draw conclusions for the witness."

"I don't need to, your honor, the recordings draw their own conclusion. No further questions."

"Do you wish to cross examine, Mr. Johnson?"

"I believe I do," Charles Johnson said. He stood slowly, walked to the witness stand, "It occurred to me you were trying to say something, Agent Steel. Could you elaborate for us please? There is no pressure now."

"Yes sir," Steel said. "After I listened to the recordings, I realized a big hoax was taking place. These recordings came from one source that had Detective Ramos' fingerprints all over it.

He sent Police Officer Davis down to murder the Assistant Director, but not with the intention of having him killed, but to discredit Chief Morales. That was why he made the quick phone call. How did he know the precise time to call the Assistant Director, and warn him if he had not sent Davis? I was manipulated to participate in the scheme."

"Thank you, Agent Steel, that clears up things a bit, no further questions." Johnson said.

"Wish to cross examine?" Judge Lawyin asked.

District Attorney Williams stood quickly, passed Johnson who had a slight smile on his face, and turned to the witness. She looked at him hard, "That is a lot of conjecturing, isn't it Agent Steel. You obviously had knowledge of the attack, or you would not have relieved the Assistant Director of the thumb drive after he was shot."

"I told you my story, and I am standing by it."

"Yes, I think you would when you are being accused of abetting attempted murder. It doesn't hurt you to lie."

"She's badgering the witness again, and making suppositions," Johnson shouted from his desk."

"You will refrain from the badgering of the witness," Judge Lawyin said.

"No further questions," Williams said.

"Cross examine?" Judge Lawyin asked.

"No questions," Johnson said.

Christopher Charles

"I would like to call Mr. Joel Garnell to the stand," Williams said.

The back door to the courtroom opened, and two marshals escorted Joel Garnell to the door. He walked alone to the stand. He looked around nervously. He knew he had been setup. His right shoulder, still a mess, would take five more operations before it would be right.

He was in constant pain without his pain pills. He saw Harriet, and quickly lost his nervousness. She didn't have to shoot him. He wasn't going to cut her friend.

He felt the bible shoved into his hand, and he automatically said the oath he would tell the truth. His attorney had already talked to him. He knew what to say. He took the stand and looked at the District Attorney.

"Mr. Garnell tell the court what happened at the Brown Mansion?"

"My boys and myself went to the mansion to pick up Miss Brown and her people for questioning."

"You all were carrying large caliber automatic weapons. Isn't that a little heavy against a defenseless team of three women, and two men? I think Miss Brown carried a revolver for protection."

"It's better to be prepared. Besides I'm the one that got shot by that cannon of hers."

"I think we need to play the recording to refresh your memory," Williams said.

Recording:

"Joel how much are we getting from Morales?"

"Twenty thousand in cocaine," a man said,

"We can double that by tomorrow night."

"You mean after we take some for ourselves," another man laughed.

The man yelled, "You take him, go to the gate. Let them in, but don't let them out. You got that?"

The sound of a door opening and closing.

The Recording stopped:

"That doesn't sound like you were just picking up?" Williams said.

"That's what it was," Joel said. "I don't care what it sounds like. That she-devil also blew my arm apart for no reason."

"Mr. Garnell, did you have a knife on Nadine Quiver throat?"

"That big guy comes in shooting the place up. I took her in self-defense. I wasn't going to hurt her."

"Is that why she had to have stitches in her neck?"

"She fainted and fell on my knife. That's not my fault."

"Did Chief Morales hire you for the amount of 20,000 in cocaine to assassinate Miss Brown, and her people?"

"He hired me to bring them to him for questioning, something about the recordings I think."

"Twenty thousand in cocaine seems a rather high amount to bring someone in for questioning."

"There were six of us splittin."

"Chief Morales hired you to kill Miss Brown, and her people for the 20,000 in cocaine. You were not there to pick up anyone."

"She's leading the witness again," Johnson yelled from his chair.

"Sustained!" Judge Lawyin said. "I will not tolerate this again. Strike that last statement from the record, and the jury is instructed to disregard it."

"I have no more questions," Williams said.

"Cross Examine," Judge Lawyin asked.

Christopher Charles

"It is not necessary," Johnson said.

"I would like to call Miss Harriet Brown, but her testimony will be lengthy since she is the originator of the recordings. I would like a continuance until Monday."

"Granted, until Monday at 9 AM," Judge Lawyin said. "I will not tolerate more badgering and leading of the witnesses by either side. Please keep this in mind Monday." She hit her gravel on the wood and left the courtroom.

District Attorney Williams turned around to Harriet, Clark, and Ramos, "I want a meeting with you three in twenty minutes in my office." She turned, picked up her papers, and headed for the door with Detective Ramos following her.

Harriet pulled at Clarks arm, "We need to talk now."

Clark turned, "Okay, do you want to go somewhere?"

"Somewhere we can't be heard. How about my limousine?"

"Lead the way."

Youngsu had already left the courtroom earlier. When they reached the curb, the limousine pulled up. Rose, Mc Craw, Harriet and Clark climbed inside.

When everyone settled, Harriet said, "Take us to the District Attorney's office, Youngsu." Then turning to Clark she said, "We know where the stock pile of drugs is located."

"You know what?"

"Where the cartel hid their eight hundred million dollars-worth of cocaine."

"The reason the drug cartel killed Bryant Kelly Head of DEA and Jeffery Adams head of the Los Angeles Home land security?"

"Yes sir, they were dirty as the drugs brought out," Harriet said. "I didn't know who else was dirty, so we didn't tell anyone else where they were. Since they obviously tried to kill you, and the fact they will probably try to hang this on Detective Ramos, I thought it best we tell you immediately."

The Assistant Director shook his head slowly, "You could have prevented those killings if you had spoken up earlier."

"To who, sir? Even your office was dirty as was evidenced by the attack on your life."

"I see your point," Clark said. "And you are right! We need to act on this immediately or its going to affect Detective Ramos."

"Rose, give him the Long Beach container numbers." She turned back to Clark, and quietly continued, "Both of them were warned, sir."

Rose went into the limousine computer and produced the four container numbers. She handed them to the Assistant Director, "It might be better if you received a tip from an outside source. Maybe I could call you while you are in your meeting."

"That might be a good idea," Clark said.

The limousine pulled up in front of the District Attorney's office building.

The two of them, Harriet, and Clark left the limousine, and entered the building. Walking into the District Attorney Williams' office, Ramos and Williams were already there.

Williams motioned for them to take a seat. When they settled, she said, "We have a problem. Charles Johnson is trying to turn this trial around to make Detective Ramos the one that should be behind bars. If he can distract the jury enough with this, he will have effectively moved his clients away from the facts."

Clark's phone rang, he looked at Williams', "I need to take this." He listened a moment, "Give me a second." He quickly turned to Williams, "You have a piece of paper?"

She pulled a piece of paper from her notebook and handed it to him.

Taking the piece of paper, Clark said, "Go ahead, I am ready." He began writing fast. Then he said, "Let me read it back to you." Suddenly his phone went dead. He looked up, "I just got a tip on where the cartel's cocaine is located. I will need to move on it."

"This will only take a moment," Williams said, "But taking the cocaine off the list will help our case. Morales' attorney Johnson is obviously shifting the emphasis from his client to Detective Ramos. He has something we do not know about. It could be the cocaine. If it turns out to be real, you probably should notify the press."

"Maybe the tip is coming from Morales," Ramos said. "This could backfire on us."

"I cannot see any advantage to him," Williams said. "Getting the cocaine issue off the shelf only helps us, but he does want the trial to go back to the murders at the Brown estate for some reason. He is going to try to tie Detective Ramos into it somewhere. This has to be the reason he accepted the recordings. So far they have not helped him."

"I agree with you," Clark said. "You three should go over the events of that time and see if there is something we might have missed. Now, I have to be going. I need to see if this tip is real." He stood, moved towards the door, "Keep me in the loop."

Williams watched him go a few seconds, turned back to the group, "Let's go over your testimony. We will try to avoid all issues concerning anything further back than where Morales is involved. We need to keep the focus on him."

Long Beach Container Storage Yard

Three FBI cars drove into the yard. One car remained at the gate as the other two moved to the administration office. They had their warrant and requested the four storage containers.

The administrator shook, but he managed to compose himself. He had the two FBI cars follow him on his cart deeper into the huge yard filled with storage containers.

Ten minutes later, they pulled up in front of the four containers sitting side by side. He pointed to them as the officers quickly left their cars, carrying automatic weapons.

They took up positions around the containers.

The administrator watched Clark snap the locks off the first container with the bolt cutters and allow the doors to fall open. Inside were two by three-foot boxes filled with bags of a white powdery substance.

One of Clark's men broke the box open. He retrieved one of the bags, opened it, and placed a portion into a beaker. He took out a test kit and poured a solution into the beaker. It registered positive. He turned to Clark, "Cocaine sir."

Clark smiled, "Check a few more crates to be sure they are all cocaine." He walked to next container and snapped the lock off. His men quickly removed a few boxes. They tested positive.

He called his office, "You can call the press. Yes, it is cocaine. I'll save the last two containers for them."

Later the channel seven six o'clock news showed the two remaining containers as the Assistant Director Clark opened them. The test for cocaine revealed the boxes contained cocaine. It was the all-time largest bust of cocaine in the United States.

Monday, at nine sharp, court resumed. Everyone stood when Judge Lawyin entered the court. She took her seat as everyone took his seat. She waited a moment, then she asked, "Is the state ready to begin?"

"Yes, your honor," District Attorney Williams said.

"Then bring your first witness?"

"I would like to call Miss Harriet Brown to the stand," Williams said.

Harriet walked to the stand, took the oath to say the truth, and took her seat.

When she settled, Williams asked, "How many attempts have there been on your life?"

"Four so far," Harriet said.

"Could you describe the four accounts?"

"The first one occurred when I was alone in my office."

"What is the name of the office?"

"Brown Detective Agency, it's located in Pasadena."

"What happened there?"

"Being late, and the only one there, I had closed, and locked the office. The back window of the office opened up to the parking lot. I saw two headlights suddenly flash into my window. I heard two-car doors slam, and two people walking around toward the front door. I was not expecting anyone. Scared, I could hear their car running outside.

I opened the window as a foot slammed into the front door rattling it. I was out the window by the time they had smashed in the front door. I forgot my purse, but I managed the keys to the limousine. When I realized they might chase me in their car, I took the keys from their car, and ran to the limousine. I memorized the license plate and drove off as they came running out of the door.

Without the keys, they had to leave their car. I called 911, and Mc Craw. When Mc Craw arrived, he learned they had already towed the car away. The late Jed Black was the investigating police officer. We learned later, he was from Los Angeles Police Department. We had no idea why he would be the investigating officer in Pasadena. We also found the car in the Los Angeles Police Department's car pool."

"How did that make you feel about the Los Angeles Police Department?"

"It did not make me think I could trust the Police Department."

"Okay, tell us about the second attempt on your life?"

"I decided I needed some protection after the first incident and purchased a revolver. I took the necessary courses and shooting range instructions from Officer Mathews of the Los Angeles Police Department. I received Marksman on my shooting ability. When I took the Simulation Course, Police Officer Mathews told me to go through the building following the marked path.

I shot at the correct target, when suddenly someone shot back at me grazing my shoulder. I didn't know someone was going to shoot back. I began ducking behind the walls when another bullet took off a piece of the wall I managed to get behind. I saw the shadow of a man running up the stairs. I followed keeping my revolver pointed up.

When I reached the second level, I saw a bad-guy poster jump out from the room on my right. I nailed it and ran into the room with my finger ready to pull the trigger. I found the room empty. I looked out into the hall, and saw the man run into the left room at the end of the hallway. I immediately ran across the hall, and lined my revolver up against the wall, and down the hallway towards the open door where he had disappeared.

Another bad-guy poster jumped out from the room across from him. I ignored it and concentrated on the door opening on my side of the hall. I saw the left arm of my assailant reach around the doorway. I heard his gun as my gun went off. I took a bullet in my side, and he took my bullet in his left shoulder. The force of the bullet threw him back inside the room.

I immediately ran to the opposite wall and pointed my gun at the door. I knew I had wounded him. It was a standoff for the moment until I started shooting into the wall. I began to go lower on the wall until he screamed he was coming out.

I told him to throw his gun out. He did, and I told him to throw the other one out. He did after I shot into the wall again. He slowly crawled out of the room. I kept my gun on him until

Officer Mathew ordered me to put my gun down. He ordered twice more before I complied.

The man seeing his chance started to crawl towards his guns when I ran over and kicked them away. He managed to stand, and limp towards a hidden opening at the end of the hall and disappeared.

Officer Mathews and his monitor man came up the stairs, but the loss of blood cause me to pass out. I woke up in the hospital. I understand my driver, Mr. Youngsu, called 911, and the ambulance."

"Did the police find the man who tried to kill you?"

"Yes, the police found him in an alley in Los Angeles. Someone had shot him in the head."

"Going back to the police maze, wasn't Officer Mathews monitoring the shooting."

"It seems the man shooting at me wore something that made him invisible on their screens. He only saw me."

"Did you find any device on their computers?"

"No, nothing, but someone killed Officer Mathews on his way home. A truck ran him over in a crosswalk."

"Okay, let's move on to the third attempt on your life," Williams said.

"I wanted to pick up some clothes from the mansion, but it had been a crime scene, and was locked up. I asked Detective Ramos if he would meet me there to open the gate for me.

He agreed. I took my driver, Mr. Youngsu and Mr. Mc Craw with me. We parked in the bushes to await Detective Ramos. When I called him, I was already at the mansion. A few minutes later, a police car showed up instead. I didn't trust the police at this point. I sent Mr. Youngsu and Mr. Mc Craw out to disarm them.

When Detective Ramos arrived, I stopped him from going up the drive, and set up a plan to interrogate them. I was going to be the wild tough one, and he was going to play along as their buddy. He drove up the drive, I followed him at a distance. You heard it all on the recording. We got a confession out of them. They planned to arrive before us to set up an ambush. You heard them. They were going to kill the four of us including Detective Ramos.

I also had Youngsu check Detective Ramos's car for a bug. He found one and placed the bug in the police car. We would let them listen to their own people. No one thought it was a drone directional bug."

"You fired their guns for two reasons?" Williams asked.

"Yes, I fired their guns into a tree to collect their bullets. I knew my father was killed by a police revolver."

"Did the bullets match?"

"We had them checked, but their guns did not ki l him or the others."

"Okay let's go to the fourth attempt on your life," Williams said.

"Chief Morales had been given bail. We feared for our lives and set up spyware on his house. We had also gone to ground meaning we looked for a place to hide. We had been hiding in the guesthouse on the mansion property. I still had the key. It would be the last place anyone would look for us. We stayed there awhile, but I was becoming more uneasy the longer we stayed, and decided we had to move.

I sent Mr. Youngsu and Nadine Quiver out to hide the limousine, and Rose Blanchard, Mr. Mc Craw, and myself looked for another place to hide. During the process of moving, we were not listening to the conversation taking place in Chief Morales' home.

When we settled into our new location, Rose brought up recordings of the previous three hours. When I heard Chief Morales had called a hit on our guesthouse, I was immediately relieved we had moved. I called Nadine, but she didn't answer."

Christopher Charles

"Let's hold it here a moment to listen to the recording," Williams' said as she pressed the button on the machine she brought up from her table.

Recording:

"Where do we send them?"

"I've been thinking," a man's voice said. "Where would I go to hide a large black Limousine? That is their one mistake. It does not blend in well anywhere except a hotel, but even there the limousine is still exceptional, and easily remembered."

"You going to keep me in suspense? Where?"

"Why at her father's home," the man said, "A very natural place to keep it, and the last place anyone would think to look."

"Joel here!" a voice said from a phone.

"Chief Morales, make the hit at the old Brown Mansion in Brentwood."

Pause:

"Look it up, George Brown in Brentwood, take out all of them. I want no mistakes."

Pause:

"When the job's done."

Pause:

"What did you promise him?" A man's voice asked.

"Twenty thousand in cocaine."

"Where are you getting that?"

"I have it here."

"You keep cocaine here?"

"For an emergency like this one. I thought about giving him a bullet."

Recorder Off:

"Is that the voice you heard?" Williams asked.

"Yes, the voice identified himself as Chief Morales. I knew we had a problem. We had left spyware in place at the guesthouse, but no one was in there yet. Mr. Mc Craw, and myself headed for the guesthouse. Twenty minutes out from the mansion, Nadine called. She said they were at the guesthouse, and out of gas. They had gone back to retrieve one of her bags she had forgotten.

By this time, the six assassins had moved everyone into the guesthouse because it was smaller, and easier to control their prisoners. Now we could pick up their conversations. I told Nadine we would be there in an hour and a half to buy us some time. I told her I would call her back when I was ten minutes out. I didn't think they would kill them until I called her again to confirm.

We thought about calling Detective Ramos, but we did not want a hostage situation. We would try to gain some advantage first. The recording told us they were sending two men to the gate to ensure we would not escape. We had just arrived at the gate and set up an ambush. Mc Craw took out the little man and acquired his automatic weapon. The second man aimed his automatic weapon at Mr. Mc Craw, when I placed my revolver to his neck. He dropped his gun.

Mr. Mc Craw tied, gagged, and placed the two assassins in our trunk. I placed a call to Detective Ramos and apprised him of the situation. He was on his way and told me to wait for him."

"Let's stop here a moment, and listen to the recording again," Williams said.

Recording:

A man asked, "Joel how much are we getting from Morales?"

"Twenty thousand in cocaine," another man said, "We can double that by tomorrow night."

"You mean after we take some for ourselves," the man laughed.

"You take him," the first man said. "Go to the gate. Let them in, but don't let them out. You got that?" The door opened and closed.

Recording Stopped:

"Now please continue," Williams said.

"Well, Mr. Mc Craw began moving towards the house. He took one of the automatic weapons, and I followed him towards the guesthouse staying in the bushes. The sun had set, and the shadows had developed. We didn't see any lights on in the guesthouse, but that was not unusual because we had kept them off while we were staying there. You know, we were not supposed to be there.

We worked our way around to the back. When we reached the back door, I placed a call to Nadine. While the assassins focused on the phone, Mr. Mc Craw entered the house with me behind him. We worked our way to the living room. I flipped the lights on as he laid down a row of bullets at the feet of the assassins. They dropped their weapons.

Mr. Youngsu had been working on his binding. At that moment, he came to his feet, and kicked their leader, Joel. It sent him to the floor where Nadine had fallen. Joel came back to his feet with a knife on Nadine's throat. Mc Craw had to keep his automatic weapon on the other three leaving it to me to help Nadine. I told Nadine to faint. Already frightened, it wasn't hard to do.

She fell forward. The sudden weight caused him to lower his left arm exposing his right shoulder. I fired. The bullet struck him in the shoulder flinging him backward. He dropped Nadine leaving her with a four-inch cut on her neck. She was later treated at the Urgent Care with suture tape to hold the tissue together."

"Was there any doubt in your mind who sent you the assassins?" Williams asked.

"No, it was Chief Morales."

"Let's hear more of the recording," Williams said.

Recording:

"Johnson here."

Pause:

"Your man did well, thanks."

Pause:

"I told you we will have your money in two weeks."

Pause:

"I know that's why Morales is alive."

Pause:

"And me?"

Pause:

"Look, we get you your money, and its business as usual."

Pause:

"Yes, there's going to be a trial, but the opposition will be gone, and we expect the judge to cooperate."

Pause:

"The trial is in a month."

Pause:

"You don't have to threaten me, sir."

A click is heard as the phone closed:

"Who was that?"

"Our friends from Columbia, I was reassuring them."

"How much time do we have?"

"Two weeks to find the money," a man said.

"We're going to need longer," another man said, "We don't have the resources."

"Maybe our FBI friends can be of help. They have the resources to find the money."

"Once they find it, how do we get it?"

"One thing at a time, first we need to make them want to find it."

"How are you going to do that?"

"Let me think about it."

"Okay, let's hear what they have,"

A recorder is heard in the background. It stops, and the voices continue.

"It didn't sound like she had all that much on me. She sure nailed the others."

"If she cannot testify against you, the material on the drive can be dismissed as hearsay. Who recorded it? It could be someone else. I didn't hear your name mentioned."

"I see your point, eliminating her people makes the information useless."

"Too bad you don't have your drones anymore."

"Yeah, they had there uses. What about the drone man, Chapman."

"He's a problem. We don't know where he is."

"Can you find him?"

"Maybe closer to the trial date I can demand the right to question him. That will give you an opportunity for an accident."

"Okay what's next?"

"They took the evidence from the police locker. I suspect they have the bullets that killed Brown and his staff."

"They probably do, but the bullets do not fit my gun."

"You saw to that?"

"What do you think?"

"Okay that leaves the attempted murder of the Assistant Director?"

"I didn't pull the trigger," a man said. "One of my officers went crazy and made the attempt. He was only supposed to acquire the thumb drive from the Assistant Director for my inspection. I certainly did not tell him to kill him. He was supposed to pick up the drive from Agent Steel. Steel by the way was only protecting the thumb drive when he removed it from the supposed dead body of the Assistant Director."

"It would be better to eliminate your officer before the trial." Johnson said. "Then it is all supposition."

"Okay, the money, any ideas yet?"

"Let's shift everything to the cartels," a man said. "Get the FBI involved. Let's tell them about the money, and the lost product. We'll be cooperative. They will check out all the sources for us. Ramos has a tie with them. Maybe we could lean on him for the information."

"You mean admit to our association with the cartels," a man asked.

"Admit to your investigation of the Cartels. Bring Ramos up to date. Have him pursue the money. He'll bring in the FBI, and their resources. We don't have to recover the money only find it to take the pressure off our backs. Once it's out in the open, they'll know we didn't take it."

"Okay, I like it. Now we need soldiers."

"I would think about now the drug supply on the streets is about dried up," a man said, "There should be many willing soldiers just waiting for the call."

"Yeah, I know a few who could do some recruiting for us."

"Our first target should be the Brown group," the second man said. "They can do us the most damage. It should not be that hard to locate them."

"She drives a black limousine. That should be easy to spot."

Recording Stopped:

"Where did that recording come from?" Williams asked.

"We had spyware on Chief Morales's home after he was out on bail, and there had already been several attempts on my life. We felt he would try again. The information saved us again."

"I have no more questions," Williams said, "The prosecution rests, but I reserve the right to call her to the witness stand again."

"Is the defense ready?" Judge Lawyin asked.

"Yes!" Johnson said as he walked towards the witness stand carrying a recorder. He made his steps deliberate. When he reached the witness stand, he looked hard at Harriet, "You've put together very good theater. They should give you an Oscar."

His face turned serious as he said. "You seemed to have left out part of the drama. You fail to mention the drone that blew up the dump truck, and how you saved Hernandez's life from the cartels. Allow me to play your recording. I don't know how you were able to acquire them, but they are very revealing." He flipped the switch on the recorder.

Recorder:

"Black here! We haven't got the money yet. Tell them we're leaving the merchandise in the ship containers for now."

Pause:

"We'll get the money! Tell them that!"

Pause:

"I said we didn't make delivery! That was the DEA being cute."

Pause:

"You can think anything you want. You can even take the merchandise back, or you can wait until the money surfaces."

Pause:

"Yeah, I know eight hundred million."

Pause:

"You're dealing with me, not Brown. Yeah, I'm on my way there."

The Man's phone rang. He opened it.

"Black Here!"

Pause:

"About time you called. Did you get Mc Craw and company?"

Pause: "

"A dump-truck?"

Pause:

"We blew up a dump truck?" His voice went up an octave. "We spent a million and a half to blow up a dump truck."

Pause:

"Did you kill anyone?"

Pause:

"How about Hernandez?"

Pause:

"When you do know, call me!" The phone closed. "Gees, what am I dealing with?"

The phone rings again.

"Yes sir, I am heading there now."

Pause:

"You don't need to replace me, sir. Just a few setbacks."

Pause:

"The money? It will surface. We're checking the old man's bank accounts."

Pause:

"You want me to go to the Bahamas?"

Pause:

"I thought I was coming there."

Pause:

"Yes sir, the cartels want their money."

The phone clicks off and goes silent. A dialed tone is heard.

"Black here! Get me a flight on America Airlines going to the Bahamas."

Recording Stopped:

Johnson turned back to Harriet, "Does that sound like the cartels are trying to kill you?"

"Yes, Mr. Black was the cartel's man in Los Angeles."

"What happened to Mr. Black?"

"We followed him to the Los Angeles Airport, and I called Detective Ramos. When he arrived, we stopped Mr. Black from boarding the plane. We had the recording, and he carried more evidence in his briefcase."

"What happened to Mr. Black and the evidence?"

Detective Ramos gave Mr. Black, and the evidence from the briefcase to the transporting police officers. He could not take him in his car, and the evidence had to stay with the prisoner."

"You still didn't say what happened to Mr. Black and the evidence," Johnson said.

"A truck on the freeway ran into the police car. The two police officers were severely injured, and Mr. Black killed. The driver to the truck disappeared."

"Did the accident kill Mr. Black?"

"No, a severe blow to his head did after the accident," Harriet said.

"Now the big question, who knew Mr. Black was being transported to the police station?"

"My team, the police officers that were injured, Home Land Security people, and Detective Ramos knew."

"What happened to the evidence?"

"It was missing from the accident. We assumed the truck driver took it."

"Exactly, the cartels were not bringing Mr. Black home because he did well. Now they had him dead, and the evidence removed."

District Attorney Williams stood, "I don't see where this line of questioning is leading."

"The District Attorney has a point," Judge Lawyin said. "Can you clarify?"

"It's not hard, your honor, I am trying to show the Columbian Cartel has been playing a very large role in the recent murders that have implicated my client, Chief Morales, and the attempted murders on Miss Brown."

"Very well, you may continue," Judge Lawyin said.

Turning back to Harriet, he asked, "Do you think the Home Land Security tipped the cartel syndicate off to the arrest of Mr. Black?"

"No, they were not aware of evidence we had gathered," Harriet said. "They only detained him to allow Detective Ramos to arrest him."

"It appears the only one left with knowledge of the arrest were you and Detective Ramos. Is that correct?"

"Yes sir, but …"

"Let's move on," Johnson said. "How did you meet Officer Mc Craw?"

"I met him at school," Harriet said. "He was taking the same class as I did?"

"What class was that?"

"Police protocol," Harriet said, "I was working on my detective license."

"And Mc Craw?"

"I learned he was there for disciplinary reason."

"I understand you hired him. Why would you do that?"

"He protected me from getting hurt when two men attacked me in the parking lot."

"Do you know what happened to those two men?"

"They had a traffic accident. One shot himself, and the other, run over by a car, and killed in a dark alley downtown. I didn't have anything to do with it."

"Do you really believe they were accidently killed?"

"No, someone deliberately killed them."

"Who would that be?"

"Looking back on it, it was probably the cartel because they failed to kidnap me."

"Why do you believe they wanted to kidnap you?"

"I think they believed I might know where the eight hundred million dollars disappeared to," Harriet said. Tears were coming to her eyes. "I didn't know they were trying to kidnap and kill me then."

"You also left out the drive-by shooting," Mr. Johnson said. "Why did you do that?"

"It was not relevant to Chief Morales' case."

"But it is very relevant. Please tell us what happened," Mr. Johnson said.

Harriet wiped the tears from her eyes, "Detective Ramos wanted me to meet him at the outside restaurant on Colorado Bouvard in Pasadena. Still a bit shaken, this was right after the training stimulator incident.

Mr. Youngsu parked the limousine in front of the restaurant and opened the door for me. I sat down with Detective Ramos. He had already ordered me a cup of coffee.

We were just into our conversation when I saw this black car suddenly speed up. The rolled down windows on the right side had two automatic weapons sticking out of them. I immediately jumped out of my chair and ran to the bulletproof limousine. I pulled my revolver from my purse as it fell to the ground. Standing behind the limousine, I aimed over the roof using it to steady my revolver.

The automatic weapons spoke, a spray of bullets bounced off the limousine, and hit three people. One hit a little girl in the stomach. I leveled on the driver as he moved into my sights. I pulled the trigger. The bullet pierced the back window and struck him in the left shoulder knocking him against the dash. It caused the black car to veer left. It crashed into a parked car knocking the shooters forward.

Mr. Youngsu leaped from the Limousine, ran to the black car, pulled the automatic weapon from the man in the back seat, and hit him with it. Then he pulled the other man from the front seat and took his automatic weapon away from him. He knocked him hard to the ground stopping any further protest.

Then he leaped over the car and pulled the driver out. He was bleeding badly from the shoulder wound. He had to apply a tourniquet to prevent him from bleeding out." She looked up at Johnson indicating did he want more?

"Did you identify the shooters?"

"Columbia Nationals."

"You mean assassins?"

"Yes, very definitely assassins, the little girl survived."

"Where was Detective Ramos all of this time?"

"Face down on the concrete hiding behind the limousine," Harriet said. "He didn't know the limousine was bulletproof."

"Would you agree the Columbia cartel assassins were brought into the country for one reason, and that was to kill you?"

Harriet eyes began to tear up. She took out some Kleenex and blew her nose. Then she looked at Mr. Johnson, and whispered, "Why?"

"Let's continue, maybe we can find the answer," Mr. Johnson said. "Who knew you were going to meet Detective Ramos at the outside restaurant?"

"Detective Ramos asked me to meet him there, so he knew," Harriet said. "Mr. Youngsu, my driver knew. Rose and Mr. Mc Craw might have known. That's about all. We did find a phone number on one of the phones we took off one of the assassins. It went to a Mr. Schmidt, we later learned he was working for the cartels."

"Yes, we know it was a cartel hit, but who set you up? Who suggested you have lunch outside to make sure you were a target?"

"I don't know?"

"Sure, you do, but you do not want to admit it," Johnson said.

She began to tear up in earnest and shook her head.

"The only one who could have placed you there at that time was Detective Ramos."

"He would not do that," Harriet said through her tears.

"He knew when to hit the ground, where he stayed until your Mr. Youngsu had things under control."

"That's supposition!" Williams yelled standing.

"Sustained," Judge Lawyin said. "You will not lead the witness."

Johnson handed her two sheets of Kleenex from his pocket. He waited for her to wipe her tears, then he said, "Let's move on to when you went back to the mansion to retrieve your clothes, and the policemen arrived," He allowed this to hang a moment.

Harriet nodded.

"And you acted out your little drama with Detective Ramos?"

"Yes, but it was to find out why the policeman had come," Harriet said.

"Yes, we know, but did Detective Ramos see your Mr. Youngsu take the drone missile guidance bug and place it in the police vehicle."

"A…A yes he probably did. Mr. Youngsu was not secretive about it."

"When you departed from the mansion, did you call or tell anyone you made the switch?"

"No."

"Then the only remaining person to know of the switch was Detective Ramos, is that correct?"

"I guess so." Harriet said.

"It was very easy for Detective Ramos to call in a drone missile hit on the four police officers' patrol car."

"He would not do that? He had no reason to."

"Certainly, he did. They were loose ends the cartels needed removed."

"Again, he is leading the witness," Williams yelled from the floor.

"Sustained, let's not draw conclusions for the witness," Judge Lawyin said.

Johnson allowed that to settle, then he said, "Allow me to play this for you?"

Christopher Charles

Recorder:

Phone rings:

"Yes,"

"Bryant Kelly here, Is this Adams?"

"Yes sir, sorry sir, I am a little spooked."

"Why is your man, Morales, calling, and threatening me with a hit?"

"I had no idea he called."

"How serious is this?"

"I told you I had to come up with the money in twelve hours. That was two hours ago, sir."

"How does that concern me?"

"I think you know, sir."

"You tell your man Morales to take care of this now. Use any means he feels is necessary."

"Yes sir, drones?"

"I said any means necessary."

"Yes sir."

The phone clicked, and then phone dialing:

"Morales here!"

"Why in the hell are you threatening the head of the DEA with a hit?"

"I got a tip, sir. The tip also included you. Therefore, I assumed it was real."

"Take care of the problem immediately."

"Any restrictions?"

"Eliminate the problem using any method necessary."

"Yes sir."

Recording Stopped:

Johnson gave her a moment, then he asked, "How did Chief Morales pick up the assassin tip?"

"I believe from Detective Ramos."

"And where did he get it from?"

"From me, we had spyware on Mr. Herman Schmidt's hotel room where we picked up the phone numbers of Mr. Bryant Kelly of the DEA and Mr. Jeffery Adams of Home Land Security in Los Angeles."

"Did you place your spyware in their houses as well?"

"Only Mr. Adams' house," Harriet said, "Mr. Kelly was in DC."

"Let me play this for you," Johnson said. "It was in Spanish, but I had it translated to English."

Recording:

"This is Mr. Pieon. I am in Los Angeles. Who are the targets?"

"Bryant Kelly Head of the DEA, Washington DC, and Jeffery Adams Los Angeles Home Land Security."

"You are to stay in your hotel until this is finished."

The phone clicked, and the recording stopped.

"That was the assassin?"

"Yes sir."

"Was the English translation correct?"

"Yes sir."

"What happened to the Assassin?"

"He went back to kill Mr. Schmidt. A drone missile killed him and Mr. Schmidt."

"All of these killings seemed to be the result of the missing money your father was responsible for. Could you tell the court how much was missing?"

"I believe eight hundred million dollars, but I do not know where it is."

"I am sure you don't, but he and his household were killed because of it, is that correct?"

"Yes sir."

"Many believe the Cartel killed your father, but why would they do that unless they had already retrieved the money?"

"I don't know, sir. It has never made sense to me."

"The recording shows the cartels never received the money. Jeffery Adams and Bryant Kelly did not have it. Otherwise, they would have given it up to avoid being killed by the assassin. Does that make sense?"

"Yes sir," Harriet said.

"Someone obviously has the money. This somebody has allowed people to be killed over it. The threats on your life is a direct result of this, but not from the cartels, and certainly not by Chief Morales who warned Jeffery Adams and Bryant Kelly of the assassin."

Williams suddenly stood, yelling, "How long is he going to be allowed to lead the witness, until he gets a confession out of her?"

"Sustained," Judge Lawyin said, "I have already warned you several times. The Jury is instructed to ignore the last statement."

"I have no more questions, but I would like the right to call Miss Brown back," Johnson said.

The judge turned to Harriet, "You may sit down, Miss Brown." Harriet quickly walked back to her position behind the prosecution table. "I would like to call Detective Ramos to the stand," Johnson said.

Detective Ramos stood, looked around, and walked slowly to the witness stand. He was not expecting this. Still under oath, he took the chair.

Charles Johnson waited until he settled, then he asked, "Was the late Mr. Brown working for the US government or the Cartels?"

"Actually both, he was our undercover man representing the Columbian Cartels in Los Angeles."

"Were they aware of his position with the US Government?"

"No one was aware except me," Ramos said. "We kept it that way for his protection. Even our own government people did not know?" Pausing, he continued, "Well, I think Bryant Kelly knew. He was head of the DEA, and I think Jeffery Adams of Home Land Security, but that would be all."

"It appears they were connected to the Cartels," Johnson said. "So, it has to be assumed the cartels were aware of his connections."

"The cartels allowed him to broker the cocaine deal," Ramos said.

"The DEA did give Mr. Brown the eight hundred million dollars for the cocaine, is that correct?"

"Yes, he had the money," Ramos said. "The cartels checked it out. It was to flush out a year's supply of cocaine from the cartel. Once it was exposed, the DEA was going to sweep in, take possession of the cocaine and money. This would cause the cocaine business in Columbia to fail."

"What about the money?"

"It was real," Ramos said. "Then suddenly it disappeared. I thought the money may have been found when the FBI got a tip and found the four containers of cocaine."

"And."

"The money is still missing."

"How long were you Mr. Brown's Handler before he was murdered?"

"About two weeks," Ramos said.

"That seems rather short. Who was his previous handler?"

"Matlin Mc Crew!"

"How many years had she been his handler?"

"Five years plus I believe."

"She was killed from four bullets to her back, is that correct."

"That is correct. The bullets came from the same gun that murdered Mr. Brown and his staff. The two are connected."

"Did you know the bullets that killed Matlin Mc Craw, and the lab reports are missing from the evidence room?"

Ramos looked at him a moment trying to understand where this was leading. Finally, he said, "I saw the report. The bullets were from the same gun."

"Matlin, brutally murdered in her home allowed you to become Mr. Brown's handler. Then two weeks later, he, along with his staff are also brutally murdered. The only one to escape is his innocent daughter, Harriet. There have been numerous attempts on her life seemly to correct this. You seem to be involved in most of them."

"What are you driving at?"

"How did the cartel assassins know she would be at the outdoor café at that precise time?"

"You will have to ask them, or Jose Morales?" Ramos said.

"Also, it now appears you are the only one left alive with the knowledge of the transactions between the cartels, the Drug Enforcement Agency, and the 800 million dollars. Detective Ramos, everyone else is dead, except for his daughter, Harriet. I counted six attempts on her life. God only knows what has kept her alive."

"What are you suggesting?" Ramos asked.

"I am not suggesting, Detective Ramos, I am stating a fact, you killed Matlin, Mr. Brown and his household, and took possession of the eight hundred million dollars."

Williams jumped to her feet, yelling, "Really! Mr. Johnson!"

Judge Lawyin pounded her gavel four times before the courtroom quieted down. She turned to Mr. Johnson, "You better have proof of those accusations!"

"I do your honor," Johnson said. "I would like to place in evidence the bullets taken from the FBI evidence locker that killed Mr. Brown and his household. Fortunately, Detective Ramos was not able to destroy this evidence."

The door in the back of the courtroom opened. The marshal brought in two evidence bags carrying the bullets in one, and Detective Ramos' revolver in the other. He deposited them along with the lab report on a desk of the District Attorney's and left the courtroom.

Johnson walked over to her desk, lifted the two bags towards the jury, "These are the bullets taken out of Mr. Brown and his staff, and this is Detective Ramos' gun taken while he was in court today with a warrant. The Los Angeles Police lab processed the two and found a match. His gun fits the bullets that killed Mr. Brown. I have no further questions." He handed the judge a copy of the lab report.

District Attorney stood, "I need time to evaluate this new evidence."

"I will give you 48 hours," Judge Lawyin said. "We will be back here in two days at 9 AM." She banged her gavel, stood, and walked from the courtroom with a smile on her face.

An hour later Henry Brown, Harriet, Assistant Director Clark, Detective Ramos, and District attorney Williams and her secretary were in the District Attorney's office.

"What in the hell happened out there," Clark asked. "You've got Detective Ramos being accused of mass murder."

District Attorney Williams looked at Ramos, "How is it the bullets that killed the Brown family came from your gun?"

"I don't know," Ramos said. "I haven't fired my revolver for at least twelve months except at the police shooting range to keep my rating."

"How many bullets did you fire then?" Williams asked.

"I believe there were six shots," Ramos said.

"Who was the instructor?" Clark asked.

"Officer Mathews, but he was killed right after that in a traffic accident."

"Convenient," Clark said.

"Then how many bullets are there?" Harriet asked.

"I believe only six," Ramos said.

"There should be seven," Harriet said. "They are missing one. Maybe the morgue still has it. They obviously changed the bullets to fit Detective Ramos weapon. They could not use the seventh one." Standing, she headed for the door as she yelled, "Maybe you ought to get a warrant for Chief Morales' gun."

"We already have it," Assistant Director Clark yelled running after her. "I'm coming with you in case you need some persuasion with the coroner."

Outside, the limousine waited with Rose and Youngsu inside. Clark and Harriet climbed in, twenty minutes later, they were in the coroner's office.

Doctor Albert Sly, sixty plus with gray hair showing over his balding head, stood from behind his desk when they came in. He recognized the Assistant Director, "I thought you might be coming here today. I've been listening to the trial. You haven't been doing very well."

"We need to know to whom you released the bullets to taken from Mr. Brown's body. This is his daughter Harriet Brown."

Doctor Sly opened his book, turned a few pages, "Here, an officer Davis picked up the bullets. He was in such a hurry he didn't wait for the last one. He said he only needed six."

"You still have the seventh one?"

"Yes, right here." He turned and took a small bottle off the shelf. "I was wondering when you would be coming to pick it up."

Clark started to reach for it, when Sly said, "You need to sign out for it."

"You sure this is from Mr. Brown's body?" Clark asked signing the book.

"It has his DNA on the bullet. Your boys should be able to pick it up."

"I will need you as a witness in two days," Clark said. "Do I have to subpoena you?"

"I'll be there," Doctor Sly said. "Do you want me to bring my book?"

"Yes please, and how he was killed. Be there before nine to go over your testimony."

"I'll be there."

"Good, now I have to get this off immediately." Clark said placing the small bottle in his pocket. They had two days to have the bottle, and Chief Morales' gun sent to the FBI lab in DC, analyzed, and sent back. It would be tight. He had Morales' gun in the FBI evidence locker. He no longer trusted the Los Angeles Police Department.

Two days later, court reconvened at 9 AM. The lab report had not come in yet. Chief Morales and Mr. Johnson sat at their table feeling secure. They were unaware of the seventh bullet.

Harriet, the Assistant Director Clark, and Doctor Sly sat behind the District Attorney's desk. Detective Ramos sat on the end of the aisle. He would be called first. Clark kept looking back at the door expecting one of his agents to bring in the lab report any moment.

District Attorney Williams knew she had to stall. Clark had already apprised her of the situation.

Judge Lawyin entered the courtroom. Everyone rose and waited until she took her seat. She banged her gavel, "Court will resume." She turned to Mr. Johnson, "Is the defense ready?"

"Yes, your honor?"

She turned to the District Attorney, "Is the prosecution ready?"

"We are waiting on some more evidence, your honor," Williams said.

"Can we start without the evidence?"

"Yes, your honor."

"Then let's start with your first witness," Judge Lawyin said.

Williams stood, "I would like to recall Detective Ramos to the stand."

Detective Ramos slowly stood, walked to the stand, took the oath, and sat down.

When he had adjusted himself, Williams said, "Let's go back to the missing bullets, and lab report from the murder of Matlin Mc Craw. You said the bullets taken from her body matched the bullets taken from Brown massacre. Is that correct?"

"Yes madam, they were a perfect match."

"Then you could say the person who murdered Matlin also murdered Mr. Brown and his staff."

"There was no doubt the same person committed both."

"Would you say the motivation was the missing 800 million dollars?"

"Yes, the money has not surfaced yet. Whoever committed the murders were trying to secure the money."

"Where was the last time you fired your revolver?"

"At the Los Angeles gun range where I shot six bullets into a target."

"Was this a requirement?"

"Yes, to retain my position in the department."

"Do you have proof you fired six shots into the target?"

"I still have my rating, and I am still allowed to carry a weapon," Ramos said. "Officer Mathews signed all the paperwork. He said he would mail me a copy. It never arrived."

"Where is Officer Mathews now?"

"He was killed in a traffic accident."

"Was it really a traffic accident?"

"He was in a crosswalk when a truck ran him down. The driver to the truck was never found."

"Is it possible Officer Mathews dug out your bullets, and the bullets we see here are those bullets?"

"She's leading the witness," Johnson shouted from his desk.

"Allow me to restate the question," Williams said. "How is it possible your six bullets ended up in this court?"

"I only fired my gun at the gun range," Ramos said. "The only way my six bullets could be here is for someone to dig them out of the range target. I have not fired my gun otherwise for over a year."

"Who is the most likely person to do this?"

"Officer Mathews."

"Is he the same officer who watched Miss Harriet Brown become target practice for an assassin in the simulator?"

"Yes, the very same man."

"Now he is conveniently dead?"

"Yes, killed by the hit and run driver."

"No further questions," Williams said.

"Cross examine, Mr. Johnson?" Judge Lawyin asked.

"Yes," Mr. Johnson said as he walked to the witness stand. He stopped in front of Ramos, looked at him hard, "Are you admitting you killed Matlin Mc Craw?"

"No, I am only stating the bullets were from the same gun."

"Are you trying to destroy the memory of a good officer in your feeble attempt to claim you are innocent of slaughtering Mr. Brown and his staff, and now Matlin Mc Craw?"

"I am innocent of the charges," Ramos said. "The only explanation is the exchange of bullets from the evidence locker."

"Now you are accusing the officer in charge of the evidence locker to be crooked too? How far are you going to take this?"

"You just need to follow the evidence," Ramos said.

"I think the evidence from the forensic lab is accurate, or are you going to challenge them too?"

"I am innocent of the charges," Ramos said.

"I have no further questions, your honor," Johnson said.

"Do you have another witness," Judge Lawyin asked.

"Yes," Williams said, "I would like to call Doctor Albert Sly Los Angeles Coroner to the stand."

Doctor Sly worked his way to the stand carrying his book. He took the oath and seated himself.

When he was ready, District Attorney Williams asked, "What is your name?"

"Doctor Albert Sly of the Los Angeles Coroner's office."

"Did you do the autopsy on Mr. Brown and his staff?"

"Yes madam."

"How many bullets did you take out of the bodies?"

"Seven bullets?"

"How many bullets were picked up by the Los Angeles Police Department?"

"Six."

"How come only six bullets were picked up?"

"The police officer who picked them up said that was all he needed."

"What was the name of the police officer who picked up the six bullets?"

"I have it here in my book," Doctor Sly said as his opened his book. Going down the page, he looked up, "Officer Davis picked up the six bullets."

"Is that the same Officer Davis that is being held for the attempted murder on the Assistant Director of the FBI?"

"I believe it is the same officer?"

"Could he, a confessed attempted murderer, have easily switched out the bullets from bodies of Mr. Brown and staff, and replaced them with the bullets of Detective Ramos?"

"I suppose he could have done that."

"What happened to the seventh bullet?"

Doctor Sly looked through his book again, "It was checked out to the Assistant Director Clark two days ago."

"Thank you Doctor Sly. I enter Doctor Sly's book into evidence, no further questions."

"Cross examination?"

"Most definitely yes!" Mr. Johnson said. He walked slowly to the stand. Then standing in front of Doctor Sly, he asked,

Christopher Charles

"You want us to believe you have had the crucial seventh bullet all these weeks, and suddenly you produce it."

"Yes sir, I was waiting for someone to sign out for it."

"How many years have you been a coroner?"

"Twenty-five years."

"Then surely you knew the importance of the seventh bullet in a case such as this. It was your responsibility to inform the police department of its existence immediately. Unless of course there is no seventh bullet, and you just created it."

"Officer Davis did not want to wait for it. He didn't think it was important, so why should I?"

"Detective Ramos was in charge of the case; did he make any attempt to retrieve the seventh bullet?"

"No one made an attempt until the Assistant Director came for it two days ago."

"Now for the big question, where is the bullet? I don't see it entered into evidence."

"I don't know, like I said, I checked it out to the Assistant Director."

"Perhaps there is no seventh bullet, and this is a feeble attempt for some publicity. I have no further questions."

"Leading the witness," Williams shouted.

"The Jury will strike the last sentence," Judge Lawyin said. Then turning to the District Attorney, she asked, "Any more witnesses?"

"I would like to recall the Assistant Director Clark back to the stand."

Doctor Sly worked his way out of the witness stand shaking. He managed his seat in the audience as Clark took the stand.

"You are still under oath," Judge Lawyin said.

"Yes, your honor," Clark said. His phone vibrated. He looked down and flipped it open. The text message said: "Seventh bullet here, on my way." He smiled as he looked up at the District attorney.

Harriet noticed Mr. Johnson talking to his male secretary. He stood, and quickly left the courtroom. Harriet followed behind him. She bumped into him when he reached the outer door and dropped a bug in his coat pocket. He recovered, and helped her to her feet, then he ran out the door.

Harriet opened her phone, "Rose, I dropped a bug in Mr. Johnson's secretary's coat, see if you can pick it up." She waited a moment.

"I have him, he's breathing heavy."

"Pick me up in the limousine."

"We're right around the corner. We'll meet you outside."

Harriet went through the outer doors and made her way down the steps. The limousine pulled up to the curb. Rose and Mc Craw were already in the limousine knowing the arrival of the FBI agent was going to be close.

Harriet stepped inside, "I think he's going to try, and stop the FBI agent bringing the seventh bullet."

Rose looked at her screen as the red dot moved out ahead of them. "He's driving!"

"Get closer!" Harriet said. "He may try to ram the agent's car."

As they approached the next block, they saw the secretary's car ram into a federal car coming the other direction. It struck the car in the rear wheel sending it sliding across the street.

Youngsu immediately pulled over to the side of the street.

"Mr. Mc Craw detain the secretary," Harriet yelled, "Rose with me, Youngsu turn this limo around."

Christopher Charles

The three of them jumped from the car and ran to the accident. Mc Craw had the secretary up against the car when he stumbled out. Harriet and Rose reached the dazed agent.

"You okay?" Harriet asked,

The agent nodded. He recognized Harriet, and held up the seventh bullet package?

"Let's get him to the limo," Harriet shouted. "Mc Craw, bring the secretary with you."

Youngsu had the limousine turned around waiting for them. They all climbed inside as the limousine pulled away leaving a traffic mess behind.

Court Room

"Could you restate your name for us?" Williams asked.

"FBI Assistant Director James Clark."

"What would be your take on having the man who attempted to murder you pick up the six bullets from Mr. Brown and staff's bodies?"

"I would say the man is not interested in preserving the law."

"Would it be to his advantage to replace the real bullets with the bullets taken out of the target?"

"His loyalty is obviously to Chief Morales. If the real bullets came from Chief Morales' gun, it would be to his advantage to switch them out."

"How hard would that be for him to do?"

"Once Officer Mathews gave him Detective Ramos' bullets he shot at the police firing range, it would be very easy to switch them."

"The bullets are here as evidence, but what is missing from the lab report?" Williams asked as she handed him a copy of the report.

Clark looked the report over closely, "I do not see any DNA reported on these bullets."

Williams handed him the sac of bullets, "Please examine these? Then give us your opinion what these bullets were shot into."

Clark opened the bag and took one bullet out. He looked at it carefully. "This bullet is extremely collapsed like one would find if it struck the hard board behind a target. It would not be this flat if it came out of a body that is much softer. In fact, it is very hard to read the rifling on this bullet because it has become so compressed." He needed to stall. He knew his agent should be there any second with the lab report. Where was he?

"Then you would say these bullets are from the police target boards?"

"Yes, they would not be from a softer body." Clark said. He looked up as Harriet came through the door followed by his agent. Behind him came Mc Craw with Mr. Johnson secretary.

Mc Craw deposited the secretary beside Mr. Johnson and Chief Morales, "Your boy failed."

Judge Lawyin pounded her gavel several times to quiet the uproar coming from the audience, and the jury. 'I'll have order in this court, or I'll be clearing it." Then glaring at Harriet, she yelled, "Young lady, come to the bench."

Harriet walked up to the bench with the District Attorney beside her.

Judge Lawyin looked at her hard, "What is the meaning of this intrusion into my court?"

Harriet looked up at the judge, "Mr. Johnson's secretary intentionally ran into the FBI agent's car bringing the FBI DC laboratory results of the seventh bullet. He meant to keep the agent from coming here."

She smiled to herself, turned to Mr. Johnson, "You will keep your secretary confined. He will-be handed over for obstruction of justice. Miss Brown, you will take your seat, and we will continue." Looking at the District Attorney Williams, she asked, "Are you placing your findings into evidence?"

"Yes, Your Honor, I would like to enter the findings of the FBI DC forensic laboratory results after it examined the seventh bullet with Mr. Brown's DNA on it along with the Chief Morales' gun." She took the laboratory report from the Agent and brought it to the Judge.

Judge Lawyin opened the envelope. She read the paper inside. After a few minutes, she said, "Chief Morales's gun fired the seventh bullet and the DNA matches Mr. Brown DNA."

"I have no further questions," Williams said.

"Cross Examination:"

"Most definitely," Mr. Johnson said as he walked towards the witness stand. "I sent my secretary back to my office to pick up some papers for me. Unfortunately, he had a traffic accident. They hauled him out of his car by brute force and brought him back here. His car is still holding up traffic."

"He may return to remove his car, Mr. Johnson, but he will still be held over," Judge Lawyin said. She could feel the pressure slowly being relieved.

Mr. Johnson reached the witness stand. The Assistant Director was looking at him intently. He could feel the anger in the man. Standing back a few feet, he said, "It appears we have a difference of opinion as to whose gun killed Mr. Brown, and his staff. You only have one bullet, but we know for-a-fact there were seven bullets. I would think six bullets outweighs the one, wouldn't you agree?"

"I see you as a conniving predator, sir, twisting the meaning of people's words."

"A simple yes or no, sir." Mr. Anderson said looking up at the judge.

"You will answer with a yes or no," Judge Lawyin said.

"Then, definitely no."

"No further questions," Mr. Johnson said.

"You may be seated Mr. Clark, and we will go into summations. Are both sides ready?"

"I am ready, your honor," Williams said.

"Mr. Johnson?"

"I am ready."

"Good, we will start with the prosecution," Judge Lawyin said.

The Assistant Director took his seat as the District attorney quickly reviewed her notes. Slowly she walked to the jury. She looked at them a few seconds, then she said, "We started with attempted murder, manslaughter, and the obstruction of justice, but now we have first degree murder that turned into mass slaughter by one, Chief Morales. Coldly he shot Matlin Mc Craw down in cold blood and followed this with the slaughter of Mr. Brown and his staff leaving his daughter, Harriet Brown homeless, and then persecuted by this man. Somehow, she survived six attempts on her life.

His only defense has been his attempt to place the blame for these evil deeds on her only friend in the police department, Detective Ramos. Trying to defend herself, she exposed the depth of the corruption in our legal system. This monstrous man needs to be found guilty, so he cannot prey on anyone else. He is very good at wiggling. You cannot allow him any wiggle room. You must bring back the verdict of guilty on all counts." She turned and took her seat behind her desk.

Charles Johnson walked slowly to the jury, "My client has been accused of these despicable crimes. He feels for Miss Brown, the attempts on her life by the cartels, and the sudden loss of her father, but we have seen the real villain here in one Detective Ramos. We have shown repeatedly his involvement in the actions my client is being accused of. You must find my client innocent to allow the court to file charges against the real villain, Detective Ramos." He turned and walked back to his seat.

Judge Lawyin turned to the Jury, "You will decide if Chief Morales is guilty of murder in the first degree that may bring with it the death penalty, attempted murder, manslaughter, and the obstruction of justice.

You will decide if Mr. Charles Johnson is guilty of attempted murder, conspiracy to commit murder, attempted murder, manslaughter, and the obstruction of Justice. You will decide if Officer Peter Davis is guilty of attempted murder, wounding a federal officer, obstruction of justice. You will decide if Joel Garnell is guilty of conspiracy to commit murder, kidnapping, attempted murder, and dealing in drugs. You will decide if FBI Agent Ted Steel is guilty of conspiracy in the attempt to kill a federal officer, and if Cal Chapman is guilty of conspiracy in the deaths of four police officers. The jury is dismissed." She pounded her gravel twice and left the room.

The marshals came in took Mr. Johnson and Chief Morales into custody. Harriet and company filed out of the courtroom. She was exhausted.

The Assistant Director Clark came up behind Harriet, squeezed her shoulder, "Thank you for pulling us out this one. I owe you two now."

Harriet tried to smile, "Maybe I will try to collect one day."

Her team walked down the steps and stepped into the waiting limousine. They knew the jury would be awhile.

"Let's go back to the beach, Mr. Youngsu," Harriet said, "Maybe I can finally have a good night's sleep."

The next morning, they received a call the jury was coming back to the courtroom.

Youngsu drove them to the courthouse. Dropping them off, he said, "Good Luck, Miss Brown."

Harriet nodded, and led her people up the steps. Inside they took their usual seats.

Harriet sat beside Clark behind the District Attorney's desk. The Jury walked in and took their seats.

Judge Lawyin entered the courtroom; everyone rose. She sat down, pounded her gavel, "Court is in session." She looked over at the jury, "Has the jury come to a verdict?"

"Yes, we have," the Forman of the Jury said. He handed a sheet of paper to the bailiff who took it to the judge.

She read the verdict a few moments, then she asked, "Will the defendants rise?"

Mr. Johnson and company all stood.

Clark took Harriet's hand, and squeezed it.

Judge Lawyin handed the verdict back to the Bailiff indicating the Forman was to read it.

The foreman took the paper, cleared his throat, "Chief Morales, guilty on all counts including first-degree murder for the killing of Matlin Mc Craw, Mr. Brown and his staff. Mr. Johnson guilty on all counts. Mr. Davis guilty on all counts. Mr. Joel Garnell guilty on all counts. Ted Steel guilty on all counts. Cal Chapman guilty of conspiracy but with leniency.

Judge Lawyin turned to defendants, "The marshals will remove the prisoners. One week from today court will be in session for the sentencing." She pounded her gavel, "This court is adjured."

Clark released Harriet's hand as she smiled up at him. It felt like a very heavy pressure suddenly lifted from her body. No one would be trying to kill her. She rode back to the detective office in the limousine.

They had Mc Craw dropped off to buy some refreshments that included beer. Today he saw justice for the murder of his wife, Matlin. He was still emotional, but he would have to allow others to extract his revenge. He allowed a tear to drop.

Chief Morales and Mr. Johnson sat in the same jail cell awaiting transfer. Neither of them said a word.

Finally, Morales mumbled, "I should have killed that Brown Bitch."

Johnson looked up, "That's something that has been bothering me. Why did you try so hard to kill her when you knew she didn't have the money?"

"That's the point. I missed the money by seconds the first time with the Matlin woman, and I thought I had it the second time, but Brown had transferred it. Now, I was not going to chance losing it a third time. I figured Brown had left some clue with her. She was going to find it sometime. I had to eliminate that possibility. I would have found it eventually. You really can't hide that kind of money for long."

"I assume you had an inside man."

"Sure," Morales said. "He became a loose end. I removed him coming up the steps. A little hasty as it turned out. The money did not transfer."

"I suppose Bryant Kelly Head of DEA, and the other one Jeffery Adams Los Angeles Homeland security were in on this?"

"How did you think we got the money? It was my job to pick it up here."

"I assume you knew the location of the product," Johnson said.

"Knew right after the money arrived but had to figure a way to get the money from Brown first. I delayed things a bit by removing his handler from the equation. It only spooked Brown to hide the money, a miscalculation."

"The product in the warehouse?"

"A fake delivery to draw out the money. I told them it wouldn't work."

"What's our survival chances?"

"The cartels did not do well this year. There's going to be reprisals."

"I thought you had connections."

"It may not be enough this time."

Thirty minutes later, Harriet and company arrived at the Brown Detective Office.

The first time in a very long time. It was eerie to open the door, but this wore off quickly as they all began milling around recounting their lives over the past few months.

Detective Ramos stopped by bringing more beer, and refreshment that included take out. He gave Harriet a big hug and thanked everyone for keeping him out of prison.

When things settled down, Harriet walked up beside Detective Ramos, "There is one thing that has been bothering me."

"Yes."

"Morales' attorney, Johnson, asked me a good question I could not answer."

"What was that?"

"The drive-by shooting at the café in Pasadena. How did the assassins know I would be there?"

"My car was bugged. They heard me make the date with you. Remember, you had Youngsu remove it later."

"Humm, that sounds reasonable. That takes you off the hook Detective or should I say Captain Ramos."

"Thank you, I think." He smiled, turned, and took another beer from the case. He had been wondering that himself.

An hour later, he left. It became very quiet. Everyone was in his or her own thoughts sitting back relaxing.

Henry Brown came by, congratulated everyone, and offered to take Mc Craw and Nadine home. Nadine, more than willing, she had not been home for some time, and suddenly felt very tired. Mc Craw moved into the drunk stage, so he needed to be-driven home.

Rose needed her car and took advantage of the offer to pick it up, leaving Youngsu and Harriet alone.

Harriet went into her private office. She sat back in her chair looking at the photograph of her grandfather and herself. It seemed to be slightly out of the frame. She tried to adjust the picture. Not working, she finally took the picture out of the frame, and looked at it. She noticed something on the other side. Turning it over slowly, she saw some writing and numbers.

Looking at it closer, it read:

"I don't know who to trust. I am getting pressure from all sides. I need to stop everything until I can figure this out."

Below this was ten bank account numbers from different banks in the Bahamas. Immediately she knew what this was. She had found the money. Taking the picture, she ran into the next room, "Youngsu, we need to go to the FBI headquarters now!" She was already moving out the door.

Youngsu quickly closed up the office. He opened the door to the limousine for Harriet.

Harriet climbed inside, and placed her phone to her ear after she had dialed the Assistant Director's number:

Phone:

"Yes, yes, but I have to see you immediately," she said.

Pause:

"Yes, it's that important!"

Pause:

"Your office, I'll be there in twenty minutes."

She closed her phone:

Twenty minutes later Youngsu pulled to the front of the building and watched her walk up the steps. He parked the limousine a block away and turned on his receiver. He had not had time to remove the spyware on the FBI building.

Harriet left her revolver with security and took the elevator to the seventh floor. She stepped out of the elevator, walked to the receptionist, "I am to see the Assistant Director Clark."

The secretary looked up, "You are to go right in."

Harriet quickly walked into Clark's office.

Clark, already there, had a big smile on his face. "Come on in," He said taking her hand. "This reminds me of old times. Are you going to place a bug on me?"

Harriet tried to smile, but it was not working. Softly she said, "I need to tell you something important."

Clark took the smile off his face and led her to the chair in front of his desk. Sitting, he looked at her, "Now, what is so important?"

"Is there a reward for finding the eight hundred million dollars?"

"Did you find it?"

"I have to know under what circumstances you would take the money back."

"What do you think the reward should be?"

"How about ten percent?" Harriet said.

Clark smiled. Here was his chance to complete the whole thing. He had already retrieved the drugs, now the money. It all lay with her. She found out something. These thoughts only took seconds. "Ten percent is way too high, I would lose my job."

"Five percent," Harriet said.

"Still too high," Clark said. "That's forty million dollars."

"Then one percent, and I am giving it away for almost nothing."

"You're still over eight million. How about 800,000 dollars that is not your money to start with."

"How about 800,000 and the mansion estate?" Harriet asked. "It has been mine for five years."

Clark thought a moment, then he said, "Done!"

"Do you need to verify this with anyone?"

"I am probably the only ranking officer left on this case," Clark said, "But I will have my secretary draw up the papers immediately."

"Then I will wait for the papers to be drawn up," Harriet said, and sat back in her chair.

Youngsu waiting in the limousine smiled to himself.

Clark left the office and talked to his secretary. She immediately began typing a document. Fifteen minutes later, she had the paper done, and handed it to Clark. He brought it in and signed the document in front of her.

Harriet looked at it, "We need two witnesses to sign."

Clark left the office a second time and brought in two agents. They each signed the paper.

Harriet looked the document over carefully. Satisfied, she signed the paper, "We will need at least two documents."

Clark again left the office and had two documents made.

Finally coming in, he asked, "Okay what do you have?"

She took out the picture, handed it to him, "You will find the money in the ten accounts listed on the back of this picture. My father used ten different banks to disperse the funds to make it look smaller, and more difficult to find."

"Clever man, we were looking for eight hundred million in one chunk," Clark said. "I'll have the money sent to you after it is retrieved, and you may take possession of the mansion anytime you wish since the deed is already in your father's name. Is that satisfactory Miss Brown?"

"Yes, thank you for doing business with me." She stood and walked out of the office. She picked up her revolver and met Youngsu at the curb waiting for her. A week later, she received a check for 800,000 dollars. She gave each member of her team including Nadine a hundred thousand dollars for a job well done. Mr. Brown allowed her to keep his portion to run the office. After all, she had increased her overhead with the mansion repairs, and new personnel.

Post Script:

Chief Morales, and Mr. Charles Johnson were found dead, strangled with dental floss the first week in prison while they awaited their sentencing. It seems the Columbian cartel did not like the loss of the eight hundred million dollars and their product.

To be Continued in Detective Harriet Brown Two: